D1580409

# KILLER'S COOKBOOK

# KILLER'S COOKBOOK

by

Nicholas Stuart Gray

London
**DENNIS DOBSON**

To my friends
Fanny and Johnnie
with love

First published in Great Britain by
Dobson Books Ltd.,
80 Kensington Church Street,
London W 8.

Photoset Printed and Bound by
Weatherby Woolnough,
Sanders Road, Wellingborough,
Northants.

ISBN 0 234 77668 4

# Contents

Appendix: Items marked with * in the text, will have recipes in the appendix.

# FOREWORD

An entertainingly written, wittily garnished dish such as *Killer's Cookbook* should find its place unerringly on every whodunit lover's shelves. We have long respected the more serious works of this gifted playwright and author whose 'Star Beast'* we consider should be numbered among the great short stories of the world. Thus we approached this new venture with the trepidation of the untravelled English when tackling their first dish of *Grenouille à l'ail*.

Happily our fears proved groundless for this latest confection gratified our taste buds to the last mouthful which we metaphorically sopped up with scraps of bread.

Fanny and Johnnie Cradock.

*In *Mainly in Moonlight*

*Chapter one*

## APPETISER

'Furthermore,' Emma said, 'if the silly bitch sets one foot on the door-step, I will poison her.'

'The sacred laws of hospitality . . .' began Robin.

Emma cut through her husband's words in a voice so high-pitched with rage that a bat would have been pushed to emulate it. She said she was not joking.

Her entourage stirred uneasily. It had reason to know that when that note was used, the chances were that Emma meant what she said. Or thought she did.

'And Giles can take a week's notice,' added the lady, going an incredible half-tone higher, 'and leave the house . . . *now* . . . before dinner!'

The man singled out for the glare of her angry eyes relaxed. So did the rest of Emma's audience. In spite of the tumbled fury of words, the bat-voice and blazing eyes, they all knew she would never send anyone foodless from under her roof, whatever the provocation.

Giles rapidly assumed a complicated expression, composed of equal parts of charm, guilt, stainless integrity, and simplicity.

'My dear,' said he, 'if I'd known you felt so murderous towards the poor soul. . . .'

'What's poor about Maybelle Warwick?' snarled Emma, pacing round in a small circle like a demented gazelle. 'She's rolling! What about her ghastly American car . . . like a cardboard charabanc! And her hot-house penthouse in Byanston Square! And her damned Saluki, that got slung out of Cruft's for biting the judge . . . !'

'Don't be petty,' said her husband. 'Our own beloved Chin-Chin was slung out of the cat-show for the same error.'

'Error, my foot!' cried Emma. 'He meant every tooth-mark. It was Mrs Bates judging, and she pinched his tail. Just because she breeds Angoras . . . great fluffy fools. . . .'

She stopped abruptly and glared at Robin.

'You think you've side-tracked me from Giles, don't you, clever!'

'It was a try.'

'Well, it failed. I've every right to be angry, and you know it.'

1

'Just come down off the ceiling, love,' said Robin. 'You're making a mountain out of a mole hill. Just because Miss Warwick is coming to dinner. . . .'

'Not by my invitation! I wouldn't give her house-room! I wouldn't give her a drink of water if she was dying of the Black Plague . . . !'

'Nor would I,' said Robin. 'I'm not inoculated against it.'

He leaned back comfortably in the huge armchair, and blew a mouthful of smoke in the general direction of the fireplace. Emma eyed him uncertainly for a moment, and then turned back to the others.

Her secretary was still standing by the chair she had vacated when the storm burst. Lynn's quiet, rather beautiful, dignity had not deserted her, although she was twisting her hands together in the only outward sign of alarm she ever showed in emergency. Her eyes were not on her employer, however, but on the man who was now embarking on a fairly feeble line of defence.

'How could I guess you'd take it so seriously?' said he.

'What do you mean, guess! You must have *known*! And what's more,' said Emma, 'if you think you can just stand there, looking hurt and pure, trying to shift the blame on to me. . . .'

'Oh, please . . . have a heart . . . darling Emma. . . .'

'And don't try to wheedle!'

'Any port in a storm,' said Giles.

Emma turned her back on him quickly. She stared through the wide window, over the terrace and balustrade, to where trees threw darkness over the lawns. She was not, it seemed, admiring the September twilight, for she tapped one foot and said in a choked voice that it was no good trying to make her laugh.

'Well, sweet reason, love,' implored Giles. 'I had to find *someone* for tonight, didn't I? It's not my fault that the photographeress of "Kalendar Kittens" has 'flu. . . .'

'Cat 'flu?' asked Robin.

'She didn't specify. But, whatever brand, she couldn't bring it here and pass it round the table, like salt. Could she? So, quite rightly, she cried off. With regrets,' said Giles, 'and fulsome apologies. Then I . . . not wishing to leave us a woman short, and having to find one who isn't burdened with a husband or something . . . I thought. . . .'

'That, from a whole world teeming with females, black, white, yellow, old and young, the one ideal guest we all long to see is Maybelle Warwick. Why?' said Robin.

'Well, because it. . . .'

'I must say,' put in Lynn, in her gentle and rather deep voice, 'it doesn't seem a very bright idea, Giles. With all these television people coming, too.'

'But, sweetheart, that's just exactly why it's a brilliant idea!'

With this impassioned declaration, Giles strode to a superb walnut card-table, circa 1740, snatched a cigarette from a box, dug a lighter from his pocket, and went back to look pleadingly at Lynn, and then at the other two people in the room.

'Surely,' he said, after a steadying pull of smoke, 'all this chit-chat about the deathless feud between Emma and Maybelle has gone on too long? It's getting weary, stale, flat, and totally unprofitable! Besides, it was all done years ago, in the Forties, by the two Hermiones . . . much *better* done. It did seem to me that we could put paid to the whole silly thing, if everyone knows that Maybelle Warwick dines here.'

'You might start it on a second round, with extra fuel,' said Robin.

'Even a knock-down, drag-out cat-fight would be better than a welter of malicious gossip.'

'My dear young man,' drawled Robin, from the depth of his armchair and the height of twenty years' seniority over Giles, 'whatever makes you think that a . . . cat-fight . . . wouldn't exacerbate the gossip?'

'You know quite well what I'm driving at,' said Giles, running both hands through his rough fair hair, and adding harassment to his mixture of expressions. 'At least, if everyone behaves nicely, it will make a story for the press. . . .'

'If!' said Robin.

'Everyone will behave beautifully,' Giles assured his doubting hearers. 'And it will make headlines. Which is what, among so many things, I'm paid to achieve for Emma. It'll be a positive story, not a snippet in a newsy column from some woman's-paper dolly . . . with her pen dipped in acid to report the latest bitchy remark made by Emma about Maybelle, or vice-versa. . . .'

Emma spun on him as though he had stuck a pin in her neat round bottom.

'What has that Warwick mare been saying about me, lately?' she demanded.

'Darling, he was only generalising,' soothed Lynn.

'And would be wise to stop,' said Robin, 'before he out-generalises himself utterly.'

A temporary lull fell on the action, while the protagonists gathered breath for further argument. A quick, wry look passed between Robin and Lynn. Then Giles and Emma both opened their mouths to begin the next bout. And they stayed transfixed, like waxwork models of themselves, as a scream sounded shrilly far away in the big house.

The place had been added to, and altered through the centuries, so that its halls and corridors were wide, the walls thick, the rooms large. Yet the scream was clear and most alarming. Its hearers, however, when they recovered from surprise, were more bored than apprehensive.

'Oh, no,' sighed Robin.

'What's he done, now?' wondered Lynn.

'God knows, and probably He alone!' groaned Giles.

'I'll kill him!' said Emma.

'God?' said Robin.

'No! That clown Derek!'

There was another scream, fainter but more despairing, breaking into a gabble of wild cries, and a far crash of splintering glass.

'If that's the Bristol salad-bowl . . .' began Emma.

'More likely a frying-pan through a window,' said Giles.

'Or himself?' hoped Robin.

'Derek? Never. It's just another row he's making with Johann,' said Lynn. 'Probably all about the proper way to peel potatoes, or something.'

'It is my personal opinion,' said Emma, looking martyred, 'that I must have done something almost irretrievable in a previous life, to deserve the things that happen to me in this one! This house is like bedlam! The amount of work . . .! All tonight's food to prepare, *and* stuff for the banquet on Friday! And now I expect Derek's fused the big electric mixer, the poor fool! Or pricked his finger and fallen asleep!'

'That's not the way it sounded,' said Lynn, uncertainly. 'Shall I go and . . . ?'

'Certainly not, dear,' interrupted Emma. 'Whatever's going on in the kitchen, you could only make it worse. You'd have Johann staring at you like a mooncalf, muttering sonnets, and sending Derek hysterical. With half an hour before guests start arriving, that's all we need! Keep out of this. I'll sort them myself.'

She swept to the door, looking calm and competent. She cast one glance back across her shoulder.

'Remember Giles is sacked,' said she.

On this stern note, she departed.

The three in the library looked thoughtful, in the sudden silence.

'Do you suppose she means it?' said Giles, after a pause. 'Sacking me, I mean?'

His handsome face fell into another complex run of expressions, conveying misery, anxiety, wounded affection, and a sort of sorrowful anger that finally forced the others away, and kept the field to itself.

'I did it for the best,' he said.

Lynn went to him, and touched his sleeve.

'She'll come round, darling. She never means all that she says.'

'She must know I wouldn't deliberately upset her.'

'She was startled. You did leave it a bit late to tell her the guest-list had been changed. It's nearly seven o'clock, you know.'

'But she's been at clothes-fitting all afternoon! By the time she got back, it was time to rush off and get ready for the evening. What chance did I have to . . . ?'

'You could,' suggested Robin, 'have left her a note and emigrated. Do stop wailing, you two. I've always thought we three are the only sane members of this household, so don't run for cover when the going gets tough, and leave me on my own. Calm down. But, Giles, this row is entirely your own fault. You must have known what would happen when you told her about the Warwick woman.'

'Of course. I knew she'd blow her top. But not so violently, or for so long.'

'Then you were unduly optimistic. Emma always goes into orbit if anything creeps up on her. And she's already a palpitating mass of nerves about the television banquet. It's quite a pill, even for her. I don't have to spell it out, Giles. She's up against high-powered personalities, world famous for telly cooking. . . .'

'Emma's famous for cooking, without the telly!' interrupted Lynn.

'Shut up, angel,' said Emma's husband, kindly. 'There's a dear girl. Emma wouldn't turn a hair if she was just doing a demonstration of some sort. But to launch a long-term series with a twelve-course banquet . . . *live* . . . is a bit much, even for madam! She didn't need any extra problems thrown in her face.'

'I'll grovel,' Giles told him. 'I'll eat mud. If I could think of any way to put off Maybelle Warwick this very minute, I'd rush to the phone. But she'd be livid. And she'd give such a tale to the Press! I suppose I've been a fool, but I did it for the best.'

'So you keep saying.'

'*I* believe you, darling,' and Lynn drew deeply on a newly-lighted cigarette.

'Thank you,' said Giles. 'But, Robin. . . .'

Lynn put the cigarette into his mouth, and he choked himself red in the face. When she had stopped thumping his back, he handed her the cigarette.

5

'Don't ever do that again!' said he, huskily. 'It was a sweet thought, though. Robin, I'm terribly sorry I've made such a mess of things. I do know the state Emma's in. Not herself, at all. You and Lynn and I . . . we all tried to talk her out of doing this banquet lark. What on earth possessed her to think of it! It's madness! A programme last week on how to plan and cook the bloody banquet . . . and this week to *give* the bloody banquet – *live!* It's masochism.'

'It's something new,' said Lynn. 'Everyone's had a go at "How to give a party for sixteen on three pounds twenty", or "Two-course Lucullus". . . .'

'And a banquet is only the same damn thing, plus about ninety-seven extra dishes! She's going to flog herself to death, and drive everyone mad,' cried Giles, 'just to show off!'

He sat down with a thump on the nearby Pembroke table, and struck his fists on its leather top.

'These endless preparations,' he moaned. 'That nerve-wracking show last week, with the recipes for Olde English noshes. She's fit to be tied!'

'It's you, love, who have upset her,' pointed out Robin. 'And don't smash the furniture unless it's really going to do you good.'

Giles clenched his hands on his knees, gnawing his lip. He said, after a moment:

'I still think it's good publicity, tonight's dinner-party. For the banquet, and the series. If I can feed a story to the Press tomorrow, with follow-up article and pictures, of the two great rival cooks exchanging recipes over the dinner-table. . . .'

It was the thing too much. Lynn and Robin collapsed.

Giles eyed their laughter gloomily. When he could make himself heard, he said:

'I may be starry-eyed, but . . .'

He lost them again.

'My dear boy,' said Robin, feebly, at last, 'if you think you're going to give that sort of tale to the Press, you're the greatest optimist since Mr Micawber! And if you succeed, you're the world's greatest P.R. *And* a better man than I am, Gunga. . . .'

The door flew open behind them, and they all swung nervously to face whatever had entered.

Brilliantly-silvered hair, gold lamé suit, golden eyes flashing, Emma glared at them.

'It may interest you to know,' said she, 'that Derek has smashed the Crown Derby soup tureen, because Johann struck him on the head with a tomato. If only it had been an axe! I've sacked them both. So, when our guests arrive, you can either send them all straight home, or go and cook eggs and bacon for the lot of them. I,' she stated, simply, 'am going to bed.'

The door slammed.

Apart from the sound of her light footsteps running up the stairs, the house seemed suddenly plunged in graveyard silence.

'I spilt the salt at breakfast today,' said Giles, slowly. 'I wasn't careful enough when I threw some over my shoulder, to see that it went *straight* across my shoulder. It was bound to bring me bad luck.'

'You're too superstitious,' said Lynn, her voice warm with affection.

'Don't laugh. There's more to it than you think,' said the young man, sadly. 'What about that time you walked under a ladder, and a lot of soapy water fell on your head? I told you not to speak till you'd seen a dog, but you. . . .'

'Now, now,' said Robin, unfurling himself from his chair.

Tall, with greying dark hair, and amused blue eyes, he looked with fatherly kindness at the red-haired girl and Giles. They looked back dismally at him.

'Courage,' he said. 'Unless the lads in the kitchen have cut their throats, all is not yet lost.'

He went across the room, swinging his left leg rather stiffly from the hip, to a polished walnut corner-cupboard. He took some bottles from the unglazed lower shelves, and set them on a silver tray that stood on a side-table. It already carried some lovely old Waterford glasses of various shapes and sizes. Robin really enjoyed using fine things. He thought that if objects were only considered in terms of their value in cash, it would be better to sell them and buy something useful. Many treasures passed through his hands, as director of a world-renowned antique gallery. He understood and studied most examples of fine craftsmanship, and was an expert on many of them.

Now he brought two filled glasses to the young man and the girl.

'Sherry for Lynn,' said he, 'and whisky for Giles. Now just watch your shaking little hands, and don't slop it all over the carpet.'

He went back, to pour sherry for himself.

'When Lynn has finished her drink,' he went on, 'without haste, and enjoying every sip, will she go to Emma . . . risking her wrath . . . with soft words, and carrying a huge goblet of "Blood on the Rocks"?'*

Lynn, duly sipping, nodded smilingly.

'An excellent idea,' she said. 'We'll all cross our fingers that she'll

7

knock it back in one, forget her troubles, and come back to us.'

'To that thought,' said Robin, 'let us drink.'

They drank.

## Chapter two

## HORS D'OEUVRES

Once a Tudor farmhouse sat peacefully in the middle of nowhere in Surrey. During the seventeenth century, there had been alterations and additions, perhaps to convert it to a dower-house, or residence for a 'gentleman farmer'. Then the Georgians got their hands on it. More – and worse – had been done to it later, but luckily these latter defects had not been too difficult to peel off. When Robin Randall inherited the place from his aunt, it had achieved a look of peace and dignity again, often at striking variance to the life within.

It was called Monksend. This struck many people as sinister.

For Emma and her staff, the kitchen was the heart of the house. Once several separate rooms, now, with partition walls removed, it was very large, L-shaped, with two windows at the front, and three at the back of the house. The original oak ceiling-beams had – to the dismay of their tiny nibbling inhabitants – been treated to a frightful dose of Rentokil, then boarded over and tiled in shining dark blue. The floors were tiled also and non-slip. Double, sliding, automatic doors led into the main hall, close to the service-door of the dining-room. At the other end of the kitchen, a door led to a wide passage containing the back door of the house, a broom-cupboard, a W.C. for cooks in a hurry, and a twisting little stairway to the floor above.

Looking down the room from the sliding doors, the L-shape was created by what had once been a complete small room, jutting out into the garden; now, with its inner partition gone, it formed a general washery, with sinks, draining-boards, shelves, taps and plate-racks.

The kitchen was at exactly the right temperature, full of delicious smells, and the small, busy sounds of cooking. It also contained two cooks, arguing in hissing undertones, still dazed from the impact of Emma. She had swept out, but her shadow was left behind.

'I warned you!' said Derek, tautly. 'I said she'd sack you.'

'You also,' Johann reminded him. 'She say it . . . loud! Often!'

'Only for spite. She didn't mean it.'

'Of course she mean it, stupid! All is your fault. Who break the tureen? Who shriek and bawl . . . ?'

'Who made me drop the tureen, you German oaf? Who smashed me on the head with a rotten tomato?'

'Is not rotten . . . ssh! Be silent! Belt up, Derek, or she return.'

'Oh, my God!'

Derek leaned weakly against the gas-cooker, and sprang away with a yell, wringing the hand he had carelessly put on a steaming pot. He then pushed a damp swag of brown hair out of his eyes, and stared morosely at a bucketful of Crown Derby fragments.

'And what,' said he, 'do we use for the soup tomorrow?'

Johann said this he should have considered before the screaming row began.

'I'll tell you something, sweetheart,' said Derek, through his teeth. 'If you don't drop that ghastly pidgin-English of yours, I'll be forced to kill you.'

'Have a bash,' suggested Johann.

For a moment it was touch and go. Then Derek gave a gusty sigh and subsided. He had made a wise decision. The other was two inches taller, and three stone heavier.

He was also a lot better-looking, in a rugged blond fashion. Of this Johann was very well aware. He also knew himself to be charming, witty, romantic, a poet who was irresistible to all. These attributes were less noticeable to the average onlooker, to whom he seemed merely a large, pleasant, hard-working young man of twenty-two. A trainee-cook of moderate talent, dogged but uninspired, and reliable, Johann was unfortunately given to fits of jealousy and despair. He could be cruel in these moods, if faced by a weaker opponent, but to do him justice, he fought hard against his failings.

Derek did nothing whatever about his. He gave in without a struggle to every emotion that beset him. He rather enjoyed their dramatic extravagance. Much given to falling in love on the drop of a hat – and out again on the drop of another – Derek was, at this moment, in love with Johann. He got no encouragement there, and it was anyone's guess how long his fancy would last. At least his volatility made sure his heart would never be quite broken.

Now a saucepan hissed and spat as it boiled over.

'Blimey!' said Derek, speeding into action. 'So much for the Sauce Gibbleorange!'*

The other shrugged his broad shoulders. And Derek calmed the saucepan, and mopped up foam, all very quickly and efficiently. Johann went on drying lettuce-leaves and watercress for a while. Then he burst suddenly into impassioned speech.

'This telly programme, Derek! Emma is no fool, to do such a show without my aid. If she use you only, it is worse than no aid at all! Smirking at the cameras, you . . . with your ugly little face, and skinnyness! No, no! Impossible. You . . . to drop the spoon she reach for . . . to run in circles . . . curdle the cream with your panics. . . .'

Into the kitchen came Robin, in the nick of time.

'Derek,' he said. 'Put that down.'

When he chose, he had great authority. The action halted in mid-air. Robin crossed the room, his limp almost imperceptible, set down the salver he carried, and took the chopping-knife from Derek's hand.

'Not just before dinner,' he advised.

Hanging the implement back on its rack, he turned a quelling blue gaze on the two men.

'Boys,' said he, 'I've brought you each a drink. So let's stop larking about, will you?'

'Oooh . . . !' yelled Derek, wringing his hands, '. . . I almost . . . I nearly. . . .'

'You never,' said Robin. 'You'd have missed him, and hit something valuable instead.'

Derek blinked bright eyes, that were a compelling lilac colour in his plain face, and suddenly giggled.

It took Johann a little longer to work out the meaning of Robin's remark.

'Don't bother,' said the latter, kindly. 'Just a pleasantry, my dear fellow.'

'Sir . . . ?' said the German, working this out with difficulty.

Derek laughed; and, after a moment's hesitation, so did Johann. Robin handed each of them a glass of wine, and watched them drink.

'Better?' he said, kindly.

The two cooks sighed, and nodded.

'Then give me some ice-cubes for this ghastly concoction of Emma's.'

Johann brought a bowlful, and Robin put some into a goblet on the tray; a goblet already half-filled with dark-red liquid. Robin murmured that he personally would prefer neat hemlock, but there was no accounting for tastes.

'Put this on the consul-table by the drawing-room door, will you, Derek?' he went on. 'Lynn's going to rush it upstairs to Emma when the ice has had time to melt a bit and take some of the sting out of it.'

Derek looked across the kitchen with a placatory smile.

'Johann, I'm sorry about all that. I didn't mean. . . .'

11

'Is all right,' said the German.

'Then all is well,' stated Robin, briskly. 'And the first guests will be arriving at any moment. Let us all turn our brilliant little brains to dinner. Make no mistake, boys . . . Emma will be down again very soon. In what state do you wish to be discovered?'

Derek grabbed the tray with its tinkling goblet, and fled.

'My fault is none,' said Johann, without much conviction, to the sceptical face of his employer's husband. 'Derek dismays me by saying I shall not in the telly series appear with Emma. I ask you, Sir Robin, why should she choose *him* for this honour, and abandon me?'

'Has she actually told you that you're abandoned?' asked Robin. 'And I've told you not to call me "Sir Robin". . . .'

'But you *are* Sir Robin, sir. Nonetheless,' said Johann, hurriedly, 'I will try to remember to remember, sir. And Emma she has nothing said to me about the. . . .'

'Then wait until she does, before shouting the odds. I daresay you'll both appear. And that should boost the TAM rating, if you keep screaming and bashing one another.'

Johann looked at him carefully, decided he was joking, and gave an unconvincing laugh. Then the laugh ended abruptly. The young cook's face crumpled into a hurt and angry glower.

'This I must say,' said Johann. 'If Derek is preferred to me . . . who was second cook at the "Gefüllter Hecht" in Düsseldorf . . . and *paid* for so being! . . . till I come here six months ago . . . I will him throttle with these hands! Even while people watch the show on the telly, I into the studio will burst . . . !'

'Very nice,' said Robin. 'You do that. Giles will be pleased. Headline publicity for the series! Don't fail to let the director know when you're going to do this bursting and throttling. They'll want a reserve camera for some zoom shots of Derek's blackening face.'

'What's that?' demanded Derek, halting abruptly between the sliding doors.

'A mere trifle,' Robin told him. 'We're just discussing your horrible death.'

'Only if I from the show am dropped,' explained Johann, earnestly. 'Otherwise you may live.'

'Ta, dear. Too kind! Meanwhile let's get down to this dinner, otherwise neither of us will live when Emma reaches us.'

Derek had crossed to the deep bay containing the sinks, and now began to peel some mushrooms there. They seemed to glow, with beautiful pink gills and white silk surfaces.

'I thought you didn't need to peel mushrooms,' said Robin, idly.

'Ah, but these aren't the tasteless sort that people grow in plastic buckets,' said Derek. 'I picked them this morning, in Old Ford field. There were lots there.'

'Good. We can have some for breakfast tomorrow. And listen, you two. I've heard enough brawling for one night,' said Robin. 'If there's another tweet from either of you, I'll have to Take Steps.'

The trainee-cooks glanced at one another. When all was said and done, they both knew who was the head of the household at omonksend. They nodded solemnly.

'I forgive,' said Johann, magnanimously.

'There's a love,' said Derek.

He shook the last piece of mushroom-skin from his fingers, and said he had a good mind to add a few fungi to the salad, raw and thinly-sliced.

'It is the salad green,' protested Johann.

'Think how lovely it would look with little bits of pink and white in its midst.'

'Is not correct.'

Robin told them to get on with it, glanced at his watch, and left them to their work. There was small danger of uproar now. It was too close to dinnertime for frivolity. They could still argue, of course. When Robin was well out of hearing, they did so.

'There's no such word as "correct" when you're creative,' said Derek, in smug tones. 'A really talented cook isn't tied to precedent. If no one had ever invented anything new, we'd still be gnawing bones . . . raw.'

'Is a sign of talent to have mushrooms with everything, like the chips?' Johann had taken to wide-eyed wonder and desire for information. 'Will not they taste odd with oysters? And with the shrimp butter? Great God!' he yelled. 'Where did I put the shrimps?'

'Probably ate them.'

Johann found a large bowlful of shrimps with a howl of relief, and settled down at a table to deal with them. He said would Derek now oblige him by observing a deep silence while he (Johann) was engrossed in the delicate business of shrimp butter.* 'And,' he added, 'you will not place your poison-fungus in *that!*'

'Why are ye cooking toadstools?' said a deep and grating voice, from the back-door passageway.

The newcomer stamped into the kitchen with heavy boots leaving lumps of mud on the hitherto spotless tiles. He then made a curious noise, like a sheep with croup.

'Excuse me laughing!' said he. 'But it's gey hard not to, when the clever boy-cooks is planning murder.'

He plodded to the sink units, and dumped a trug on one of the draining-boards. Muddy water began to ooze from it.

'There's yer hairbs!' he said in his thick Lowland Scottish accent. 'And ye'll find nae hemp or henbane for yer sinfu' plotting. Lettuces and parsley, and a few wee sprigs o' thyme . . . just what madam asked me for. If it's poison ye're wanting, ye should hae let me know earlier,' he wheezed, with another hoarse chuckle. 'Toadstools is crude, laddies. I could find surer things for ye.'

'You horrible old ape!' shrieked Derek, heaving the dripping trug on to a folded newspaper on a shelf. 'Look at that mess everywhere! You did it on purpose. Go away! It'll take forever to clear this up, and we haven't time. You're a swine, Crawford! You really are!'

The gardener, still chortling, backed away from his fury.

'Ye've a spiteful tongue for callin' names,' said he. 'I could call some back at you, if I'd the mind.'

'But you haven't! You're a brainless, crude, bigoted old bastard!'

'Ssh!' said Johann. 'Sir Robin says not shouting. Take no heed of Derek.' He turned to the gardener, with a pious expression of apology. 'He is in the temper, merely because he is dropped from the television show. He plans revenge, no doubt. To slay us all with the toadstools he picked at dawn, mixing them with real mushrooms in devilish cunning. . . .'

'I'm shocked,' Crawford kicked one boot against the other, so that a few more scatters of mud daubed the floor. '*And* amazed. How would Derek ken a Death Cap from a Chanterelle?'

Derek, who had finished swabbing the draining-board, and was now running clean water over the lettuces in the sink, smirked.

'Actually,' said he, 'I do know about Death Caps. Just you wait till the day I have to cook a light luncheon for you, mate.'

The Scotsman rubbed his hands together. It sounded like rasped sandpaper. His bony face grinned like a malicious skull. He said he would be most careful what he ate in this kitchen.

'Malice apart,' he went on, 'ye're dangerous with ignorance! It's likely ye've gathered some funnies. For *Amanita verna* is oft called the Fool's Mushroom.'

Cheered with this remark, he went chortling out of the kitchen. The back door closed. But he left behind a strong, residual stink of stale sweat, with a touch of ripe manure and insecticide. On the floor was an assortment of mud, straw, and small stones.

'Derek,' said Johann, thoughtfully, 'you should not the bad words shout at Crawford. He knows much about plants and seeds and fruit that are not good to eat. Take care how you get on his ugly side.'

'The problem,' said Derek, 'is to find his pretty one.'

## Chapter three

## IN THE SOUP

The evening went its way.

All the invited guests arrived in conformity with polite usage. The few introductions necessary were made. Everyone settled in the library to drink aperitifs, to chat more or less affably, and to nibble at salted-and-buttered almonds, black olives stuffed with anchovies, green olives soaked in the juice of fresh limes, and pieces of celery crammed with chopped mushroom in garlicky cream. The mushrooms were raw, at Derek's insistence, and very delicious.

Giles and Lynn worked hard to keep conversation on a social level, as ordinary as was possible. They found Robin a great help, but got little anywhere else. Determinedly cheerful voices would suddenly become muted, as the guests cast sideways glances at Emma and Maybelle skirmishing cautiously. As now . . . .

'So brave,' murmured Emma,' to wear yellow diamonds. Tradition-ally, yellow means forsaken.'

Giles gulped nervously. It was he who had mentioned this supersti-tion to her, months ago. He wished her memory was as good for more practical items.

'Forsaken?' smiled Maybelle, 'What a darling, old-fashioned word. Hardly ever used by my generation.'

Lynn and Giles began to chatter loudly, but Emma could still be heard assuring her rival that her own mother had said just the same. The rival laughed merrily. This lady was a most efficient and plushy show-business personality, whose cookery programmes had pleased television-viewers for some years. She could hardly be expected to like the idea of Emma stepping into her shoes, though there was little in common to provide much real similarity in their work. Maybelle went in for exotic, foreign dishes, thick with eggs and cream, and drenched in wine and liqueurs. Emma exhorted the use of good local ingredients, and the pleasures of tasting them. Maybelle was tall and dark, with handsome, somewhat Red-Indian features and deceptively calm eyes. For this occasion, she was wearing a lime-green gown of incredibly expensive cut, and the yellow diamonds just mentioned. Her taste was impeccable. It even forced her to break off the present exchange, which could only get nastier, and reply to a query from Lynn concerning the Judge-biting Saluki.

'Oh, the dear thing,' said Maybelle. 'I gave her to some friends, who really seem quite fond of her. I'm thinking of getting a curly-haired Siamese cat or two.'

'Fascinating creatures, cats,' said Robin. 'Of every variety, except the Kilkenny brand.'

Mrs B. L. Locke said, in her tired and faded voice, that a cat could look at a king. And Giles said that was probably enough to make it laugh. And he laughed himself, thinking the chatter was back on a manageable level. But he stopped abruptly, hearing Maybelle's next gambit.

She had drifted across to a heavily-built, but thin-faced man, who was one of the current powers at the B.B.C. A nod or shake of his sallow, balding head could make or break those dependant on his good-will. At the moment, he was in charge of Emma's forthcoming series, and it was vital to her that his nod should be kept going. B. L. Locke, not liked but feared. Everyone knew that the L. stood for Lawrence, but the B. was a close secret . . . though there were many guesses.

'And what have you in mind to follow *this* series?' Maybelle was asking him now. 'Is it in rehearsal yet? Just in case . . . ?'

She got a bleak look.

'I don't have to plan that far ahead,' said B. L. 'But I am never short of ideas.'

Emma, also overhearing this, bit her lip. She rightly took his remark as a veiled threat. His reputation, which he greatly valued, could suffer if things did not go well with his productions. He would not lightly tolerate any kind of failure.

Robin gave his wife an almost imperceptible, but reassuring nod. She was looking adorable, in her gold-lamé trouser-suit, her famous emeralds, and her most artless expression. She went into an immediate outburst of merry prattle with her guests, her voice as sweet as that of a child. She was, at this moment, about as sweet as a small adder with its front teeth sharpened.

The gong sounded from across the hall. This meant Derek and Johann were ready to serve dinner as soon as Emma gave them the word. It was also the signal for the french windows in the library to fly open, admitting a blast of chilly air, a flurry of strangely-clad bodies, and what sounded like cries for help.

The first outburst of dismay died away when the newcomers turned out to be Harriet and a friend.

Robin's niece was the only child of his younger brother. As far as anyone could tell, through a welter of flapping trousers, frilly shirt, ragged cloak, beads, and babble, she was tall and slender, with bare feet, and seemingly about sixteen. Little could be seen of her face through curtains of long, straight, honey-coloured hair. She looked slightly crazed.

Her companion was a fitting escort. Almost identical in appearance . . . except for his long, straight, honey-coloured moustache. A green ribbon round his head controlled long, straight and honey-coloured hair sufficiently to reveal gentian-blue eyes, gentle smile, and silver earrings. His trousers were striped and fringed, his shirt was frilly, but over everything he wore a goatskin jacket with a curious smell. He was tall, slender, barefooted, and looked completely demented.

They stood by the french windows and said the police were after them. Several jaws dropped. But not Emma's, or others who knew Harriet.

'Why?' Emma said, mildly. 'Close the doors, love. We'll freeze. What have you done?'

'Not very much,' said Harriet.

'*How* much?' asked her uncle.

'We were just bowling along in my Mini, innocent as unborn tadpoles, when this copper yelled at us.'

'But of course, you didn't stop,' said Mike Peel, who had met her before.

He was the director of Emma's series. He actually looked forward to his task, for nothing had ever been known to cow or depress him. Short, squat, black-haired, black-eyed, his energy sparkled almost visibly, like electricity about him. He was excellent at his job, and rightly popular. He was laughing now, white teeth flashing. And Harriet laughed back.

'Well . . . no,' she told him. 'He might have been one of the Fuzz we met at the Protest a couple of weeks ago. He might have remembered us.'

'For doing what?' said Betsie Bloot, the editress.

Editress, gossip-writer, radio personality ('Tell Your Troubles to Betsie'), she also replied to heart-throb letters in a magazine ('Blunt Advice from Blootie'). She was aging, ugly, very fat, and a brutal and brilliant wit. The glinting light in her eyes gave her a strange touch of beauty. The look she had for Harriet was amused and kindly.

'Ah,' said that young lady. 'Well . . . the fact is . . . we threw a bag of flour into the window of 11, Downing Street.'

Robin regarded his niece with interest, and asked what the Chancellor of the Exchequer had ever done to her. 'Nothing,' she said. 'But he had his window open.'

'We were doing a Protest against General Injustice,' she went on. 'And the cops might be keeping their eyes out for us.'

'Would their eyes recede again if you drive on when requested to stop?' said Robin.

'We had no money on us,' put in Harriet's friend, unexpectedly, 'for bribing them.'

Harriet now cast a winning glance round the fascinated assembly. To do this, she lifted a corner of her hair and revealed a wide grey eye with a red sequin stuck on its lid, and another on the tip of her nose. Except for Robin, Emma, Giles, Mike and Lynn, everyone was staring at the two young people as though they had just dropped in from Outer Space.

'Won't you introduce us?' said Harriet, in a social tone. 'This is Thumper. He designs ash-trays.'

'Mr and Mrs B. L. Locke,' said Robin, equally formal, 'allow me to present my niece, Miss Harriet Randall. And . . . er . . . Thumper. He designs ash-trays.'

He took the young couple round his guests, gracefully and calmly.

'Miss Maybelle Warwick, this is my niece Harriet, and Thumper. Mike Peel . . . Charles Picklehampton . . . Miss Amy Barr . . . Mr and Mrs Bloot . . . allow me to present . . . .'

Thumper and Harriet smiled sweetly at everyone.

Amy Barr was B. L.'s secretary, and looked it. A nervous, waif-like creature, in a smart flowered-silk dress that did not suit her, she kept looking at her employer as though expecting constantly to be asked to take notes. And Charles Picklehampton resembled a time-worn, slightly dissipated, but still superb Greek statue. The curls that framed his classic face were white, but that face was almost unlined. For forty years he had been the favourite photographer among professional entertainers, because his portraits were extremely flattering, as well as brilliant.

'Oh, how nice to meet you,' exclaimed Harriet. 'You've just got The Year's Loveliest Portrait award for that gorgeous one of Emma.'

'It was not difficult,' Charles assured her, 'with such an obedient model.'

Giles flinched. He was almost sure he heard Emma's teeth grinding. The sittings for that prize-winning photograph had been more than usually turbulent.

Mr Bloot acknowledged the introduction of the new arrivals with a curt nod. He was a mystery to everyone, and likely to remain so, for he never uttered. He merely ate. Like a locust, without pause or visible sign of pleasure. People had theories about him. The most popular being that Betsie had talked him into permanent coma. Giles said he was a ventriloquist's doll, manoeuvered by Betsie into saying hallo on arrival, and goodbye on departure from anywhere. Emma suggested he was a zombie, brought back from the grave because Betsie could find no other husband. He was quite grey. Grey hair . . . grey skin . . . and probably engaged in some grey job as a Civil Servant of some kind, though Robin plumped for accountant. He said the man was tolerated by Betsie merely to fiddle her Income Tax returns.

The gong sounded again, very tetchily.

'Oh, I'm sorry we've crashed your party,' Harriet said to Emma. 'We were trying to shake off the police, whizzing round corners and things. We came to your back gate, and crept up here through the undergrowth. We got tangled in some horrible thorns . . . .'

'My God, the roses! Did you trample them flat?'

'We were just going to skulk in the grounds for a while,' went on the girl, 'but Thumper hurt his knee falling over a stone tub below the terrace . . . .'

'My God! The Florentine urn!' shrieked Emma.

'So we came in for a bit of Band-Aid,' said Thumper. 'Then we can go off and hide in a shed.'

'My dear fellow!' said Robin, delightedly. 'You must both stay to dinner, if you've really nothing better to do. Where did you hide the car?'

'Oh, we're moronic!' cried Harriet. 'We just abandoned it at the gate. Let's go and cover it with leaves!'

'Please don't,' said Robin. 'The arrival of a police patrol would make an excellent floor-show. Anyway, I'm sure you managed to elude pursuit.'

Lynn had slipped away, to break the news of additional diners to Derek and Johann, and to fetch some Band-Aid. She had already had a word with Emma about re-arranging the seating order at the dinnertable. When she returned, she suggested that Thumper should wash his wound before covering it. He seemed surprised to be reminded of it at all.

Mr Bloot shovelled the last of a plateful of tiny pork-thyme-sage sausage-balls down his throat, and reached for a dish of even tinier jellied-mint-with-new-peas pastries. His wife was trying to pump Mrs Locke about B.L.'s methods of achieving power.

'The race is to the swift,' said Mrs Locke, mysteriously.

Maybelle assured Charles that she personally had nothing against the very young. They would grow up one day, said she, to realise how very silly they had been.

'As we've done?' he asked.

He was at least fifteen years her senior, and her calm-eyed fury delighted Emma, who observed it. Then she turned again to her husband's niece, and asked if she and Thumper would like to wash before dinner.

'Or . . . or comb your hair?' Then, eyeing Harriet doubtfully, she added: 'You're too tall for any of my clothes, but I've a sort of silk kaftan. . . .'

'Oh, do you mind us like this? We're quite clean, actually. And Thumper could take off his coat . . . .'

Giles suddenly threw in a suggestion.

'What about some sandwiches in the garden?' said he.

'Oh, yes,' cried Harriet. 'Thus avoiding all embarrassment, for everyone. We're not dressed for a party. We need more jewellery! Oh, you're a dear, old, clever-boy Giles!'

She clutched his hand to her bosom, and kissed him through her hair.

'I love you, too,' said Giles. 'Sandwiches, then?'

But Emma had noted her husband's eye on her, the smile on Maybelle's face, and the look of regret on Mike's.

'No sandwiches,' she said, firmly. 'I want the fugitives from justice at my table, just exactly as they are.'

The gong sounded for the third time. It sounded furious!

Emma went in with B. L., and Robin escorted Maybelle. Giles gave his arm to Mrs Locke, and Thumper was collected nervously by Amy Barr (prompted by Lynn); Charles partnered Harriet. Mike led Betsie to a chair on the left of Robin, and then took his own place on Emma's right. It was all very formal, polite, and calming to the nerves.

Dinner was served. Served in tight-lipped silence. Johann and Derek had really suffered during the delay after the first gong, watching the clock and the food until their eyes almost crossed. They wanted so desperately for the occasion to do justice to Emma . . . and to themselves. Yet, apart from the trainee-cooks, nothing was the worse for waiting. Whatever might be said about the social value of the gathering, its food was excellent.

The long table in the dining-room glittered with the soft light of four beautiful Stuart candelabra set evenly down its length. Crystal glass sparkled as though studded with diamond chips. The subtle glow of silver, polished walnut, and fine china pleased the eyes and soothed the mind.

Harriet chattered brightly to the steadily munching Mr Bloot, seemingly unaware that he never replied.

Emma talked mostly about coming rehearsals with Mike and B. L. But she spared time to listen to Charles telling Lynn that her green eyes and quiet voice had cat-like qualities, probably concealing intense evil. Lynn said she was deeply flattered. And the photographer begged her to let him make a portrait.

'I want *next* year's award, too,' said he. 'I see you in something black, with long white gloves . . . .'

An attempt was made to find out more about Thumper. It was Amy Barr, of all people, who suddenly asked his second name. He said he had none.

'I'm just Thumper,' said Thumper.

'He doesn't believe in multiple names,' explained Harriet. 'He says it limits personal existence.'

B. L. had put up with as much as he could stand. He now exploded.

'Rubbish! Ridiculous! Everyone has two names at least!' he snarled. 'It's the only way to tell 'em apart.'

'Oh, come!' Betsie was aggressively sniping at him. 'How many John Smiths are there . . . in London alone!'

'None that *I* know!' snapped B. L.

His wife began to say that they knew someone called Mavis Smith, but was faded out by an enraged glare.

'People have always had two names,' maintained B. L. in the voice that could reduce his B.B.C. personnel to jelly. 'Since the beginning of time!'

'Surely not,' Charles Picklehampton did not work for the B.B.C. 'Adam? Moses? The Neolithics?'

'Oh, bless them!' cried Harriet. 'Back to the caves! In future, I'd like everyone to think of me as Harriet only.'

'If the thought of you ever crosses my mind,' said Robin, 'it is always as Harriet only.'

'You,' said Thumper, 'have Soul.'

Robin bowed. It came to him that most of these people were quite easy to handle . . . on their own. It was the mixture that was so unstable. While continuing to play the host with deceptive smoothness, he kept a wary eye on his wife, so that he could turn the conversation when it began to teeter on the brim of suddenly-sighted quicksands. This got him many grateful glances from Lynn and Giles, an occasional wink from Mike Peel, and some small, evil smiles from Emma.

Needless to say, no police turned up. The one who had called to Harriet as she drove by had probably meant it more as a greeting than a command. But no one was mean enough to suggest this. The boy and girl were so obviously enjoying being Wanted.

Giles was trying to memorise all the clichés uttered by Mrs Locke, for use on future occasions. Some were actually new to him. Every now and then, he would quickly survey the guests' faces, and then his voice would falter slightly, and his bright expression became rather set. This was not like him at all. But he felt surrounded by pitfalls.

To name but a few, Betsie Bloot, who sat at his right, tried tirelessly to pump him concerning the past, present and future loves, hates, and (hopefully) scandals of Emma's life.

'But . . . . it's an open book!' he protested.

'Privately printed?'

Dinner pursued its leisurely course . . . or courses.

There were no mushrooms with the oysters; nor with the shrimp butter accompanying the curled sole-fillets. And Derek's notion of serving them in salad had been abandoned, which was fortunate; they would not have gone well with wild ducks and orange sauce. The lamb, with baby marrows and baby sprouts, was delicious . . . .

It was while munching a sprout that B. L. suddenly choked, and went purple. He lay back in his chair wheezing and gasping. Emma quickly poured him some water, but he waved it aside. Derek, who was serving Maybelle at the far end of the table, stood rigid. What could have got mixed into those tiny sprouts? But it was not the food that had upset B. L. It was Harriet, talking about sex.

'It's like eating chocolate,' her clear voice was informing the impervious Mr Bloot.

A hush fell on the assembly.

'When you fancy the stuff, nothing else will do,' went on the girl. 'And when you don't, it makes you sick.'

Mr Bloot ate his lamb.

'Daddy doesn't agree,' Harriet told her uncle. 'But he's more prehistoric than you are, darling. He wants me to marry a title and settle down.'

'You've got your lines crossed,' said Robin. 'Marriage is a fairly recent brainstorm in the career of Mankind. If my poor brother were prehistoric, he'd be in favour of tribal copulation.'

'But that's the very latest . . . .!'

'It's hard sometimes to tell if we're coming or going,' said Robin, sadly.

Lynn intervened by asking what title Harriet's father had in mind for her.

'Just any title?' cried Betsie. 'Like Mr Universe 1976, or . . . .?'

'The Lord of the Rings?' Mike Peel entered the field joyfully.

'The K-night of the Long K-nives?' said Charles.

He got a burst of protest and laughter. Then Mrs Locke asked Harriet if she wished to marry a title. And Mike asked how many were available. Harriet began to count on her fingers. She said there were two lords, to her certain knowledge, several knights, a number of honourables, some foreign ex-royalty, and countless counts, all for sale, apparently, to the highest bidder.

'And will Daddy buy one for you?' said Maybelle, flashing her teeth.

'If I wanted, Dad would buy me the lot,' said Harriet, softly.

'Better a dish of herbs where love is . . .' offered Mrs Locke.

'Oh, and talking of which,' Maybelle turned an earnestly enquiring gaze on her hostess. 'Do you actually grow *all* the herbs you use with *every*thing in your recipes?'

'Dearest girl!' exclaimed Emma, wide-eyed. *'I'm* not clever with dusty old leaves. Of course my garden provides what is needed for subtle flavouring.'

'Ah,' said Charles. 'I read Miss Warwick's article on the preserving of . . .'

Robin said quickly how well written it was. And Giles began a funny story to Betsie, and forgot the tag line. Lynn was, rather loudly, complimenting Derek and Johann on the individual Caramel Creams they were busily handing round.

Things calmed down. Everyone enjoyed the pudding. And left no crumb of the Scotch Woodcock that followed it. Now they sat admiring the silver dishes piled high with fruit; the splendid results of Emma's planning, and Crawford's skill, and well deserving their places down the centre of the table.

Bon Chrétien pears, pineapple-nectarines, some late figs; apples, Ellison's Orange and James Grieve; all with the shining swank, impossible to reproduce artificially, of having been harvested the same day. There were also some velvet-coated peaches.

'Beautiful,' said Thumper.

'Thank you, dear,' smiled Emma. 'Grown with the same love and care as the herbs.'

'. . . the lives of the poisoners,' said the loud and unmusical voice of B.L.

Emma's mouth opened, and Amy Barr, sounding as well as looking like a small grey mouse, said pipingly that B.L. was talking of a possible television series. Emma killed the small titter that had risen here and there by laughing herself.

'Dear me!' she cried. 'The juxtaposition of ideas makes me feel quite like a Borgia!'

B.L. said she would make a splendid Lucrezia, were she a dramatic actress.

Before anyone could say anything to be sorry for, Giles quickly asked what sort of people the series would portray.

'Various famous poisoners,' came the heavy answer from B.L. 'All the really glamorous ones, of course. Mystery, I want . . . beautiful women . . . reckless, heartless . . . that's the idea. The Borgia, yes. And Frances Howard murdering Overbury . . . .'

'But that was horrible!' protested Lynn.

'Oh, but the drama!' said Maybelle, lowering her long eyelashes in simulated passion. 'A woman scorned! Very nice, B.L. Who else?'

'Queen Eleanore and Fair Rosamund . . .' began B.L. 'The Marquise de Brinvilliers . . . .'

'And Snow White's stepmother!' said Charles.

'Handsome is as handsome does,' said Mrs Locke.

These two remarks put paid to the discussion.

Lynn began to wonder when Emma would collect the eyes of the female diners, and retire to the drawing-room, abandoning the men to a last glass of port. An old-world custom but one which made good sense. It gave the women time to refurbish their make-up, lessened the run on the lavatories, and allowed everyone a breathing-space.

'Well, I really must congratulate dear Lady Randall,' Maybelle was now drawling, 'on a superb meal. You cooked it to perfection, dear. Even the White Tower couldn't better it.'

'The White what?' said Emma.

Her smile matched that of Maybelle in venom.

'Darling Miss Warwick,' she went on, 'I'll pass your charming appreciation to my students. Dear boys! I left most of the cooking to them, tonight.'

'You really amaze me. Imagine leaving the most enjoyable part to underlings,' said Maybelle. 'To me, cooking isn't just a commercial business, but an art. A fine art, which I adore practising.'

'And I'm sure,' said Emma, 'that practice will ultimately make perfect . . .

Then her smile vanished abruptly.

She shut her mouth tightly on a gasping cry. For a moment more, she sat still and rigid. Then she levered herself to her feet, both hands clenched round the arms of her chair. Everyone stopped speaking . . . with the exception of Mr Bloot, who had never started. And everyone stopped whatever they were doing . . . with the exception of Mr Bloot, who took another peach. They all stared in dismay at the white, contorted face of their hostess.

'Robin . . .' she whispered, hoarsely, as he came to her side.

Then she gave another strangled cry. Derek, who had just come in with Johann, clutched the German's arm. Johann patted him feebly. And Emma fell. Glasses were swept aside as her body slid helplessly across the corner of the table.

'My God, the Waterford!' said Charles, stupidly.

## Chapter four

## FISHY STUFF

Silent but fevered gloom descended on the remnants of the dinner-party, when Robin left the room carrying the feebly writhing body of his wife. Lynn raced ahead of him, making small gasping noises indicative of shock and dismay. Giles ran to Emma's little office on the other side of the main hall, to telephone for her doctor.

At table, people pushed aside their fruit-dishes; some lighted cigarettes. Only Mr Bloot helped himself to sugar-glazed grapes. The silence became oppressive.

'Dear me,' said Mrs Locke suddenly, making a heroic effort to revive the social atmosphere, 'whoever would have thought it!'

'Thought what?' said Betsie.

'Why . . . that poor Emma . . . well, I always say that in the midst of life . . .' here Mrs Locke began to waver badly, wishing she had kept her mouth shut in the first place, '. . . I mean, who could have guessed she was ill? She's been working too hard . . . .'

'It's probably appendicitis,' interrupted Mike Peel, as B. L. frowned ponderously at his wife.

The frown turned on him instead.

'Who says she's got appendicitis?' demanded B. L.

'No one. Just my guess. It's possible.'

'That's all we need. An operation. A fortnight in a nursing-home. And what,' said B. L. in a voice of doom, 'about the Show?'

'Oh, my dear love!' cried Betsie Bloot. 'Make her crawl out of bed to do it! She can show her stitches to the viewers. They'd love it. Make "Peyton Place" look like "The Magic Roundabout"! You know the kindly British Public . . . if she could have a relapse in front of their eyes . . . .'

'Very amusing!' snarled B. L. 'Pity it's not your problem.'

Mike's cheerful voice interrupted again. He spoilt a promising scene.

'It would be splendid publicity,' said he. 'Even if the series has to be postponed a week or two. Whet everyone's appetites. Assure us a tremendous . . . .'

Maybelle flicked the rim of her glass with an elegant fingernail so that it rang like an alarm bell. Everyone looked at her, and at the shadowy smile that lurked round the edges of her mouth.

'Publicity?' said she, softly. 'You'd better make sure it's a natural illness before you start telephoning the Press. It might not help your programme if you have to tell the world that poor dear Emma poisoned herself with her own cooking, at her own dinner-table.'

There was a longish pause.

Then Harriet and Thumper sprang to their feet in unison, and glared at Maybelle. Their normally gentle eyes glinted surprisingly; the click of necklaces, and tossing-back of wild fair hair was suddenly hostile. Apparently their anger could be roused on behalf of someone other than themselves.

'Is that the story you mean to spread round, Miss Warwick?' demanded Harriet.

'And you a guest here,' said Thumper, sorrowfully.

Maybelle looked as startled as though they'd suddenly grown horns. In a way, they had. Her subtle smile vanished.

'Oh, well . . . er . . .' she said.

'Go on. Out with it,' Mike Peel suggested. 'You can't just leave it there. What made you say such a thing?'

Maybelle looked round at her fellow guests, took a deep breath, and made a graceful and deprecating gesture with both hands. She said:

'Dear people! Believe me, I wasn't trying to be funny or unkind. All I said was that Emma wouldn't wish any word of this to reach the public. No cook would. I believe I'm entitled to speak for the . . . for the trade.'

No one responded to her little titter, so she straightened her face quickly and went on. She said they all know how ready people were to believe the worst.

'Of course you speak for yourself?' said Betsie.

'Where famous people are concerned,' Maybelle swept on, ignoring this, 'the worst is hardly bad enough to satisfy the morbid taste of the public. They would laugh at Emma, you know they would. They'd roll the gossip round their tongues. Wondering what went wrong with her cooking! Wondering if they could trust her recipes! Think of all the variety shows, and the comics. Can't you hear the sort of jokes . . . the giggling!'

Mrs Locke, out of sheer nervousness, produced a voice that cut through Maybelle's so shrilly that it set everyone's teeth on edge.

'Miss Warwick,' she said, 'this was not an accident.'

In the silence that followed a general gasp, Mr Bloot's steady munching sounded like a cow walking through mud.

'Oh, my God, woman!' growled B. L.

'Surely,' said Maybelle, gently, 'no one disliked darling Emma as much as *that*.'

Four people spoke together.

Mrs Locke said that was not what she'd meant.

Mike Peel begged everyone to keep their heads.

Harriet and Thumper said they were going.

'Better not,' Charles Picklehampton told them. 'If this latest suggestion should prove true, we may be favoured by a visit from the police in a short while. They will naturally want to question everyone present. I believe this is their wont if suspicious circumstances arise,' and, in case anyone had missed the point of his remarks, he added. 'They will examine closely all our possible motives and opportunities for murdering Emma.'

He was plainly gratified by the uproar of outrage, protest, and amazement.

'Who on earth's talking about murder!' husked Betsie's voice through it all. 'We don't even know that she's dead!'

The dining-room door flew open. A wild white face, with round, staring, maniacal eyes surrounded by lank and flying hair, entered. In a high shriek it said it had killed its darling Emma.

Once more the dinner-party froze into attitudes of stunned horror, all its mouths open.

'I didn't mean it!' the scream went on, coming further into the room, and waving its long thin arms in the air. 'It was a mistake. And now I'll be hanged! I've killed her. I've murdered her! Everyone knows what a sickening row we had this morning about the honey on the ducks . . . and I said I'd kill her . . . I shouted it all over the house . . . and now I have! I'll be hanged . . . .'

Mike said rather tersely that people didn't get hanged these days.

'And do let us try to remember,' said Betsie, 'that she is not, as far as we know, dead.'

The scream changed abruptly into high-pitched moans, and Giles came into the room behind it and told it to shut up.

'You're just making a fool of yourself as usual, Derek,' he said. 'Emma is still quite alive. And the doctor is on his way. Go and get coffee for everybody. Now!'

He grabbed the trainee-cook, spun him round smartly, and propelled him out through the doorway. A sniffle faded away down the hall, and into the kitchen, where closing doors cut off the sound. Giles sighed.

'I suppose it's only temperament,' he said, 'but it does get a bit exhausting.'

Then he looked round the room, and a worried frown crossed his face.

'Oh, I say, you are having a rotten time!' he said. 'Let's go through into the drawing-room, and be more comfortable . . .'

'How can we be comfortable,' said Harriet. 'When poor Emma . . . ?'

'Well, we've got to wait till Dr Simmons comes before we know any more,' Giles said practically. 'We may as well be comfortable while we do it. I take it no one wants to leave before we hear from the doctor?'

'We did think . . .' began Thumper.

'No,' said Harriet, 'we must wait to know what the doctor says. But if the police do have to be called in, *then* we'll get out of it, because of the Protest and all that.'

'Who said anything about police?' asked Giles, in astonishment.

No one told him. He said someone was trying to have everyone on.

'Come on,' he said. 'It's nice and warm in the drawing-room. And brandy all round will be a help.'

He marshalled the uneasy guests, with efficiency, through the double communicating doors from the dining-room to the huge, L-shaped drawing-room. To everyone's unspoken relief, it was as comfortingly warm in there as had been promised.

There was a calmly elegant flavour to the room, which was to be expected in Robin Randall's home, but with deviations that gave added character. A Chinese horse reared with massive grace in an alcove, where lower shelves displayed lovely glass birds, and a bronze Egyptian cat with gold ear-rings. Some crinoline-armchairs were set about the room; but the huge buttoned olive-velvet couches and chairs were Victorian. Small tables and bureaux, glass-fronted cabinets, and two jardinieres, ranged from late Stuart to Regency times. And, because all these were to one man's taste, the room had pleasantly original homogeneity. It lacked the museum touch that sometimes spoils a beautiful room. It was cosy.

The two chandeliers were not lit, but their glittering crystals flashed reflections from the fire, as did the wall-brackets which were alight. Silver columnar candle-lamps were set here and there, where needed. At the back of the house, two long windows reached to within a couple of inches of the floor, and could be used as doors out to the terrace. Their panelled white shutters folded into recesses at the sides. At the moment, the windows were masked by Thames-green velvet curtains on brass poles.

Opposite the entering guests was a wide alcove, with a glassed door in it that led into a conservatory. The door was open, showing glimpses of green foliage, flower colours, white furniture, and feathery spray from a little fountain.

The fire was burning in a stone Georgian fireplace adding to the sense of welcome extended by the room . . . though the warmth was mainly due to tactful central heating. The dinner-party, for all its varied anxieties, felt itself soothed and distracted. It found seats to satisfy individual tastes, and sank into them. Betsie instantly sprang up again, as a heap of pale-grey fur in the chair rose screaming into the air. When everyone's nerves had calmed sufficiently to realise what it was, it turned out to be the cat, Chin-Chin. Betsie went and sat as far away from him as she could get, and Giles stroked and soothed the creature until he deigned to lie down again, and narrow his turquoise eyes. But even narrowed they still glared balefully at Betsie.

He was not the easiest of cats. The undisputed god of the household, and the only living thing whose anger was cravenly feared by Emma, he was the bastard son of a Blue-Point Siamese and a Silver Tabby. Disqualified from a local cat-show (Most Beautiful Cat Class) for biting the judge, he had proved, according to Emma, his discriminating good taste. Having dealt with Chin-Chin, Giles now organised Mike and Thumper into handing brandy round, as fast as he could pour it into glasses.

Slowly, people began to feel themselves sufficiently restored to attempt light social chat. With the inevitable exception of Mr Bloot, who found a silver dish of bonbons, and concentrated on that.

Betsie produced a small notebook from her handbag, and tried to interview Harriet on her opinion of the present Government. Crossing things out as fast as she wrote them down, she decided to change her line of questioning. But Harriet's views on the Opposition were quite as unprintable.

Mike Peel tried to bribe Giles into appearing on television, to be grilled by one of the more sadistic inquisitors on the subject of 'Loyalty to a Difficult Boss'. And Giles stammered and stuttered with the vehemance of his refusal.

'Oh, very well. *Be* faithful unto death!' said Mike. 'What about persuading Emma, when she recovers, to meet the editors of 'The Weekly Feline' and 'The Monthly Doggy World', to discuss her contributions to animal charities?'

Giles said that Emma played no favourites. She would also have to be allowed to meet the representatives of the 'Kindness to Moths Society', and the 'Researchers into Therapeutic Seances League'.

'Are those real?' said Mike, excitedly.

'Probably,' Giles gave him a mixed look, of innocence, sincerity, and total implausability. 'You'd hardly believe the nut-cases in which this sceptred isle is knee-deep. And all of them wanting to be financially supported by someone else.'

'I can believe anything I want to,' Mike told him.

'Like the White Queen?'

'How dare you!'

Mrs Locke was explaining to Amy Barr, in detail, the exact way that B.L. liked his early morning tea; and Amy was nodding gravely, almost as though she cared, while all the time her eyes kept sliding sideways to dwell admiringly on a darkly magnificent oil painting of her host. She thought it absolutely beautiful.

Maybelle regaled Harriet with a weird account of a clairvoyant who had foretold that she (Maybelle) would one day wear a crown. She wondered if it meant she (Maybelle) was going to marry royalty. Harriet said perhaps it meant a heavenly crown, though adding that it seemed a bit unlikely. Equally unlikely, said she. And Maybelle said that she (Harriet) was being just a tiny bit unkind.

If asked, half an hour later, not one of them would remember a word they had said.

'I'd so like to photograph that ghastly cat of yours,' Charles told Robin, 'if he'd only stop looking like the Monster of Monksend when-ever I . . . .'

The front-door bell rang.

'That'll be the doctor!' cried Giles, into an electrified silence, and fled.

The silence lasted while a murmur of voices crossed the hall and went up the stairs. It lasted until Johann flung open the door, and asked what to do about coffee?

'Why not try bringing it, love?' suggested Mike Peel.

'Because Derek is tying a rope to that hat-hook on the back door,' blurted the German. 'He say he will himself hang, rather than be arrested.'

'Not there, he won't,' said Harriet. 'The hook isn't high enough.'

Giles came back. He told them, with relief, that Emma had recovered consciousness some time before. But added that she had been terribly sick.

'There!' said Mrs Locke 'Something she ate, perhaps.'

Maybelle tittered. Mike Peel choked on his brandy. Johann said what about Derek? And Thumper said give him a cup of Horlicks. Johann marched from the room, saying he would rather give him a cup of arsenic.

'Has he got some?' wondered Charles, mildly, as the door closed.

Giles crossed the big room, and leaned over the photographer, who was sunk so deeply in a great armchair that only the top of his white curly head was presented to the anxious gaze of the other man. Beneath his breath, Giles begged him not to start any fresh hares running.

'Why not?' murmured Charles. 'Everyone is loving the suspense. What would *you* care to talk about? Those proofs of my new photographs of Emma? The ones she tore up, and sent back in an unstamped envelope?'

Realising that quite a few people were listening to this disclosure, Giles gave a deep, merry laugh. He said the proofs had been a little blurred . . . .

'Or too unblurred,' said Charles. 'After all, in the immortal words of another photographer, *I* am two years older than when I took the previous batch. The prize picture.'

'How old *is* Emma, now?' asked Maybelle, innocently.

Giles said she was thirty-six.

'Oh, I don't mean officially! I mean actually.'

'The same.'

'Well,' said Betsie, 'what's a couple of years, here or there? I admit to forty-seven, and everyone thinks I must be at least sixty to go that far.'

Charles said if people were going to discuss ages, he would claim the right of the oldest party present to change the subject. He got a very sweet smile from Mrs Locke.

'So . . .' he went on, 'Has anyone seen the new play at the Royal Court? The one where the man rapes his mother in full view of the audience.'

If he wished to startle the gathering, he failed. Mrs Locke said shyly that she preferred Ivor Novello. Amy Barr, surprisingly, said the play to which he alluded was not at the Royal Court, but in a sort of cellar called The Abattoir Theatre. And Thumper said it sounded old hat, anyway.

'That theme,' he stated, 'has just about been done to death.'

B.L. had been sunk in brooding thought for some time. Now he set down his glass and frowned at everyone.

'I would like this understood fully by the whole lot of you,' said he.

33

'Whatever the cause of Emma's illness, there will be no spreading of malicious rumours . . . either in writing or gossip.'

He turned cold eyes on Betsie, who stared coldly back. He looked at Maybelle, who smiled.

'Darling,' said Betsie, 'don't worry your pretty little old head! If Emma dies, we'll all be as kind or as foul as our natures permit. If she recovers, we will try to be circumspect. I speak, of course, only for myself.'

'She'll recover!' said Giles, loudly. 'She'll be all right. She must!'

Several of the women, and Thumper, made soothing noises at him.

'I'm sorry,' he said. 'I didn't mean to shout. But I . . . well, it hasn't exactly been a care-free evening for anyone.'

If this struck his hearers as the understatement of his life, no one said so. Most of them rallied to him in a way that paid tribute to his popularity. Indeed, for a while the small-talk sounded almost natural. Then the door opened; and the instant pause, the quickly-turned heads, the sudden rigidity of the whole party, proclaimed the tension.

'Robin . . . how is she?' said Giles, breathlessly.

Their host went to a side table to get some brandy. He looked strained. The lines round his mouth were even deeper than usual. But he smiled at his guests, and said that Emma was feeling a great deal better.

'The doctor is staying awhile. He's telephoned to his partner for some pills. And he's coming down to join us for some coffee. Is there coffee?'

Harriet put her finger on the bell push by the fireplace.

'But, Robin . . .' said Giles, 'does he know what . . . I mean, can Doctor Simmons tell what caused . . . what made Emma . . . .?'

'Relax,' said Robin. 'Calm down, my dear boy. Simmons can't possibly tell what upset her, unless he can find out exactly what she ate and drank this evening.'

'Ah,' said Maybelle, 'you know I had an idea that the shrimp sauce wasn't quite . . . .'

'Bloody rubbish you talk, woman!' snarled Johann from the doorway. 'There nothing wrong was with any of the food. *Es ist nicht wahr!* All lies! The wickedness is in the toadstools that Derek serve to Emma alone!'

The trainee cook looked even more dramatic than he knew. Framed in the open door, the light picking glints in the fair hair that tangled on his forehead, his china-blue eyes staring wildly at the riveted company, he looked extraordinary.

34

'Let the police come,' said he. 'For the dragging away of Derek to be hung.'

'Johann,' said Robin, in bored tones, 'would you please cease to play Kean as Hamlet, and pull yourself together. Emma did not gorge toadstools all by herself in a corner. And the police, since you mention them, would take a very dim view of slanderous accusations being hurled about.'

'Is not the slander!' shouted Johann. 'I tell you, Derek and the poor Emma have the row unbelievable because she say he is too ugly and stupid to make appearance on telly . . . .'

'Johann!'

'Sir Robin, sir, she is your wife. Is it to hush up the crime you choose? That she has the Fool's Mushroom been given . . . on purpose . . . .?'

'Excuse me,' said a voice in the hall behind him.

Surprised, he started aside, and a man came past him into the room. Robin went to meet him.

'Ah,' he said, 'Doctor Simmons.'

Before he could begin a round of introductions, Johann came back into the limelight by moving forward, and saying loudly:

'I come to ask how many for coffee.'

'Don't be silly,' said Robin. 'Just bring lots.'

'And before you go,' put in the doctor, 'one word with you, young man. I heard what you were saying, and it was pernicious poppycock. Fool's Mushroom, as you call it, is a killer. Had Lady Randall eaten any, she would now be dead or dying, instead of well on the way to recovery. Let us have no more ill-informed nonsense.'

Robin shut the door on Johann's aggrieved face, led the doctor to the centre of the hearth, and introduced the assembly to him. Simmons nodded gravely to everyone, and took the brandy that Giles handed him. He was a portly, elderly man, balding and grey. With his hairy tweeds and yellow waistcoat, he might have been a determinedly rural stockbroker, keeping blood-sports drearily going in an attempt to ape the extinct country squires. In fact, he was strictly an indoor man, with a passion for chess.

In reply to mainly sincere enquiries, he said Emma was dozing.

'She'll have something to make her sleep properly when my partner arrives,' he said. 'By tomorrow she should be quite comfortable. A nasty attack, and very alarming for you all.'

'And what did cause it?' asked Maybelle. 'Shrimps, by any chance?'

'Oh, for God's sake!' said Giles and Mike Peel, together.

'Don't go on and on, dear,' said Betsie. 'It's beginning to be the least

35

fraction boring! We all ate shrimps, and no one else was carried off writhing.'

'I really would leave it to the experts, Miss Warwick,' suggested Charles. 'Do you know anything about toxicology?'

'Do you?' said Maybelle.

Charles murmured that he had once read a book. B.L. cleared his throat pompously and wanted to know if the doctor intended to call in the police. Doctor Simmons, rather regretfully, said the opportunity had been denied him.

'From the symptoms, both observed and reported,' he went on, 'I would normally suspect some kind of poisoning. Whether accidental or not would depend on analysis of what she had been eating. But Lady Randall has refused to allow any sort of analysis. She says she felt ill before dinner. I am forced to take her word for it.'

'That's splendid,' said B.L. 'So there's no possible reason for any publicity, or discussion, or dragging in the police . . . .'

'I would be happy,' interrupted Robin, 'to drag in Scotland Yard, M.I.5, James Bond, and the Ku Klux Klan, if there's the slightest suspicion that anyone tried to harm Emma!'

People gave him surprised glances. Such vehemence was unusual from him. But, of course, the circumstances were unusual.

Charles, burrowing back deeper into his chair in a way that seemed likely to dislocate his spine, said he would be delighted to support Robin in his statement.

'It's a shame, if we aren't going to fetch in the law,' said he. 'There are those here present who, skilfully photographed in handcuffs, might win me a prize for This Year's Most Astounding Picture.'

Harriet had been crouching on a rug, and she now uncoiled and went to join Thumper by the conservatory door.

'Beloved Uncle Robin,' she said, 'I'm glad we don't have to tangle with the Fuzz. They'd only arrest us, and confuse the issue.'

Catching the doctor's interested eye, she gave him a grin through her hair.

'I promised Mummy not to be arrested again this month,' she told him. 'It's been rather a busy season for Protesting, you see. There's so many things one can't *not* protest about, aren't there?'

'Oh, decidedly,' said Simmons.

'It'll all be easier, when I'm eighteen. I can be arrested every day if I choose. But for the next twelve months,' said Harriet, 'it does seem only fair to Mummy . . . .'

'Apart from all that,' said Giles, 'can we ask everyone here not to talk about what happened tonight?'

There was a murmur of reassurance from various people in the room. And one or two noticeable abstentions.

'There's nothing to talk about,' said the doctor. 'Chit-chat about poison and shrimps, and so forth, is quite meaningless. There is nothing whatever to show that Lady Randall is anything but the victim of a stomach-ache. Natural causes. To hint at more might be heavily actionable. Just one word with you, Sir Robin . . . .'

He drew Robin aside. Giles and Charles started a loudish discussion on the release of press photographs of Emma, to drown their quiet conversation.

'Of course I wanted some samples for testing,' said the doctor. 'But your wife managed to get to the lavatory before she was sick. Several times. One cannot but admire her determination and thoroughness. She has refused, most emphatically, the use of a stomach pump. She told me it would be bad publicity for her, if there was any talk of her being poisoned at her own table. Well . . . I wonder. But there's nothing I can do, in the face of her stubbornness . . . and gallantry. But I do advise you to keep an eye on what she's given to eat during the next few days. And if you know of any possible enemy . . . .'

He stopped. Robin's face was set like stone. The doctor clasped his arm briefly, and said he was probably making too much of it, anyway.

'I've a suspicious mind,' he said, 'and your wife most likely knows best.'

'I'll watch her,' said Robin, grimly.

'Oh, I say!' came a sudden cry from Maybelle. 'Where are those dreadful children?'

'If,' said Charles, 'you mean the ones I think you mean, they went thataway.'

He waved a languid hand towards the conservatory. Mike went to the door of it, and peered in. But the dimly-lit, leafy place was empty.

'They've gone into the garden,' said Mike, sounding amused. 'Probably bolting for it, in case someone changes his mind and calls the cops.'

'Extraordinary behaviour,' rasped B.L. 'Most uncouth. But then they weren't . . . .'

Regretfully, he halted his remarks, remembering that the creatures were under the protection of his host. Even B.L. knew sometimes when to stop.

At this moment, the drawing-room door from the hall flew open. Three people were seen trying to get into the room.

37

'Let me by!' Derek was bleating, thrusting with both elbows. 'Get out of my way, you great fat Crippen!'

'Go into there you shall not,' the other man was trying to block him by sheer bulk and weight. 'Blame me, is your plan. Lie you would, skinny Judas! Titus the Oat! Litter! Trashy-cook!'

Derek kicked him savagely on the shin.

Roaring unintelligible German oaths, Johann grabbed Derek's hair.

As Robin and Giles moved into action, Lynn slithered past the two cooks into the room.

'Doctor Simmons,' she said, 'Emma is awake again.'

'Not sick?'

'No, no. Just weak, and a bit tearful. Will you go up?'

'Of course.'

He patted her twisting hands kindly, and said under his breath:

'She hasn't changed her mind about telling me anything? Still the same story?'

Lynn nodded.

'Well, you go and sit down,' said the doctor. 'Have some coffee, if it ever arrives. I'll stay with Emma till Cochrane comes with the pills. Then she'll go off soundly.'

Robin and Giles had halted to hear this interchange, and now the doctor went to the door, and addressed the frozen tangle there.

'Excuse me, please.'

Derek and Johann sprang apart, and he went quietly out to the hall, and up the stairs. Giles stalked to the trainee-cooks, glaring, and told them to stop being such clowns and get the coffee. Derek, adjusting his collar and blinking pink-rimmed eyes, said life was intolerable. Giles said it wasn't so side-splittingly jolly for anyone at the moment.

'Buzz off!' he demanded.

'Buzz I will,' said Johann. 'But buzz back I also will, if Derek to blame me try for the murder.'

'*What* murder!' hissed Giles.

'He say I funny things put in oysters. What would anyone put in oysters, I ask, that is not there already? Who would anything add, except maybe a drop of lemon-juice. The shell open, there he lie. The oyster perfect. What more could be?'

'A pearl?' suggested Charles.

'Get the blasted coffee!' said Robin.

The cooks withdrew, struck by something in his tone that suggested he might be getting tired of them. Giles closed the door with a thud, and apologised to the company for the service.

'Those two are raving mad,' he said. 'If anyone ever did get murdered in this house, it would be one of them. Or *by* one of them.'

He went to get himself more brandy.

Lynn had been saying something quietly to Robin, and now he put an arm round her shoulders.

'Tell them, my dear,' he said. 'It confirms what Doctor Simmons told us. Go on, Lynn.'

The girl looked pale and rather shaken. She sighed, straightening herself with an effort. She said Emma had wakened about ten minutes previously.

'She was very worried,' said Lynn. 'Worried what people might be saying. You know . . . laughing at her, and . . . she thought some unkind things might be said . . . .'

She gave a quick look round the room, avoiding Maybelle's eye with difficulty, and then went on:

'She was . . . not strong enough to say much. But she clutched my hand . . . .'

Unconsciously, she lifted one hand to show the little indentations on its back.

'She asked me to tell you all that she felt extremely ill before we began to have dinner.'

'Fancy!' said Maybelle.

'*Long* before we had dinner,' said Lynn, firmly.

This produced a small outburst of conjecture and speculation.

'Means she may be coming down with something,' said Mike Peel.

'Appendicitis!' groaned B.L. 'An operation!'

'What did she have for tea?' asked Maybelle, with interest. 'Home-made cakes?'

Lynn's deep voice topped the others.

'It was nothing that she ate. No illness. It was a stomach-upset. She does get them from time to time. Don't make me spell it out.'

'Poor lamb,' said Mrs Locke. 'I used to be just the same.'

'She says she's terribly sorry to spoil the party,' continued Lynn. 'She doesn't want anyone to worry about her. She's perfectly all right, now. Just tired, after . . . after all that pain and nausea.'

'It's a shame,' said Betsie. 'Tell her how sorry we are, too. And *she* mustn't worry about *us*.'

'Hear, hear!' said Mike.

'So will you please go on as if nothing had happened,' Lynn finished her reportage of Emma's words. 'That's what she asked me to tell you.'

She turned to go, but found Mrs Locke blocking her way to the door.

'Lady Randall can do without you for a while,' said the plain woman, who seemed not to need the aid of cliches at the moment. 'You heard what the doctor said, Miss Sanderson. Sit down, and get your breath. There's some coffee on its way . . . I hope . . . and you look as if you could do with a cup.'

She led the girl to a chair, and put her into it.

'Now, don't all look at her,' she told the others. 'Leave her alone. She's worn out. Just go on talking, do.'

To set an example, she seated herself on a couch beside Miss Amy Barr, and asked casually how she liked working for Mr Locke.

'Merry as a marriage-bell!' said Amy.

She then put her hands over her mouth and stared apologetically at her boss's wife. But that lady only nodded, and said she knew what Miss Barr meant. They both glanced at B.L.. But the man was haranguing his host, oblivious to any voice but his own.

'You must understand, Sir Robin,' he was saying, ponderously, 'that I'm not being callous about Emma. I have to make sure she'll be available for the programme that is now under way. After all, it's the most important thing in her life, isn't it?'

'You think so?' Robin sounded faintly amused but polite.

Yet he was clearly not his usual self, for he absently pushed Chin-Chin out of the big chair, and sat down. There was a frightful yell of astonishment and rage from the cat, that rang round the room and startled everyone. The creature stared at Robin with mad blue eyes, puffing himself out into a terrifying spectacle of savagery.

'Oh, sorry!' said the man.

He stretched a placatory hand towards the cat, but it got him nowhere. Chin-Chin said something appalling, and stalked with affrontedly swinging tail into the conservatory.

'He won't speak to me now for days,' said Robin.

'And he's gone to eat all the buds off the . . .' began Lynn.

But B.L. was not to be diverted by the antics of anyone. He stood over Robin, raised his voice, and clarified his views on the troubled evening.

'Everything,' said he, 'is settled satisfactorily. No accident with food. No crime. No mystery or scandal. Just a normal stomach-ache. Poor Emma, of course. Of course. But nothing for anyone to worry about. She'll be able to rehearse on Friday at 2 p.m. That's when you've arranged a run, isn't it, Mike?'

'Er . . . yes. And a meeting with the cast, and a sort of briefing on Thursday afternoon if Emma is able . . . .'

'She will be able,' stated B.L. And it was a statement, not a hopeful wish.

'God's in his heaven,' said Betsie Bloot. 'All's right with the world of big business!'

The coffee arrived at last.

*Chapter five*

## SLIGHT PAUSE FOR BREATH

The manner of its serving reduced the recipients of the coffee to nervous apathy.

Derek poured from lovely Georgian silver pots; Johann carried the cups round; then they offered cream jugs and sugar bowls. Mistrust and spite flickered between the two cooks like sheet-lightning. Apart from meaningless mumbles which might be construed as queries regarding the guests' views on cream and sugar, the ritual was conducted in silence. A sense of relief prevailed when the two left the room.

The first sips of coffee had barely been taken when the front door bell rang. This turned out to signal the arrival of the doctor's partner. With polite regrets for leaving his guests for a while, Robin went and escorted him upstairs.

Conversation broke out in the drawing-room. It would smack of cowardice to be the first to rise and go home. And Giles and Lynn were trying so hard, poor dears, to keep the atmosphere of a normal dinner-party going. Most of the guests backed them up to the extent of their ability.

Betsie even managed to raise a general laugh, when she told Lynn how lucky she was to be beautiful.

'The way a plain woman has to work,' said she, 'is something cruel! Look at me, dear. Like a horse – eighteen hours a day – just to keep up, never mind make progress. And someone lovely, like Emma, or you, dear, can just blink your big eyes and some man will come pounding up to help you. It's bitter! To hell with Woman's Lib,' said Betsie. 'There are times when a great big hand is very welcome.'

'I work hard, too,' said Lynn, gently.

'Yes, darling, of course. But you do get a lot more out of life than I do, for all me money and me fame! I mean,' said Betsie, 'what *have* I got!'

She was, to be frank, a little the worse for wear on brandy and tension. The laughter had quickly died away, and no one dared to glance towards the munching Mr Bloot.

A little later, there were voices and footsteps in the hall. Then Robin came in to say the doctors had gone, and Emma had settled down to sleep. The party decided it was in order now to make a move. In spite of rather luke-warm protests from their host and Giles, the guests moved. They left sympathetic messages for Emma, to be relayed to her the following morning, together with compliments about the lovely dinner ('most of it perfectly edible' – Maybelle).

Mike offered to drive Amy Barr to her flat in Greenwich, which was kind of him as he lived in Hampstead, and they went off together, Amy's last look dwelling on the tired face of Robin. The Lockes glided away in state and a Bentley. Charles said no one was to laugh, but he would save her a hire-car, and drive Maybelle home. No one laughed. She thanked him sweetly, and sent him to bring his car right up to the front door. Hearing this, Betsie instantly dispatched her still-chewing husband to bring their car right to the door.

While waiting, Maybelle turned her smile on Robin.

'Darling,' said she, 'I promise not to utter one adverse word about the shrimps, or any other – doubtful – topic. Not to anyone. Not if they offer vast payment. We all heard what poor Emma had to say about her tum, and of course no one would be rude enough to doubt it. Which is just as well, when you think of the hoot of mirth that would go round if – for instance – the rumour spread that the dear woman was trying to poison a rival, and got the plates mixed, and ate whatever-it-was herself!'

She gave a peal of gay laughter. Robin stared at her without expression. And Betsie gave her a dig in the ribs that changed the peal to a yelp.

'Your little mouth,' said Betsie, 'had better resemble that of a closed clam! People might add two and two, and come up with the idea that a less famous cook tried to poison her rival, and *succeeded* – almost. If the police had been called in, would you have let them examine that very large sequinned bag of yours? I am, of course, joking.'

The ladies exchanged sneers.

Their respective cars, not before time, drew up at the foot of the steps. Charles had just managed to be in front. Betsie bared her teeth at Maybelle, who smirked.

At long last, the party was over.

While Robin had been speeding his parting guests, Giles had been trying to relax. Sprawled among the crumpled cushions on a great Chesterfield in the drawing-room, he shut his eyes, and drew some long deep breaths. Someone had told him this was a good way to calm the nerves. It had been quite a party. Now, alone, no demand was being made on him to be cheerful, soothing, or optimistic. There were no combatants to be separated. No family row to referee. He could just slump. Giles, with a glorious sense of release, slumped.

Lynn had gone through to the kitchen. Robin had asked her to provide a Thermos jug of hot milk, to set by Emma's bed, in the unlikely event of the invalid waking during the night. The doctor was sure she would not, but. . . .'

The girl announced her errand, dropped on a bench by one of the long scrubbed tables in the centre of the kitchen, and rubbed her hands across her eyes.

'Careful, doll. You'll unhitch your false lashes,' said Derek, busily rinsing a white Thermos jug at the sink.

'She does not the falsies wear,' bridled Johann.

Lynn yawned, and said neither of them had the slightest idea what she wore, or did not wear, and to mind their own business anyway. She then announced that it had been the longest and least agreeable dinner-party she'd ever had the misfortune to attend.

'What is disagreeing with you, then?' demanded Johann, hovering over a saucepan of milk. 'You eat poison, too?'

'Don't be so stupid, dear,' said Lynn. 'There wasn't anything wrong with the food. How often do you need telling?'

'That's right,' said Derek. 'Drop it, or drop dead!'

The milk stirred lazily, and Johann snapped off the gas. He started to pour the hot liquid into the jug, and Lynn got to her feet. But the German shook his head at her, and told her to rest a while longer. Let Derek take the Thermos upstairs.

'Is good for him, exercise,' he stated. 'Maybe give him muscles here and there, so he look less like a bit of old, wet, knotted string. Go on, *Knabe,*' he told Derek, 'and take the jug to madam's room. I make some tea while you do so, and you shall have a cup if you behave good.'

'*Muchos gracias,*' said Derek.

He took the big jug and went through the doors that slid aside as he stepped on the footplate.

Johann watched him go, and then turned to look at Lynn. She was leaning over her folded arms on the table, eyes closed.

'Hey!' said the man. 'Not to drop off, now. Tell me, Lynn, why does Sir Robin say Emma has stomach-ache? Why does he command us not to mention poison in the . . . ?'

'Johann, you are so irritating! You *know* Emma wasn't poisoned.'

'Who says?'

'*She* says! And she should know. She felt ill long before she ate any dinner. So there's no question at all of. . . .'

'Huh!' said Johann, scowling. 'Is the first I hear that Emma have funny stomach.'

44

Lynn straightened her shoulders. She said with muted force that it was most unlikely Emma would go round telling the whole world of her natural minor ailments.

'Minor?' said Johann. 'To drop unconscious and shrieking at table? With guests?'

'I wish you'd drop unconscious,' snapped Lynn. 'And shrieking,' she added, unkindly. 'For pity's sake let's leave the subject. If you say one more word about it, I'll dash that bowl of lettuce in your face!'

Then she got up, saying she was going to bed and good-night. But the burly young man placed himself quickly between her and the door.

'Not be angry with me, Lynn,' said he.

He put his hands gently on her shoulders, and she shook him off crossly.

'Don't do that!' she said.

His eyes narrowed, and his whole face seemed to coarsen.

'Why do you treat me like a ravening ape?' he said. 'You think I rape you?'

'No – of course not.'

'You make a performance!' said the man, angrily. 'But I am not fooled. I know you're not the shrinking virgin. . . .'

Lynn moved backwards as he came closer, until she was brought up short by a table.

'Johann, please . . .' she said. 'Stop this, will you. It's too late, and I'm too tired for any more scenes.'

'It's for me to be angry. For me to call names. For me to accuse,' snarled Johann.

He put his face close to hers, and glared into her eyes.

'Who with are you sleeping, Lynn?'

Her mouth fell open. Then she shut it with a snap, and glared back.

'Are you mad?' said she.

Johann grabbed her again, and gave her a little shake. His hands were quivering, and it was a credit to his control that he held her lightly. When he spoke, his voice was unsteady.

'No pretend more, Lynn. You know just what I mean. Not to lie, and evade any more. This affair you are having . . . who is the man? I have the right to ask you.'

'Let go,' said Lynn, 'or I'll scream! I'll yell the house down! That's a promise.'

'But I insist that you tell me. . . .'

'I'll tell you nothing! You've no right to question me, or to touch me. You know I hate being touched.'

'I know you pretend to hate it. Pretend to be so modest – so virtuous – pure! Huh!' said Johann. 'Innocent as a lamb, eh? All lies! I know better. Tell me who is . . . ?'

'I'll count three,' said Lynn, 'and then start screaming. One!'

The man hesitated. Then, with reluctance, he released her. Lynn went past him quickly to the door. She hesitated there, and turned back.

'Johann' – she drew a long breath, and spoke more kindly – 'you mustn't go on like this. I'm sorry you feel the way you do about me. But it isn't my fault. You know I've never encouraged you. Be honest, Johann, and admit it. I've told you often that I like you – but nothing more. I've tried to make you see. . . .'

'I see very clear!' The man's expression changed from anger to despair. 'There's no way I can stop my feelings. Even knowing you are only pretending innocence! No . . . don't go, *liebchen!* Lynn . . . I've asked you to marry me. You are not truly the girl to love outside marriage. Is not right for you. So, I go on . . . asking . . . begging you to think. . . .'

'Not tonight you won't,' said Lynn. 'I think you're just indulging in a drama of tragic romance, my dear. Ask as much as you like, I'll only go on saying no. So let's just stay friends. And now, goodnight.'

The pair was so engrossed in its problems, that the sliding sound went unnoticed of doors opening to admit Derek. His voice took them by surprise.

'Bitch!' he mewled.

'What?' said Lynn and Johann, together.

They stared, open-mouthed, at the thin figure at the door. Its eyes had filled with tears of rage, and it proceeded to elaborate its theme.

'Disgusting cow! Talking like that to Johann, when we all know the filthy way you've led him on! No one could miss it, revolting bitch! Now you say "no",' he savagely mimicked Lynn's voice, 'just to see the poor bastard crawl. With his great, silly tongue lolling out!'

Johann emerged from a sort of trance.

'Enough!' he shouted.

He strode across to Derek, and Derek slapped his face resoundingly.

'Eeeh!' said Johann.

He seized the other and shook him until it seemed his head might come off.

'Eeeh!' shrieked Derek.

'Stop that!' cried Lynn. 'Johann . . . no! Put him down!'

She sounded as though she was ordering a large, badly-trained dog to heel. But her voice could not top the uproar in the kitchen. Johann was rasping a stream of German oaths, and Derek was just a thin wail under whirling hair. Yet certain unpleasant words emerged from his wailing.

'. . . bitch! Filthy . . . ! Revolting . . . ! Sleeping with Robin . . . !'

'I kill you!' brayed Johann.

Then he dropped Derek with a thump on the floor.

'What was that about Robin?'

Mumbling and sniffling, Derek scuttled under a table for safety.

'It's true,' he snarled. 'If Emma'd been murdered, that stupid bitch would have done it. Having it off with Robin. . . .'

'Don't be such a fool, Derek!' said Lynn.

Derek scrambled from under the table on the side furthest from Johann. He pushed his hair aside, looking furious and sick, and said if they didn't like hearing the truth, that wasn't his fault.

'It's time someone told that Boche zombie what's going on,' he added.

'The truth,' said Lynn, her own temper suddenly loosed, 'is that you are in love with this zombie – for the moment – and you think everyone else ought to be! Well, the rest of the world doesn't always share your tastes, which is just as well. Because you're a tramp, you think you can accuse me. . . .'

Derek burst into tears.

He rushed to the far door, that led into the back hall. He fell heavily over a stool, picked himself up and vanished, with an ululating wail. The back door was heard to open and slam. There was a clonk and tinkle as some milk-bottles were sent flying. Then silence returned.

'Into the night,' said Lynn.

Johann drew a long, shuddering breath. He went heavily to get a drink of water from a tap. He drained the glass before he spoke again.

'You make me sick!' said he. 'You and he, both. He to sleep with me wishes. You sleeping with someone else are. Both are the sluts. And I despise you!'

'Splendid!' snapped Lynn. 'It makes a nice change from all the vows of deathless passion. All the poems and letters filled with glorious devotion and flattery. . . .'

'You mock my poems?' Johann sounded amazed and outraged. 'But you told me they are of beauty . . . of merit. They rhyme.'

'Oh, they'll pass. They're all right,' said the girl, wearily.

'All right? The cries of my despair! But in them I write all that you will never let me speak. Lynn, they tell you how I love you . . . worship you. . . .'

'Goodnight, Johann,' said Lynn, at the door.

47

'Goodnight then, slut!' snapped her worshipper. 'I find out who is your lover. Then is possible will be some real killing!'

'Rubbish!'

She stamped on the floor-plate, marched through the parted doors, and collided with Giles. He coughed, recovered his balance, and put out a hand to steady the girl.

'I heard the yelling,' said he, 'and came to see what was going on.'

'It was nothing at all,' Lynn told him, firmly. 'Just a silly argument. I'm off.'

She headed for the main staircase, and Giles shrugged and followed.

By himself, in the great shining kitchen, Johann glowered round at the rows of pots and pans; copper, steel, and cast-iron. China gleamed cleanly; so did the glass fronts of store-cupboards. Very deliberately, he crossed the room and lifted a large pottery bowl containing about two dozen eggs. He raised it above his head, and dashed the whole thing to the floor.

'Ho!' said he. 'There's some cleaning-up for someone!'

He stalked away through the back hall, and up the little staircase, to his bed. He left all the kitchen lights on for Derek, so that he could find the final and messiest chore of a fairly messy day.

'Lynn,' said Giles, softly.

They were just outside the girl's bedroom, and her hand was on the brass door-knob. She smiled with weary affection into the man's earnest face.

'It *has* been a wearing day,' said Giles, understating again. 'But at long last it's over now. Don't let any of it keep you awake, love. Nothing happened, really. Just a lot of very silly talk, and an unlucky bout of sickness. . . .'

'Are you staying here tonight?' asked Lynn.

'Upstairs, yes. I could drive home, but honestly, my head's spinning and I'd probably end in a ditch.'

He looked at the dark smudges of strain under the girl's eyes. He said she should take an aspirin or something, and have a decent night's sleep.

'I intend to,' said Lynn.

She leaned forward, and put both hands on the man's chest, staring at him.

'Giles,' she said, 'you didn't . . . ? It wasn't . . . ? Oh, I'm being stupid, but I'm sure Emma ate something odd. You didn't do anything silly, did you?'

'Such as what?' said Giles, in amazement.

'Well . . . such as giving her whatever made her sick. Yes, I know. I'm

48

being a perfect fool! But . . . you did have an awful row with her, about Maybelle Warwick. She did say some terrible things to you. She sacked you! Darling, you might have thought it would serve her right, if she looked a fool in front of. . . .'

Giles firmly collected the girl into his arms, and smiled down into her face.

'Sweetheart,' he said, 'just get two things into your lovely, mad brain. One, Emma is always sacking me, and saying terrible things. Two, it would take more than a tiff about Maybelle Warwick to get me dropping venom into anyone's food. Oh, and three, you're letting your imagination run away with you.'

He kissed her then, tenderly and thoroughly.

'What's more,' he added, lifting his head reluctantly at last, 'I may borrow a couple of those aspirins for myself.'

'Come in. Be my guest,' said Lynn, opening her door.

The man smothered a quiet laugh.

'If anyone heard that!' said he.

She smiled sleepily, and went into the dark room. The door closed on the two of them.

*Chapter six*

## ENTREE ... AND EXIT

Not surprisingly, no one got up early the following day.

At about eleven, people began to meet each other mooning about in dressing-gowns. They exchanged greetings, asking what sort of night had just been spent. And most answered truthfully, that it had been middling to rotten.

Of them all, Robin seemed most himself. He told all who asked – which was everyone – that Emma had slept soundly, and would be getting up for tea. He looked with mild interest at the white faces, pink-rimmed eyes (Derek), bitten lips (Johann), languid mouth (Lynn), and the slightly remote expression of Giles. He made no comment on any of them. Robin was quite an expert on minding his own business.

True to her promise, Emma came down to the drawing-room at about half-past three, wearing a highly becoming silk kaftan, a fine cashmere shawl, and a tremulous smile. She moved with care, and accepted the sympathetic greetings of the others with gratitude, begging them to forgive yesterday's appalling exhibition. They murmured reassurance. She then gave way to what Robin called 'a fit of the Recamier', stretching herself gracefully on a one-ended couch. She prepared, like that other formidable lady, to hold court.

It was smallish, as courts go, consisting of her husband, Giles, and Lynn.

'How sweet and kind it was,' said Emma, 'of our Mrs Smart, to come back this afternoon to do out my bedroom. She's working up there like a house-pixie.'

'I would have . . .' began Lynn.

'Not your job, dear,' her employer told her. 'And besides, old Smartie is only too glad of the vast extra sum of money she'll get – not to speak of going home loaded with our gratitude, and baskets of left-over goodies, the old vulture.'

'So sweet and kind a vulture,' murmured Robin.

But he smiled, thinking of Mrs Smart. She was a middle-aged woman who came every morning to sweep and dust. She was what is generally called 'a treasure', and knew it. It would have amazed her to hear

Emma's last remarks about her. She was used to describe herself to various friends and acquaintances (in the village pub, on three evenings a week) as the main prop and stay of the Monksend household.

'I reely can't imagine how they'd get on, if I was to leave 'em in it,' was her theme. 'Ooh, a right lot they are, no mistake! Queer as ten-sided pennies, all of them. Though, rightly, it's that skinny kitchen-fellow who's. . . .'

Her comments were totally predictable always. In fact, she was very fond of her job, with its opportunities for contact with well-known people. This gave her stature among her fellows. The modern equivalent of the old-world system of servants taking precedence according to the social standing of their masters. And as horrid a system. Emma, a passionate Socialist, had no idea of the snobberies committed in her name. She would have been furious.

'I do wonder what the lads are up to now,' she was saying.

There had been so complete a silence from the kitchen department all afternoon that it was beginning to be unnerving. It was not like Derek and Johann not even to be on shouting terms.

'Honestly, I'll be glad when it's tea time,' said Giles. 'At least we'll hear the patter of their tiny feet!'

'I'd rather hear a row than a long pause,' said Emma.

But when at last the silver tea-trays were brought, the pinched faces and heavy breathing of their bearers made everyone else feel nervous. And when Derek set down some spoons with a clatter, there was a collective raising of hands to brows.

'Sorry!' he snapped.

Emma covered her eyes, and waved him away. And Lynn said if everyone would excuse her, she would go and wash her hair and have a bath.

'Go ahead,' her employer told her. '*Be* fanatical, darling!'

'Fanatical about what?' asked Lynn.

Emma made a vague gesture.

'Who knows?' said she. 'You're a dark horse.'

'Tally-ho,' said Lynn, and left the room.

Emma now professed herself unable to lift a spoon, let alone a teapot, and asked Giles to pour out.

'Since our Lynn won't even grace the trays for us,' said she.

Then she told them she knew she was being captious. Darling Lynn's little ways being so well-known to all, it was unfair to criticise. Catching her husband's eye, she added that no one *was* criticising. It was merely a fact that, when people were ill, perhaps they expected more of some other people . . . needing extra little attentions. . . .

'Derek!' she snapped, breaking off her discourse, perhaps for lack of conviction. 'What are you putting in that cup!'

'*Trink' das nicht!*' cried Johann, snatching it from Derek. 'Do not touch it!'

Derek had jumped several inches into the air. Now he said sullenly that it was only a bit of lemon.

'For me,' explained Robin, patiently. 'As usual. I take lemon in my tea. Derek was. . . .'

'It isn't ripe,' said Emma.

She herself disliked China tea, saying it tasted like soapy water. She drank only the best Indian, with a little cream. Real cream, not what the Americans call cream which is milk.

Derek now drew himself to his inconsiderable height, his face a mask of icy dignity, and said it had been all right when he'd cut it. Nice, and soft, and fully ripe.

Emma made a mocking noise. She said you didn't go by the feel but by the smell. Derek said it had been unnecessary to smell it. The thing was ripe. This got him a lecture on how to judge the condition of lemons – also grapefruit, peaches, avocados and melons – by their scent alone.

'No one but a fool would pinch them, you'd think,' stated Emma, in peroration. 'Yet people do, until the fruit is all squishy and rotting. Then they think "ha, ha – this is nice and soft and ripe!" '

'Not lemons.' Derek seemed hell-bent on an argument. 'No one pinches lemons.'

'Then how did you know it was soft, without smelling it?'

'It looked right.'

'Shut your fish-like mouth, there's a dear, good boy,' smiled Emma, 'and go and get a decent one for Robin.'

Derek shut his mouth and went. In the kitchen, he deliberately chose another lemon for its colour, holding it as far from his long nose as possible. He brought it back to Emma, declaring his method of choosing it. She sniffed it, pronounced it perfect, and blew him a kiss.

'Horrid little fellow,' said she, 'you think you've put one over on me, don't you? Well, you haven't, beloved! By sheer coincidence, no more, your wild guess matches my skilled diagnosis. Because you can't be wrong *every* time, can you, darling!'

'You must now see,' put in Johann, unexpectedly, 'why it would the madness unthinkable be to let him set foot inside the television studio. He make a right circus of the banquet. . . .'

'Circus is right,' said Derek, 'if you're in there clowning.'

'That will do, thank you,' said Robin.

As Giles poured, the trainees handed round cups, avoiding one another in passing. Emma sighed, rather heavily, and said as soon as she'd finished her tea, she might well copy Lynn's example and have a bath with lots of oil and hot water – to ease some of the stiffness from her bones. Robin said it was a good idea, and that she should go back to bed afterwards.

'Well, I'm for the garden, and a breath of air,' Derek informed them.

He left the room, and Johann, muttering something about prancing apes, followed him out. The patter of their feet died away across the hall.

'Far be it from me,' said Robin, 'to disparage your gifted assistants. . . .'

'They'll both have to go!' snapped Emma. 'I'd rather train a couple of Eskimoes.'

'Specialising in new recipes for blubber?' said Robin.

Giles and Emma laughed. Then Emma's face changed. She looked weary and irritable. The telephone had started ringing from her little office across the hall.

'Oh, Giles!' she said, crossly. 'Surely you let everyone know I'm not available today?'

'Yes, I did. I'm sure I did.'

'It might, of course, be a call for me,' suggested Robin, gently. 'I'm expecting one. And someone might have rung the wrong number.'

Giles struck himself a violent blow on the forehead, and reeled with the pain of it.

'I've gone mad!' he cried.

'Not you, too?' said Robin.

The telephone bell had stopped ringing, and Johann now swung the door wide and announced that the B.B.C. with Madam wished to speak. Giles gave an exclamation, and hurried towards him, looking abashed, contrite, and harassed. It was one of his more involved expressions.

'I'll take it,' he said. 'It's entirely my fault, Emma. I'm sorry. I forgot to put them off. I'd arranged for them to call you this afternoon. It's about that cloak for the programme. I'll tell them to call back tomorrow or something. . . .'

For all her pallor and her weakness, Emma beat him to the door.

'I'll deal with it,' said she. 'It won't take a moment.'

She went out with Johann.

Giles caught Robin's eye, and said again that he was sorry.

'I'm not myself today,' he mourned.

'Obviously,' said the older man, dryly.

53

'Well, it was all those carry-ons yesterday! I feel unstrung. My brain's twisted,' said Giles. 'I'm doing things without thinking. Forgetting things. . . .'

He stopped abruptly. His jaw dropped, and he looked hopelessly at Robin.

'Remembered something?' said the latter.

Giles nodded. He gave a slight gulp.

'Yes,' he said, 'well . . . it's your parcel. . . .'

He paused again.

'Do go on,' said Robin.

'It arrived. Earlier. I put it in your study. I meant to tell you, but I forgot it completely until this minute. It's probably important. . . .'

'How big?'

'What?'

'About how big was this parcel?'

'Oh . . . about . . . this big.'

Giles gestured with his hands, and Robin finished his cup of tea unhurriedly and got up.

'Probably the Hilliard miniatures,' said he. 'Did they arrive by messenger?'

'Yes,' said Giles, sadly. 'From the National Gallery. I signed for them.'

'Definitely the Hilliards, then. I'd better go and take charge of them . . . just in case.'

'In case of what?'

'In case you just happened to toss them into a wastepaper basket. I'd hate to see national treasures consigned to a dustbin and thence to the Municipal Dump. The Gallery wouldn't like it, either,' Robin added, calmly. 'Even if the miniatures aren't genuine, which isn't yet known, they're very fine copies.'

He gave the stricken Giles a fleeting grin, and left the room. Just outside the door he came face to face with Johann.

'Oh, Sir Robin . . . I mean, sir . . . Excuse, but madam is having the row terrible with telly fellow on the phone in there!'

The German waved a large hand towards the closed door of Emma's office across the hall, and burbled on:

'She say fake sable cloak, or no banquet! She speak of broken contracts. But me,' he said, 'I do not listen to overhear.'

'It's to your credit,' said Robin. 'Excuse me.'

Johann stepped aside, and Sir Robin Randall went quietly limping up the staircase. No one could have guessed, from expression or behaviour, how greatly he had looked forward to seeing and handling the precious miniatures. He was not a man who wore his heart anywhere near his sleeve.

Behind him, Johann shrugged his shoulders, stuck his head into the drawing-room, and wagged a finger at Giles.

'You should interference make,' said he, reprovingly. 'Is not for madam's good, this shouting at B.B.C.'

'Mind your own damned business!' snapped Giles, goaded at last beyond bearing. 'Go away! Right away! Go and annoy your admirer in the kitchen.'

'Derek? He is . . . whizz! . . . into gazebo, for sulking.'

'Well, whizz off and join him!'

Johann started to splutter some comment, but a hearty shove cast him to one side. Framed now in the doorway stood Mrs Smart.

'Cut along, sonny,' said she. 'Get on with your work, and stop wasting time.'

The young man glared at her. But he knew her too well to think of arguing with her. He contented himself with a snort and a sneer, and departed.

'There!' said Mrs Smart. 'There's foreigners for you! Nasty tempers, and nasty people. I wouldn't trust any of 'em, not even white ones, down a dark alley with a razor in his hand!'

Giles said he wouldn't trust anyone down a dark alley with a razor in his hand.

Mrs Smart told him he was a caution. She patted her unlikely red hair, that clashed vividly with the colour of her lips. She was wearing a green blouse and skirt, a yellow cardigan and a large apron swathing her lower half. She beamed at Giles, and said obscurely that it was a poor heart that never rejoiced.

'Oh, quite,' said he.

Then he gave a small groan, heaved a sigh, and looked at her pleadingly.

'We're not ourselves today, Mrs Smart,' he informed her. 'Don't take too much notice of anything we say or do. We're all edgy. Lady Randall's illness has upset us. You've heard all about that, I'm sure.'

'Oh, yes, sir! They told me in the kitchen. Ever such strange stuff! Make your hair stand on end to listen. Murder and poison and police and hanging . . . you never heard such rubbish . . . !'

'Didn't I just!' said Giles. 'Well, you can see we're not going to get much sense out of Johann for the moment. And Derek is . . . whizz! . . . to the gazebo for sulking. So will you, like a poppet, clear away the tea-things? They'd drop the lot, the way they're going on.'

Mrs Smart said it surprised her that one bit of china was left unbroken, the way they always went on. She then said she'd be happy to help in any way possible.

'As ever. I've never been one to hold hard and fast by me rights,' she stated. 'What I say is, we're all human.'

Giles cast her a doubtful look. Then he quickly thanked her for her co-operation. He said he had to nip up for a quick look at a contract, but was sure she could deal with everything superbly. She smirked, and said she thought so, too.

Half-way up the stairs, Giles could hear her saying it never hurt anyone to do a little extra for everybody. She was, presumably, talking to a teapot.

She also had a few words for the clock on the mantelshelf. Pushing a strand of hair from her forehead, and pouting at her reflection in the looking-glass that backed it, she told it that the world would be a horrid place if everyone thought only of themselves. Though she could name some! She then turned away and ate two cucumber sandwiches. She piled some ashtrays together. She was carefully choosing among some delicious little cakes, when she heard a low ringing sound. She went to a gold telephone on a side table, putting the cake back on its plate and licking her fingers.

'Hallo,' said she, formally, lifting the receiver. 'Sir Robin Randall's residence.'

'It's me, Mrs Smart,' said Giles's voice on the line. 'I'm only on the house-phone from my study. Could you be an angel, and find my address-book? No, no, it isn't lost . . . it's on the right-hand garden seat below the terrace. I left it there . . . Lady Randall called me in a hurry. I need a number rather urgently. If you would . . . I'll hold on while you get it. . . .'

'Just a sec,' said Mrs Smart, cheerfully.

She snatched up a cake, not the one she had originally handled, and went through the conservatory to the terrace at the back of the house. Murmuring to herself, through crumbs, that the main thing in life was to do for others what you wished they would sometimes do for you, she went down the nearer flight of shallow, stone steps to the lawn, and across the grass to a half-curved, lion-supported, marble seat. The leather-covered book had slipped off the back of it into a clump of lilies, but was easily to be seen. Mrs Smart pounced on it, and scurried quickly back to the drawing-room.

'Here we are,' she told the telephone. 'What name, sir?'

'Bless you,' said Giles. 'It's MacNeill, David MacNeill – and it's a number starting with 235.'

She riffled through the pages of the little book. And said ah yes, here it was. She articulated the numbers as though for the benefit of a backward horse. Giles thanked her and she said it was nothing, and that she'd bring the book up to him.

'Not to worry. . . .'

'Oh, I'm not one to fuss about me poor aching feet,' said Mrs Smart.

As Giles rang off, she licked icing sugar from her purple lips, and trotted upstairs, smiling a saintly smile. She just missed a head-on collision with Johann as he charged downwards. She gasped something about great clumsy Huns, forgetting her halo. And he plunged past her, round under the staircase, and into the kitchen.

The lady tossed her head.

'Coming to something,' she told the banister rail, 'when they acts as if they owned the house!'

Giles was already speaking on the phone when she went through the open door of the office, and she laid the book on his desk with exaggerated caution, received a nod of thanks, and trotted off downstairs again.

While collecting the teacups on to the silver trays, she told them that life was mostly care and trouble, and all that mattered was seeing other people through some of it. Then, she said hopefully, they just might be talked into giving you a hand with yours.

When she carried a tray out to the kitchen, there was no one there.

'Aliens!' she said, with deep contempt.

'Twits!' she said, in case she had left anyone out.

'My God!' she added, loudly. 'What can you expect from a pig but a grunt!'

With this tremendous thought, she went back for the other tea-tray.

Just as she was putting a chocolate whirly-cake in her mouth. . . .

'Help yourself, do,' said Emma, just behind her.

Mrs Smart yelped, and spun round. She mumbled something.

'Go on, dear. Take whatever you fancy,' said Emma, dropping exhaustedly on to the couch she had recently vacated. 'Thank you for coming back this afternoon. You're an angel. Take those cakes home with you. You can eat them all after supper, or something.'

'Well, that's ever so kind. . . .'

'They'll go well with the evening's telly.' A note of bitterness seeped into Emma's voice. 'Sickly cream with sickly television! Stale, stomach-turning stuff! Produced by charlatans to entertain fools!'

'Now, now, dearie!' protested Mrs Smart, shocked. 'You shouldn't.

Reely, you should make allowance. Sometimes it's ever so good. Here, now. . . .'

She came to Emma, and pushed a cushion into a comfortable shape under a silk shoulder. She tucked the ends of a shawl round Emma's feet. She looked with genuine concern at the pale face of her employer.

'They've properly upset you,' she decided. 'What have they been and said?'

'I've upset them a lot more,' said Emma, grimly. 'I told them I wanted *two* imitation sable cloaks. One for the rehearsal. That rocked 'em. Teach them to be funny!'

'Who?'

'The B.B.C., rot it! Arguing with me about clothes. When everything's been settled for *weeks*. Now they try to tell me it would be cheaper to hire a real sable cloak than to have a fake one made. As if I'd ever wear real fur! Good grief,' said Emma, hotly. 'I'm not a fool! Anyone's a fool who tries to compete in looks with the original owner of a fur. No human born can wear a dead animal's coat, and not look an oaf.'

'Emma . . . ,' said Robin, in the doorway.

'They've had all the time in the world to get the cloak finished,' Emma pursued her train of angry thought. 'I suppose they've got a strike of the people who take pins out, or . . .' She noticed her husband. 'Oh, darling . . . I've had such a flaming row with. . . .'

'It doesn't matter.'

'Doesn't *matter!*'

'Not now, Emma. . .'

Suddenly aware of a note in his voice she had never heard before, she turned on the couch to stare at Robin. He was standing stiffly, with a clenched fist against the door-post. His face looked grey.

'What's the matter?' said Emma, in a whisper.

'It's Lynn. She's dead, Emma. I've just found her. In your bath . . . dead, Emma.'

'Lynn? Drowned . . . in my. . . .'

'No,' said Robin. 'Her head . . . ! She's been killed.'

After a moment of total silence, he said:

'Now I'll call the police.'

## Chapter seven

## REMOVE

'Slow down a bit, Darling,' said Detective Chief Superintendent Stillman.

'I'm not speeding, sir.'

'Maybe not, but you are doing forty in a thirty area. Some smart-alec will leap out and book us, and then we'll look proper charlies. Drop down, Darling, like a good fellow.'

The car slowed.

'Silly old fool!' said Darling. 'Who'd go booking a police-car on the job!'

All this, however, he said to himself. Aloud he merely murmured, 'Yes, sir.'

'Silly old fool!' said Sergeant Woolsey, from the right-hand corner of the back seat. 'We're supposed to get there as quickly as possible. I'd have had an escort and a siren!'

He also was speaking to himself. Aloud he said they were just going through Guildford.

'I can read signposts,' said the Superintendent.

'Silly old fool!' said Detective Sergeant George Woolsey and Police Constable Ronald Darling – inside their heads.

'And I know what you're thinking,' said their superior. 'That I'm a silly old fool.'

'No, no, sir!' said the two young policemen, hastily adjusting their minds in case he really could read them.

The car turned left, along a one-way street and down a little hill, and out on to the main road for Dettington. Superintendent Stillman closed his eyes, and wondered what sort of case he was heading for, this time. He reckoned it would be a proper headache. And tricky, too, from all he'd heard about Lady Randall and her set-up. He'd met it all before and never with any pleasure; artists, writers, actors . . . and now, probably, cooks. Temperaments, hysteria, muddle. Any touch of artiness, in his opinion, made people more trouble than a cageful of baboons. Grimly he considered the prospect. It would be a real problem to get any sense out of anyone.

'Why?' he said, aloud. 'Now why couldn't they give me a nice, open-and-shut case of straight bigamy? Something simple.'

'It's a shame,' said his sergeant, and added to himself: 'The poor old sod isn't up to it. He's past it! He'll muck up the whole thing, and retire with a failure to end off his career. Bloody hard luck!'

Young Woolsey was an intelligent man. He knew the Superintendent's record, and respected it. There had been successes – back in the past, and probably by chance. He liked Stillman. He thought the old boy painstaking, steady, and well-meaning. It was not his fault, thought Woolsey, that he'd grown old and dull. Too slow, too humdrum, and far too unimaginative to cope with the sort of thing awaiting him a few miles westward.

The Superintendent was thinking much the same. He glanced at his watch. It was just on half-past six. He sighed sadly. At home now there would be a comfortable old armchair, a real fire, a cup of tea to tide him over till his wife had supper ready, and a lovely pile of rose-growers' catalogues to browse through. His notebook would be to hand, with its growing list of roses without which no one could live – yet which would need about four acres of garden to accommodate them. Even the names were a joy. Rosa Mundi . . . Magenta . . . Moonlight. . . .

George Woolsey looked thoughtfully at his senior officer. He hoped the old fellow was not going to drift into senile slumber. They were almost at the end of their run from London, and he had no wish to start shouting 'Wake up!' in front of the driver.

'Just down the lane here,' said Darling, who had memorised a map before leaving the Yard.

He pulled off the main road, and took to what seemed by comparison a cart track.

Round a few corners, under a line of ancient beechtrees by the verge, over a bridge which allowed a glimpse of some small tributary of the Wey, they came at last to a run of tall brick walls, and an open gate. A policeman stood here, and stepped forward. But when he saw the uniformed driver, he saluted, and waved the car in. Swinging up a gravel drive, Darling brought them to a halt in a wide circular courtyard where several other cars stood nose to tail.

The Superintendent opened his eyes (to the relief of his Sergeant, who was just drawing breath for some galvanising remark) and looked at the stone steps and white-columned front door of Monksend. His quiet dream of roses fled. Reality strode grimly into his mind, which received it with distaste.

'Here we go, then,' said he. 'Say your prayers!'

'Yes, sir,' said Woolsey, and added to himself: 'For *you*, sir.'

He jumped out of the car and went round to open the other door for Stillman. Then he ran up the two wide, shallow steps; before he could find or ring a bell, the door was opened by a constable who had obviously seen their arrival through a hall window.

'Detective Sergeant Woolsey,' said Detective Sergeant Woolsey, rapidly. 'With Detective Chief Superintendent Joseph Stillman. From the Yard.'

'Oh, ah. Been expectin' you,' said the other.

He sketched a salute to the Superintendent as he came to the door and turned to a grim-faced young man who had come into the hall from a door at the far end.

'They're 'ere, sir,' said the constable.

'At last!' said the young man. 'I mean, good.'

He watched with a mixed expression of relief, expectation, and deep gloom, as the Yard men entered the hall. The front door was closed behind them. In the drive, the lights of their car went out.

Stillman had a pleasant greeting for the constable, then he caught Giles's eye, and went over to him, introducing himself and his Sergeant. Giles's expression changed to one of solid gloom, as he surveyed the thin, elderly man, the quiet, gentle face, curly grey hair, and spectacles badly mended on one side with sellotape. The Superintendent gave a little cough, and Giles pulled himself together.

'I'm – very glad to see you, sir,' said he. 'I'm Giles Warrington. I work for Lady Randall.'

'This is a very sad business,' said Stillman.

He looked slowly round the hall, taking in the lay-out of doors and staircase. Giles made an effort to concentrate and be helpful. He said the police doctor had arrived some time back, and was now with Lady Randall in the drawing-room.

'He's been upstairs, of course. He did – all that could be done. There wasn't any more . . .' said Giles. 'He thought he'd attend to Emma till you came. Oh, and Superintendent Fisher is in the library. He had a look round, and took some statements from everybody, and now he's just waiting for you, Mr Stillman.'

Exactly on cue, from a door at the right of the hall, came a thickset man dressed in Irish tweed jacket and slacks. He had a reddish face, white hair and sideboards, and a sense of humour that showed round his eyes and mouth. He held out his hand.

'I'm Henry Fisher,' said he. 'You made very good time from London, sir.'

'I've a very good driver. How do you do, Superintendent. This is my Sergeant, George Woolsey.'

Giles was listening rather impatiently to this exchange of courtesies. Now he broke in:

'Mr Stillman . . . I expect you'd like to talk to Sir Robin and Lady Randall? They're in here. In the drawing-room.'

He went to the double doors at the far end of the hall.

'Just a moment, sir, please,' said Stillman. As Giles turned, he went on gently: 'Of course I want a word with them in due course. But first I'd like to see where this . . . sad occurrence took place. In her bath, I was told.'

'More or less,' said the local Superintendent.

'Really? Well, well. Would you be kind enough, Mr Warrington, to ask the police doctor to join me as soon as he can?'

Giles nodded. He looked worn out. He asked if Stillman needed him, upstairs.

'I've . . . been up there,' he said, hesitantly. 'Just to make sure . . . that I couldn't do anything. But . . . if you want me to show you . . . to explain. . . .'

'No, sir, thank you,' said the Superintendent, kindly. 'Mr Fisher will take me up. If you'd just ask the doctor to spare me a few minutes?'

'Yes, yes, of course.' Giles looked flustered and out of his depth. He bit his lip and said: 'Sir Robin told me to tell you that the library is at your disposal, sir.'

Stillman thanked him, and he went into the drawing-room apathetically.

'This way,' said Fisher.

He began to climb the curving stairs at the left of the hall, and Stillman and Woolsey followed. The former was consciously preparing his mind, as usual, for the first sight of tragedy. However often he had to view these pathetic scenes, he could never grow used to them. He greatly deplored violent death, in every form. It was so rarely caused by genuine accident. One in a thousand cases might happen because of a heart attack, or a burst tyre. For the rest, people were stupid, made mistakes, were absent-minded, played the fool – or lost their heads and killed.

'If only everyone would think more,' mused the Superintendent.

At his heels, his Sergeant looked impassive and austere; inside, he was a seething mass of raw nerves.

'He'll muck it! He's going to bloody muck it!' he was thinking, tensely. 'Talking like everyone's old auntie! "Please . . . if you'll be so kind . . . thank you, sir . . . pray permit me . . . !'" Gawd, that's not the way. Boss 'em around. Make 'em jump. Get some answers while they're good and scared. Maybe clear the whole thing up in half an hour. But he'll ball it up. It'll be a fiasco!'

'This way,' said Fisher, again.

He had turned to the left at the head of the stairs, and crossed the wide landing to open a door. He nodded to a police constable who stood watchfully there, and the man stood back to let the officers enter.

'This is Sir Robin's bedroom,' said Fisher to the Superintendent.

'Really?'

'Well, the bathroom is between his and Lady Randall's room.'

'Is it, indeed?'

'This particular bathroom is.'

Fisher stepped aside to allow Stillman an uninterrupted view of the bedroom. The lights were already switched on, and he stopped to take a careful survey. There were two large windows in the wall opposite the door, which would in daylight command a very fine view of the garden, and fields and trees and river beyond. Very nice, too, thought Stillman.

'I wonder – if I were as rich as these people –' his thoughts drifted, '– would I furnish a room like this for myself? Instead of sharing all Ruthie's frills and chintz?'

Ruthie was Mrs Stillman. She liked what she called 'happy colours', and plenty of the 'woman's touch'. She would not have cared for this room.

It was large and square, and very plain. The walls and carpet were white, and the ceiling was deep grey-green; it contained few ornaments, but these were striking. An oil-painting of a tortured sky, with wet, bright colours in the foreground; some silver; some dark prints; old, severe, shining furniture; a few fine pieces of jade; a bowl filled with yellow roses; two bookcases. . . .

Ruthie would have *hated* this room.

'Good grief!' breathed Sergeant Woolsey. 'That's a Turner.'

'It would be,' said Fisher.

The Sergeant sighed. Then he followed his seniors into an adjoining room, through a door at the right.

Here they all stood for a few moments in silence.

'Unusual, eh?' said Fisher.

Stillman took it that he was referring to the bathroom. Not to that which lay on the floor, with a large towel laid compassionately over its slender length, leaving only the head revealed.

In his customary manner, the Superintendent gazed slowly round the room, filing a mental picture for his later use if required. From where he stood, a window in the left wall would look out on the same view as that from Sir Robin's room. Opposite Stillman was another door which was slightly ajar. The sunken bath lay just right of centre. It was made of dark-green marble, and was perfectly round. Its taps were shaped like white alabaster dolphins, to match the soap-holders. The walls of the room were faced with plain white marble; and the ceiling was marble, too, the same colour as the bath. A thick white carpet covered the floor, with a fluffy golden rug just where some little steps led down into the bath. Right along the wall under the window was a wide, white shelf, carrying bottles and jars, a tall vase with late orange gladioli, and a huge blue alabaster bowl. There were drawn yellow velvet curtains at the window; a golden rail with towels on it; and a large green armchair. To the left of the admiring Stillman, part of the room had been walled off, and through its door could be seen a small window, and a golden-yellow WC. In the right corner of the bathroom, was a very charming stone Aphrodite, only a little smaller than life-size; unexpectedly, but permissably, her only attire was a necklace of yellow crystals. She seemed to be looking down with gentle serenity at the pitiful thing on the floor, that had so recently been Lynn.

'Sir Robin found her in the water,' said Fisher. 'He got her out, of course. He thought – well, hoped – she might still be alive. But you can see her head.'

'Yes,' said Stillman.

'He covered her, and went to telephone us. He'll tell you himself.'

'Yes.'

'I brought our team,' said Fisher. 'But I haven't had them up here. They're waiting on your instructions, Superintendent, of course.'

'Ah. Thank you. Sergeant, will you be kind enough to go and ask the photographer and the finger-print chaps to come up now?'

'Yes, sir.'

Woolsey hurried from the room. He supposed it was nice to be spoken to so politely, but he would rather have received a brusque order, to establish his senior's authority in front of the local officer.

The Superintendent walked carefully round the room looking at its furnishings and decor. Fisher watched him with interest, almost as though he expected an instant explanation of the girl's death. If so, he was disappointed. At last there was the sound of movement in the next room.

'Ah,' said Fisher. 'Here's the mob.'

Two men came into the bathroom, from Robin's bedroom. Stillman greeted the local team, after being introduced to them by Fisher, and waved them into action. Sergeant Woolsey stayed in the doorway.

A man came past him and approached the Superintendent so silently and mousily that the effect was slightly sinister. A small, spindly man whose ears stuck out on either side of his head like the handles of a Grecian urn, but not as becomingly. He had a tiny, white face, and meagre hair. He was quite insignificant, almost invisible. Until he spoke.

'And what,' said he, 'do the mighty London brains make of it?'

His deep bass voice echoed round the room, making some glasses chime on the shelf.

'Er – this is Doctor Knight,' said Fisher, hurriedly. 'Doctor – Detective Chief Superintendent Stillman – and Sergeant – er. . . .'

'Woolsey,' said Woolsey.

The little doctor repeated his original question in exactly the same words. Stillman looked at him placatingly and said it was a bit too soon to tell, wasn't it?

Knight snorted, and slid silently across to stand by the body of Lynn. His pale eyes had no expression at all as he gazed down at it. He said resoundingly that by now even the inadequate and superfluous country coppers might hazard a guess at violent death.

'Well, yes,' said Stillman. 'And I think I would agree with them.'

'Too gracious,' said the doctor.

With a stricken glance at the two London policemen, Fisher crossed to the little man.

'*We* called in the Yard,' he said. 'After due consultation with the Chief Constable. . . .'

'Parkes? Major Jopplestone Henry Parkes wouldn't chance giving a straight opinion if an old hen died of constipation!' said Doctor Knight.

Woolsey choked, and gave an unconvincing cough to cover it.

'London germs!' came Knight's accusing roar.

'Not at all. Merely nerves,' said Stillman. 'Now, if we could just establish a few facts? Oh, and perhaps you might bear in mind, Doctor Knight, that local authorities often prefer to bring in outsiders on a murder case. For an objective view. After all, a local policeman might have killed the girl.'

After a moment, the doctor said this was highly improbable.

'But possible?' said Stillman.

'Oh, I suppose, in theory. . . .'

'Thank you,' said the Superintendent.

65

Fisher cleared his throat cautiously. He said if murder had indeed been committed here, it was best to cope with the matter as efficiently as possible.

'Thank you for your loyalty, Dr Knight,' he added. 'It's appreciated. But it's quite unnecessary, in this case. We chose to call in the Yard for precisely the reasons the Superintendent has given. Now, can we go on from there?'

They did so.

Stillman knelt to examine the body, carefully lifting the tragic head. He saw the hideous wound in the wet hair. . . .

'Poor thing,' he said. 'She'd just washed it. I can smell shampoo.'

'When I first saw her,' said the doctor, 'she was wearing that bath-cap. I took it off to examine her, and her hair was just as you see it now.'

He had indicated a bright orange cap, lying near the wall. It, too, was stained and torn. The Superintendent beckoned the photographer towards it. Then he pointed into the sunken bath, at something beneath the scented cloudy-green water where marblings of blood still floated.

'That?' he said to Fisher.

'I imagine so. We left it there for you to see. I don't think Sir Robin noticed it at all. He didn't say anything about it. But his mind was on other things, naturally. And it isn't all that easy to see unless you're looking closely.'

'Better get it out, George,' Stillman told his Sergeant. 'Very careful. Though I don't suppose there'll be anything like fingerprints on it.'

He looked again at the bathcap, and the photographer kneeling by it for a close-up.

'Funny,' said Stillman. 'My wife's got red hair, and she says there's only one colour a redhead doesn't wear.'

He took a final long look round the bathroom, and went towards the door in the farther wall, saying he supposed this led into Lady Randall's bedroom. Fisher, following, confirmed his guess.

Judging, rightly, that the bathroom had been designed to amuse the lady, and did not reflect Sir Robin's personal taste, Stillman was half prepared now to see a room resembling a set from a Hollywood epic about the fall of the Roman Empire. He was surprised at the calm elegance of what he found.

There were enormous, mirror-fronted, built-in white wardrobes all along the wall opposite the bathroom door. In the middle of them, a recess with a window and a cushioned seat. To the left were two tall sash-windows, also with seats; and, between them, a very delicate columnar plinth of alabaster. Against the inner wall, to the right of the hall doorway, stood an enormous half-tester bed, with brass posts and canopy, hung and covered with Dutch-blue damask. There were dark amethyst walls and ceiling; a pearl-grey carpet and white rugs; a white dressing-table; white chairs, and one great lilac armchair. There were lovely Regency wall-mirrors and candelabra and chandelier. Red roses in silver bowls; shell-pink and white gladioli in glass vases; carved white shelves carrying fine china and glass; a delicate drift of spicy scent.

A dressing-gown was spread over the foot of the bed, with slippers on the rug below. On one of the white bedside tables was a small pile of books. Apart from a normal scattering of odds and ends, the room was tidy. The bedclothes had been neatly turned down, ready for use. Fisher commented on this.

'It seems,' said he, 'that madam spent most of the day in bed. After she got up for tea, the daily woman came up and neatened things ready for her to retire again. That's a Mrs Smart,' he said. 'She came in this afternoon because Lady Randall had been ill. Mostly she only does mornings.'

'I see. And was this Mrs Smart in here when . . . ?' Stillman gestured towards the open door of the bathroom.

'She says not.'

'Well, I'll get her story. . . .'

'You will, indeed!' said Fisher. 'She's bursting to tell all she knows, and a good deal more to the "*real* detectives from the Yard"!'

He grinned, treasuring this insult.

But Stillman had gone over to the bed and was looking down at something among the piled pillows. A limp heap of pale-grey fur, which suddenly lifted a baleful face, and was staring back at him with two completely round turquoise eyes.

'It just woke up,' said the Superintendent. 'How could it sleep through all this disturbance?'

Fisher said he did not suppose for one moment it *had* been asleep.

'Lying there listening,' he hazarded. 'Waiting to be noticed and admired. Strange beasts, cats. Almost looks as if he knows what we're saying.'

'If he's been here all afternoon,' said Stillman, 'I wish he'd tell us what other people have been saying.'

But Chin-Chin was not in the mood for telling tales, if indeed he knew any. He eyed Stillman for a minute or so, and then pretended to relapse into slumber.

The Superintendent, who was no expert on cats yet greatly respected them, moved away. But George Woolsey had a passion for the feline race, and was suddenly overtaken by the mad desire of such fanatics to touch and stroke. With a foolish smile on his rugged features, he bent over the bed and stretched out a big hand.

The cat shot upright, extended itself to become a huge mad-eyed monster, opened its mouth to the full, and gave a scream that skirled through the room like a siren.

'Don't!' said the Sergeant.

'Stop teasing the beast, George,' said his senior.

'Ah,' said the local police officer, before the outraged Woolsey could draw breath to protest, 'I've been warned about that animal. Fussy, he is. Only likes a few people, and screeches if anyone else gets near him. Some voice, he's got, eh?'

He opened the door into the hall to its widest, and Chin-Chin stalked out.

Stillman said they'd better go on now, and have a look at the rest of the rooms. At which point the doctor slid noiselessly towards the door and said he would like to depart.

'I've urgent matters to attend, elsewhere,' he boomed.

The crystal chandelier tinkled overhead, and some rose-petals fell round a bowl.

'Amongst the temporally living,' added Doctor Knight. 'I can do no more for this murdered girl.'

The last adjective hummed deeply through the room, and Stillman looked thoughtful.

'Isn't it possible,' he said, 'that she may have fallen into the bath by accident, and hit her head and drowned?'

'Out of the question, Mr Stillman. I've had a good look at the weapon, and there's no doubt what it was used for. No possible doubt. She was killed by a savage blow on the back of the head, that smashed the occipital bone. Whether she was actually in the bath at the time, or fell in afterwards – or was pushed in – you will no doubt decide, with your expert detecting faculties. The post-mortem will establish that she didn't drown, which will match my own poor guess. Now I'll be off.'

'By all means, sir,' said Stillman, amiably. 'No doubt I'll be asking your advice again, at some near date.'

'No doubt,' said Knight.

He turned to Superintendent Fisher, said he'd know where to find him, added that he would send an ambulance to take the body to the morgue, and left. The Sergeant glared after him.

'Saucy swine!' he snarled to himself. 'Why didn't the old man chew his great flapping ears off!'

'Saucy swine!' thought Fisher. 'This London fellow's a meek old thing. Wonder if he's any good?'

Pondering, the two officers followed the Chief Superintendent on a tour of the other rooms that were distributed round the first-floor hall.

Between the outer wall of Emma's bedroom and the chief guest-room there was a lavatory, and another bathroom. The latter, of considerably simpler design and decor, was as comfortable and warm as Emma's own. The main guest-room was luxurious and welcoming, in green stripes, and dark-yellow carpet, and huge double bed. It had no outstanding personal touches, for these had been left to the guest who stayed there. But there was a bookcase, filled with a mixture of fact and fiction. And several charming, and easy-to-like water-colours on the walls, stopped it from being too impersonal.

Fisher said that the dead girl had been using the second guest-room. And added that, for an influx of visitors, there were three very pleasant bedrooms (and all mod. cons.) upstairs in what used to be called 'the attics'.

'What are they called now?' asked Stillman.

'The top floor,' he was told gravely. 'It sounds less slummy.'

Then they went to the room where the dead girl had spent . . . how many of her last days and nights? Stillman asked about this.

'She was living here,' said Fisher. 'For the past six months, I'm told, since she took on the job. Secretary to Lady Randall. Part of the perks. And very nice, too – as long as it doesn't include being murdered! She used to go home sometimes to see her parents. I've got their address, down on the Kent coast. Yes,' he answered a look from Stillman, 'Sir Robin telephoned there, to say there'd been an accident. Her father's on his way.'

The Superintendent nodded sombrely. He wandered round Lynn's room, opening all the cupboards and drawers with infinite care and caution.

He thought it a restful room, if one could forget the reason one was in it. There was a wide bed, with a padded headboard. The furniture was walnut, gently gleaming against white walls and carpet. Curtains, bedcover and cushions, were in various shades of green and dark-blue. It was all very neat. An orderly girl, mused Stillman, except for the manner of her departure. And for that, she could hardly be blamed. Even her handbag, lying on a chair, did not contain the usual chaos that most women carry about with them. Just a few cosmetics, a comb in a pink leather case, a cheque-book also in a leather case, a purse with a few pounds and coins in it, a driving-licence, a key-ring

69

with four keys and a golden horse-shoe attached to it . . . for luck . . . ?

On a small writing-table, a Crown Derby dish held pen and pencils, paper-clips, erasers, a paper-knife, and several books of stamps. There was writing-paper and envelopes below in a long, shallow drawer. Stillman stood by the writing-table for quite a few minutes, frowning a little. Something seemed to be troubling him. The girl, he brooded, had been Emma Randall's social secretary. But there seemed no traces here of the sort of work she did. No note-books, no loose papers of any kind, no letters, where one might expect to find them. Or anywhere else, for that matter. Stillman prowled quietly about the room, opening and shutting things. Then he shook his head. It was all too neat and tidy, somehow. He went back to the dressing-table.

A glowing red hair was still clinging to a brush there. He looked at the bottle of scent ('Tweed'), creams and lotions with first-rate brand-names, two clean horn combs; a bowl of yellow daisies; a dish containing pins, safety-pins, and a thin gold chain. A gold wrist-watch lay ticking sadly. In a big silver comfit-box was a pair of gold earrings, and a pair set with pearls. Also, in a small special drawer, and in its own jewel-case, a very fine pearl necklace.

'Dear me, dear me,' said Stillman. 'Poor little soul. Let's see the other rooms.'

On the landing, towards the front of the house, the door of Robin's study stood open. Fisher switched on a light, and stood aside to let Stillman enter.

At the right of the window was a large desk, with a tooled-leather top. On this, books, papers, notebooks, and writing materials were piled fairly lavishly. In its drawers were ledgers containing dates, prices, and names of great craftsmen, together with labels, balls of string, and staples. Also on the desk was a diary, an address-book, a telephone and its attendant tomes, and one silver-framed photograph. Not a gorgeous studio portrait of Emma, but the enlargement of a snapshot that showed her squinting slightly into the sun, hair blown over her eyes, and mouth open as though shouting. She was wearing a huge macintosh and a pair of gum-boots. Stillman wondered why Sir Robin gave this a place of honour. Because it had been taken on some memorable April day? Because he liked it? What did his lady think of it?

The panelled walls were ivory-coloured. There were three magnificent oils, and nine jewel-like miniatures. Any one of these would have bought a garden for the Superintendent with space enough to grow all that his heart craved.

For furniture, there was a revolving chair, and a big armchair; hand-

70

lamps, with a powerful goose-necked one on the desk; a Sheraton escritoire; bookcases, whose contents mostly concerned art and were written by people whose names, supposed Stillman, would be well-known to their own world. There was a small, drum-topped table; a pair of Chippendale wall-mirrors. The carpet was deep and silky, ancient, and Chinese. Ruthie would have thought it a dull room, lacking colour and prettiness.

On the floor under the window was a heap of paper, string, and padding. The two little paintings, side by side on the drum table, were so enchanting that even Ruthie might have hung them by the television set in the lounge at home.

Between this study and Lynn's room was Giles's office.

It was merely an office. No pretensions to anything but utility. It held all that a busy Public Relations man could need. Typewriter, reams of paper, envelopes, stamps. Two diaries – one enormous, filled with Emma's public engagements, and one with 'Things for Giles to Re-member' written in gold letters across the front. This had obviously been a present to him from someone. There were well-worn telephone books; a gigantic stack of photographs of Emma, all glamorous studio studies, these. About twenty fat books of press cuttings, and an index for them. In a cupboard, neatly packed piles of office materials. There was a leather-framed calendar on the big oak table that served as a desk. Beside the calendar sprawled a lop-eared toy dog. There were chairs, flame-red carpet, sheepskin rugs in front of the window and the fireplace; brass candlesticks; two telephones; walls covered in oatmeal hessian, which probably made for sound-proofing; red corduroy curtains; a copy of Roget's Thesaurus on the table. And that was that.

'I'll bet this chap's kept fairly busy,' commented Fisher. 'Run off his feet, I rather imagine.'

'He must like it, or he wouldn't stay,' said Stillman, smiling. 'More interesting than the average daily grind, at any rate.'

'Such as ours?'

'Well, I'd call ours quite interesting, but sad in many ways. Like now.' The Superintendent then said he would like to inspect the staff quarters, if Fisher could spare the time to show him these.

Beyond the main stairwell, and under the upper flight, an arched opening led down two steps to a corridor. This was in the oldest part of the house, left more or less untouched, and still charmingly cottage-like; two-storied, gable-windowed, and oak-beamed, with iron latches on its oak-plank doors. The kitchen of Monksend had once been its lower floor. Stillman went down the steps, interestedly.

On his left, he found first a bathroom, white-tiled, warm, but incredibly untidy. And next was a WC, not quite so cluttered. Then there was the top of a staircase, and the doors into two bedrooms. Both these latter were large, with sloping roofs and small-paned windows. One was reasonably neat, though the cover of the bed was slipping off, and a few articles of clothing were spread on chairs, and a pair of slippers lay far apart. The built-in cupboard held few clothes, and the drawers of the chest were half-empty, except for small piles of starched clean aprons and caps. There was a big sea-chest under the window, which held a cheap suit-case, a pair of climbing boots, an ice-axe, and some books of poetry in German, and some in English. All round the room were books on cookery, also in these two languages. There was a pile of postcards and letters on a table, all with German stamps. The window was wide open, and the place was very cold.

The other bedroom was a shambles. It was clear that the two trainee-cooks were expected to do their own chores. This bed was unmade, looking as if it had been slept in by a very large dog. More a nest than a bed.

There was a dark-blue vase, with a carefully arranged spray of twigs and grasses in it, that needed dusting badly. A good try, though. There was also a very mixed smell, of scent, after-shave lotion, old socks, and unopened windows. The cupboard and drawers were filled with cheap trendy clothes, shoes, and ties, all carefully placed on hangers and trees. The books that lay on the table and bed were mostly Science Fiction. On the chest-of-drawers was a triple looking-glass, a magnifying shaving-mirror, and some make-up.

'It's all in the mind,' said Fisher, obscurely.

Both the bedrooms had basins with hot and cold water, and heated towel-rails.

Stillman said he had seen enough for the time being. They went back along the corridor to the landing. And then they climbed the narrower staircase that curved up above the main one to the upper floor.

The three rooms here were pleasant, but completely impersonal. These were the two extra guest-rooms, and their bathroom with all cons. One room had a suitcase in it – a rather nice, plain leather one – and a dressing-gown on the back of the door. Also a well-cut dark suit in the wardrobe, a dinner-jacket suit, and some shoes. A comb on the dressing-table, a toothbrush in the mug on the basin, together with shaving tackle, and a book (*On the Beach* by Neville Shute) on the bedside table, showed the room was in use.

'Mr Warrington stayed here last night,' said Fisher.

'Well then,' said the Superintendent, 'if you gentlemen have seen all that you want, for the moment, we might as well go downstairs. Don't let me hurry you, if there's anything else you need to see. But I think I've got as much as my head will hold for the time being.'

'The casual way you looked round would hardly supply an ant's egg to a fish!' said Sergeant Woolsey, in a muddled way, inside his own head. He was feeling muddled. He thought it was much too soon to be looking at people's rooms, long before one had even got round to suspecting any particular people. As they went downstairs, he asked his senior sceptically if he had noticed anything suspicious anywhere. The Superintendent said suspicious of what, for instance?

'Well – like – like preparations for murder . . . ?'

'There were a few oddities,' said Stillman. 'But I saw no bloodstained knives, or recently fired guns, if that's what you mean.'

Woolsey said it wasn't quite what he'd meant, and mumbled into silence.

At the bottom of the main stairs, they were led by Fisher across the wide hall, over black-and-white squares, to the little office near the front door, where Emma Randall's more personal activities were arranged and recorded. This, it appeared, was where the dead girl had worked.

The little room was painted pale lilac, with royal purple ceiling and carpet. It had a white desk, flat-topped, with curly legs. There were two padded chairs, and two white telephones. It was all most charming. Feminine, in the best sense of the word. Ruthie would have approved. Various books were neatly packed into a revolving bookcase. A silver-framed calendar, with a handle to roll the dates round, stood on the desk. There was a leather-bound blotting pad, and a desk-diary. The Superintendent turned the pages of a half-completed letter, and pursed his lips.

'Something interesting, sir?' asked Fisher, eagerly.

'Not really, no. Answer to an invitation. But . . . Lady Randall's private appointments are all entered in this diary. Social dates, hairdresser, and so on. None of Miss Sanderson's. Did she keep no personal records? What did she do with her time off?'

Fisher said he had no information on the subject.

'Someone will have to go to Kent,' said Stillman.

'Me, damn it!' snapped Woolsey, mentally.

'You, George,' agreed Stillman, to the young man's alarm. 'And now, Mr Fisher, I'd better go and have a word with the Randalls. Thank you for showing me round, and for your patience with my slowness. I wonder if you'd mind waiting in the library for me? You've already had a chat with Sir Robin and his wife, I believe? It will be interesting to compare our notes after I've seen them. The Randalls, I mean, not the notes.'

'I'll get mine sorted out neatly,' said Fisher. 'I'll be quite glad of a quiet smoke, and a chance to think.'

He nodded briskly, and went off across the hall.

'Now we're going to display our sweet natures to the nobs!' thought Sergeant Woolsey through his teeth.

Not everyone can do this, but after his short association with the Superintendent, he found it easy.

'Don't be nervous, son,' said his senior, looking with mild surprise at his gritting teeth and scowling brow. 'They won't bite.'

'Let 'em try!' snapped the Sergeant.

He rapped the drawing-room door with unnecessary force.

Giles ushered the two men into the room, and introduced them.

Emma sat upright on a chesterfield, against a heap of cushions. Her eyes were blank with shock, and reddened by tears. From her side, Robin got up and greeted the policemen with apparent composure. While he shook hands with them, he said he hoped they would regard everything and everyone in the house as being at their disposal.

'But I don't think they should question Emma too lengthily,' said Giles, looking anxiously at them from where he stood by the fire. 'She ought to be resting. . . .'

'My dear fellow,' said Robin, 'don't fuss.'

'Rest!' said Emma. 'Are you mad, darling? Mr Stillman will tell us just what he wants us to do, and when to do it.'

'Thank you, madam,' said Stillman.

'But, Robin, she's so tired. . . .'

'Darling,' said Emma, 'for God's sake, belt up! I'm not going to bed, anyway. How could I? In the next room. . . .'

She choked, and covered her face with her hands. Giles began stammering something about the spare room, and faltered into silence under Robin's frown.

'I'll let you know when we're through in the bathroom, of course,' said the Superintendent. 'I do think it's a good idea about the spare room, if I may say so.'

'All under control,' Robin told him. 'Mrs Smart has dealt with it.'

Emma emerged from cover, gave Stillman a faltering smile, and said everyone would do everything they could to help him.

'You must find out what happened to Lynn,' said she. 'I suppose it was some horrible accident, but . . . whatever could have caused it? I mean, how on earth . . . ?'

'We'll just have to see, won't we, madam. The best help you can give me right now, is to stay here, all of you, nice and warm and quiet, till I've finished talking with Mr Fisher in the library. Oh, and thank you, sir, for letting us use the room. It'll be very convenient. Now, you won't object, I take it, if I send an officer in here to get your finger-prints? I need them from everyone resident in the house.'

'Whenever you like,' said Robin.

'I know,' said Emma. 'It's to see if any strange prints are anywhere. I've read detective stories, too,' she told her husband.

'I'd like to ask you,' said the Superintendent, 'just what Miss Sanderson's work here involved. For instance, she dealt with all your social engagements?'

'Yes, that's right. She answered letters for me, when they weren't to do with professional matters,' said Emma. 'Giles did all the professional stuff. And Lynn made phone calls for me, and arranged dates with my masseuse, and that sort of thing. She was so good at it. I had to sack the girl I had before. The muddles she got into! The muddles she got *me* into! It's been bliss since Lynn. . . .'

She stopped, and gulped.

'I'll come back later, if I may,' said Stillman, gently. 'Then you can tell me what you remember of this afternoon's events.'

He hesitated, took a step or two towards the door, and then said almost casually across his shoulder:

'Can any of you tell me anything about a yellow statue of a lady sitting on a big bird? About fourteen inches high. Quite heavy. It was upstairs in. . . .'

'Chi-tan-huang. Yellow jade,' said Robin. 'The Queen of the West and her Phoenix. About two hundred BC. Why?'

'It's in my bedroom,' said Emma.

'It was found in your bath, madam. It was used to kill Miss Sanderson.'

'God-almighty!' said Robin, through Emma's horrified cry. 'Was it damaged?'

'I don't think so, sir. She was, though.'

The Sergeant closed the door after him with a thud, as he followed his senior from the room.

## Chapter eight

## ANSWER? A LEMON ICE?

Outside, in the main hall, stood Mrs Smart with a loaded tea-tray in her hands. To the Superintendent's greeting and enquiry, she told him where the library was. She also told him her name, and said she knew he'd be wanting her assistance soon. She would be ready and waiting, she assured him, to do all that was required of her, no matter what. Stillman thanked her, and she beamed after him as she watched the two men go into the library.

'I'll take them a cup of tea in a minute,' she told the milk-jug. 'Nothing like a bit of home comfort in time of trouble.'

She trotted into the drawing-room, giving vent to soft crooning noises indicative of sympathy. But it seemed the Randalls and Giles preferred their troubles without the aid of the fifth cup of tea she had brought for them since the discovery of the tragedy. She took the tray back to the kitchen, murmuring that she grudged no effort to help, even if it was not appreciated.

Once in the kitchen, she dumped the tray on the nearest table, looked round the room at its occupants, and said while there was life there was hope.

No one answered.

There were two long wooden tables set in line down the middle of the room, with stools that could be tucked out of the way underneath, or brought out for use. Johann was slumped on one at the far end of the farther table, his head buried in his arms.

Derek, at the sink, was unhurriedly skinning and filleting soles.

A large young man stood near the door that led into the back hall. He looked so obviously a policeman that it seemed over-stressing the matter to put him in uniform. He was jotting something down in a notebook, with a ball-point pen that was almost out of ink. He had already filled a good many pages, and crossed out most of his efforts.

No one took the slightest notice of Mrs Smart. Even the constable now looked on her as a chatty bit of background landscape.

She sat down, and poured herself a cup of tea. She did not normally use the Wedgwood china for her personal refreshment, but felt this was an Occasion. No minor accident could possibly be noticed in the present atmosphere of disaster.

'My Henry isn't going to like this,' she stated. 'It's tonight he gets his steak-and-kidney for supper. It'll be a big shock to him.'

'He knows you're unavoidably detained,' the policeman felt in his breast-pocket, without much hope, for another pen.

'Ah, and he won't like being rung up at his work, neither,' said Mrs Smart, with an air of complacency. 'Fancy being hauled into the foreman's office, and told your wife's suspected of murder!'

'Come off it, ma!' said the constable. 'Who suspects you? And who says it's murder? We don't know yet. . . .'

Johann lifted dull and despairing eyes, and said of course it was murder.

'How do you know?' said Mrs Smart and the policeman, together.

'Is obvious to the most stupid. He killed her.'

'He?' Constable Dowling suddenly glimpsed a great coup for himself. Crime solved by keen young P.C. . . . promotion . . . 'Who is *he*?'

'Who knows?' said the German, quelling these hopes. 'Is probably *him*!'

He pointed a shaking hand at Derek.

'Don't be naughty,' the accused said. He was now sitting at the draining-board, chopping some shallots. He looked mournful and added: 'Why ever should I kill her? Much more likely you did it. And you know what I mean to do about that.'

'Is your wicked jealousy. You hate her,' croaked Johann. 'And for why, I ask? That you may have me for yourself . . . which you shall never do. Never! Not though you murder every woman on the earth.'

'Is he likely to try?' asked the policeman, intrigued.

'Who knows!' said Johann, again.

'Well, I do for one,' said Derek.

'A thing that could kill my Lynn. . . . !'

'You poor soul,' said Mrs Smart. 'Here, dear, drink this, and you'll feel better.'

She put a luke-warm cup of tea in front of Johann, who gave a cry of misery and anger, and swept it to the floor.

'Good job you gave him one of the kitchen mugs,' commented Dowling.

Mrs Smart suggested to Derek that he should mop up the tea, on the grounds that he had upset Johann. He rejected the idea utterly, on the grounds that only a fool would offer tea to a man who drank only coffee. The policeman intervened. Mrs Smart went to get a cloth and bucket, saying she knew where her duty lay, even to doing chores that were not her rightful affair. P.C. Dowling said her attitude was saintly. She agreed.

'When I've done this,' said she, 'I'll make another pot for the officers in the library. They'll be panting for a cup by this time.'

The officers in the library had gone through the data in their possession. After pooling their notes and speculations, it all boiled down to the fact that they knew there had been a certain homicide, the weapon that had caused it, and the names of everyone who had been in the house at the time, or thereabout, when it had taken place.

'Between four o'clock roughly, when she left the drawing-room,' said Fisher, 'and half an hour later when Randall found her dead in the bath.'

He tapped his notebook, and said there was a statement from everyone in the house . . . a very brief one . . . of where they had each been during that half-hour.

'Where they *say* they were,' he amended. 'Naturally, they all claim to know nothing at all about the girl's death.'

'Naturally,' said Stillman.

The local Superintendent lay back in a deep buttoned-leather armchair, and lit his pipe again. He blew smoke round his face until he looked like the Djinn of the Lamp in a pantomime. He said everyone had been in a bit of a state when they talked to him, so he would not vouch for any accuracy.

'Except Sir Robin,' he said. 'He was cool and collected enough. Seemed more concerned about his wife, than with having a murder in his house.'

'People sometimes react oddly to such things,' said Stillman.

He flicked over the pages of his own notebook on the table in front of him.

'Often they just don't believe it,' said he, almost as though he was speaking to himself. 'As if they suddenly found themselves on a stage, and didn't know the lines or the plot. They wait for instructions. It's shock, of course. Some seem not to care, but it doesn't necessarily mean anything.'

He stopped, and put his finger on a phrase in the notebook.

'That bath-cap. . . .'

There was a loud tap on the library door. Sergeant Woolsey strode to it, and held it ajar. He started to say that no one could come in, but Mrs Smart shouldered past him, and advanced into the room with a tray.

'Here now, Mrs!' said the Sergeant, scandalised. 'You can't just. . . !'

The tray was set on the central table with such decision that spoons rattled on the saucers. The china was the blue-and-white striped kitchen ware. Mrs Smart did not regard policemen as Wedgwood types.

'There,' said she. 'Nice and hot. You'll think better with this inside you.'

'Most kind,' said Stillman. 'Thank you, Mrs . . . Smart, isn't it?'

'The daily,' said Fisher.

'Mrs Dora Smart,' said the lady, 'who helps out. I don't have to, you know. It's my pleasure. Henry would as soon I didn't go to work at all. But what I say is, it would be a poor world where no one was willing to help out. Shall I pour? I know you men! All slopped in the saucers, and wet spoons in the sugar. Don't tell me!'

No one dared to. Cowed, the three men accepted large cups of tea and lumps of sugar.

'And now,' said Mrs Smart, 'you'd like to know who done this dreadful murder.'

After a moment, Stillman said cautiously that they'd be glad to hear anything useful that she could tell them.

'It's that Mr Hawley,' she said, 'He's confessed.'

The Sergeant gave a sigh of relief. Thank God, it was going to be easy. The old man would not come unstuck, after all, Then he stirred fretfully at what the old man was now saying.

'Do you believe this confession, Mrs Smart?'

The woman gave a muffled titter. She said of course not. Derek was just larking about, silly fellow.

'Any idea why?'

Mrs Smart said no one in their right mind would have any idea why Derek ever did anything.

'Proper ninny, and no mistake,' she enlarged. 'One of those . . . you know. . . .'

She winked lewdly at Superintendent Fisher. He blew a cloud of smoke as though for protection.

'But he wouldn't hurt a fly, really,' Mrs Smart went on. 'Scream if he saw a mouse! Not the sort to go round killing people. Girlish,' she said, 'if you take my meaning.'

Stillman said he took her meaning.

'Lizzie Borden was girlish,' said the Sergeant, unexpectedly.

He drooped, as everyone turned and looked at him.

Mrs Smart said if no one was going to arrest her, could she go home normally?

'Henry won't like having to get the fish-and-chips from the corner,' she told them. 'It's his steak-and-kidney night. And if I'm not there to hot up the fish, even, he'll go spare. I mean, if you're going to third-degree me, could it be now?'

'I'm so sorry,' said Stillman, 'but I've got a few things to do first. I really think I must speak to Lady Randall and Sir Robin again. She'll be glad to get it over. If you could be kind enough to wait half an hour, I'll be as quick as I can.'

'Here we go again!' moaned Woolsey, inside his brain, 'Apologising now to the hired help!'

Mrs Smart said she hoped she knew her duty. She would always put herself out to help the police, no matter what people said about them. And nothing was too much for her to do for Lady Randall.

'Such a lovely person,' she told them. 'Got a little temper, of course. But that's her artistic nature. Stands to reason she won't take any non-sense lying down, and why should she? She could buy and sell the lot of them! Except Sir Robin, of course. He's got plenty of his own. Rolling . . . fair rolling, he is, and no mistake.'

'Do they get on well? The Randalls,' said Stillman, casually.

'Well, he's not one for showing his feelings much,' replied Mrs Smart. 'I've never heard him say anything nasty to her, but then he wouldn't with me around, would he? She goes for him sometimes . . . real nag, nag. But she don't mean half she says. And I, for one, don't blame her for anything she do say. Got plenty to put up with in this house, she has, and so I tell you.'

She gave an extraordinary toss of the head. It left the men baffled, but was, in fact, meant to convey loyalty and defiance.

'And now,' she said, in a shrill voice,'some rotten swine has tried to murder her . . . twice!'

With a strong sense of the dramatic, she marched to the door, and left the room. The policemen were frozen, with cups in their hands and their mouths open.

The Sergeant recovered, sprang to the door, and prepared to order the lady back at the top of his voice. But his senior spoke first.

'Let her go, George. I'll talk to her later, when she may not be showing off quite so much.'

Woolsey came back. He said optimistically that the case might prove fairly easy to solve, after all.

'We won't have to do a thing,' said he. 'This lot will tell us exactly who did what . . . and how . . . and why. . . .'

'The difficulty,' said Stillman, sounding depressed, 'will be to stop them.'

Fisher knocked his pipe out in an ashtray on the table, and asked if his presence was needed any longer.

'Well, perhaps not,' said Stillman, 'I'd like to come and talk it over again with you in the morning, if I may. I'll know better then where I am, and what needs doing. I can pick your brains about it all. Tonight it might be best not to alarm the people here by having too many officers about the place.'

'He *should* alarm them!' thought Woolsey, despairingly. 'He should frighten the pants off them!'

Stillman asked if the two constables now on duty in the house could stay there overnight.

'Or, if they're going off-duty, perhaps they could be replaced? I'll be much obliged if you will arrange this. I think it's necessary.'

'Old fool!' thought Woolsey, through his teeth. '*Think*? This is bloody murder!'

Fisher, co-operating cordially, went out into the hall with Stillman. Sergeant Woolsey collected his own and Stillman's note-books from the table. The latter was lying open on top of the one Fisher had left with his own notes in it. Woolsey glanced down at some words in Stillman's neat writing:

'Randall? Lady Emma . . . Lynn Sanderson . . . jealousy? Whose? Concerning whom? The bath-cap. Confession! Must have "Madame Hardy". . . .'

'*What!*' said the Sergeant.

He did not know that green-centred white rose. He shrugged, and followed the other officers into the hall. Here he joined his senior in bidding Superintendent Fisher a polite good-night. Then he and Stillman went back to the drawing-room.

Robin and Emma were still ensconced on the chesterfield. Giles sat by the fire, and stared blankly at the blaze, his hands loose between his knees. He did not turn to look at the two policemen, not even when the elder of them spoke his name.

' . . . dislike disturbing you,' Stillman said. 'But . . . Mr Warrington. . . .'

'Wake up, Giles,' said Robin, rising from the couch.

'Oh, what! Yes?'

'I'm sorry, sir,' Stillman told him. 'But I'd like to talk to Sir Robin and Lady Randall, if you don't mind.'

'No . . . not at all.'

'On their own, Mr Warrington, please.'

Robin put his hand on Giles's shoulder. He said all of them had been

81

extremely fond of Lynn, but must tackle getting the dreadful business cleared up.

'Of course the Superintendent wants to talk to us all, each in turn,' he explained, in reassuring tones. 'It makes sense. So run along, like a good lad. There's a fire in the library. Go in there and have a drink. If you don't want to be on your own, go into the kitchen, and have a drink or some coffee there.'

'That would really be best,' Stillman supported him. 'We'll come and find you, when we're ready for a chat. I don't like turning you out like this, you know. But it's sometimes easier for me to concentrate, when I've fewer people to . . .'

He glanced at his Sergeant, who had given vent to an exasperated grunt. But Giles got to his feet, and gave him the ghost of a grin.

'Of course,' said he. 'You want to hear us contradicting one another's statements. And avoid the danger that we may gang up on you.'

'Quite correct, sir,' said the Superintendent.

'Dead right!' added the Sergeant, hoping he sounded menacing.

Giles left the room, saying he would be in the kitchen when required.

'Now, Lady Randall,' said Stillman. 'Er . . . may we . . .?'

'Oh, I'm so sorry. Do please sit down, both of you,' said Emma.

They did so, Woolsey produced his note-pad, and poised a pen hopefully.

'What can I tell you?' said Emma.

Stillman looked at her glazed eyes, and registered the fact that she was clutching the hand of her husband, who had taken his place beside her again. He saw how white she was, so that her make-up appeared garish. Yet she was lovely in spite of it. He wondered if she knew it. He wondered if her emotion was slightly over-done.

'I'm trying not to cry again,' said Emma. 'I don't really want to, because I'm too angry for tears. It's just fatigue. And . . . I'm so bewildered! I know I can be beastly to people when I'm busy and worried . . . but have I really offended someone so badly that they want to kill me?'

'To kill you, madam?'

'Of course, Superintendent. I was poisoned yesterday.'

'Really, madam?'

The Sergeant wrote busily. This was the second time reference had been made to an attempt on the lady's life. Most interesting.

'I know I told everyone it was the curse,' went on Emma, gathering momentum as she spoke. 'Well, I had to! It would have been mad to let that lot know the truth. But I knew all the time it was some sort of poisoning. Food-poisoning! What a fool I'd have looked. That War-wick cow would have spread the giggle forever. I couldn't let that happen, could I?'

'Would you tell me about it, please?'

Stillman got the story. When appealed to by Emma, her husband confirmed the details.

'And . . . if something toxic was given to you, madam, deliberately . . . who do you think might have done it?'

'I don't know! I swear I don't know!' cried Emma. 'I didn't think anyone disliked me *that* much! But it must have been deliberate. And given only to me . . . no one else was ill. And now! Look what's happened now! Mr Stillman, you must find out who killed Lynn. I feel so awful about it . . . that she's dead because of something I've done. Some enemy of mine . . . who thought she was me!'

'We don't know that,' said Robin, repressively.

'Of course we do! She was in my bath. Wearing my cap.'

Ah,' said Stillman. 'I was coming to that. How did you know she wore your cap?'

'I told her,' said Robin. 'It surprised me a bit. It wasn't like Lynn to borrow other people's things. And my wife says she never asked to borrow a cap.'

'Weren't you surprised, sir, to find the young lady in your bathroom at all?' said Stillman.

'Extremely. I would hardly have gone in, if I'd known she was taking a bath there, would I?'

'And why did you go in? Did she call out?'

'Not that I heard. I was in my study, looking at some paintings, and I heard someone go stamping through the upper landing like a bison and down the stairs. I went out to see what was going on, and saw Johann half-way down, and Mrs Smart coming up. I assumed it was just some sort of normal uproar. Then I saw my bedroom door was open, so I went in. I found the bathroom door wide open, too. I looked inside, and found Lynn.'

He paused. Gently, the Superintendent asked him to go on.

'She was floating, face downward. She had my wife's cap on. For a moment, I thought it was . . . ' he stopped again, took a deep breath, and continued: 'and then I realised it was not.'

'How?'

Robin looked blank, and the Superintendent apologised.

'I didn't mean to take you up so abruptly,' said he. 'I just wondered how you knew so quickly, when she was face downwards in clouded

83

water, with her hair hidden in a cap.'

'I have been married to my wife for ten years.' said Robin, stiffly. 'I would know her under any circumstances. It was only for a moment that . . . .'

Again he came to a halt. Stillman apologised again.

'I have to ask these things, sir,' he said. 'In any case, sir, you had left Lady Randall downstairs. You could have no reason to think she'd suddenly decide to have a bath, at such an unusual time of day.'

'Now he's prompting him what to say!' said Woolsey, irritably, to himself. 'Oooh . . . he *is* going to come an unholy cropper!'

'Actually,' said Robin, 'my wife had told me she might take a bath.'

'Did I? Oh, yes,' said Emma.

'Indeed? And why did you leave the drawing-room, sir, in the middle of your tea?'

Robin explained about the parcel from the National Gallery.

'I'd been looking forward to seeing the miniatures,' he said. 'And, anyway, the gathering had broken up a bit, what with Emma having a row with the B.B.C., and . . .'

'Darling!'

Emma interrupted, rather indignantly, to justify her dealings with that body. The Superintendent heard about its impudence regarding her clothes for the forthcoming series. He heard about the forthcoming series. He heard about the imitation sable cloak (or cloaks). He heard how Emma had routed opposition. He made sympathetic and admiring noises in the right places. Then he said:

'So, after Miss Sanderson went upstairs, you, madam, went to talk on the telephone in your office. Sir Robin went to his study, to look at pictures. That's all quite clear. Do you happen to know where anyone else was? For instance, could you see anyone from the office while you were talking?'

'Yes,' said Emma, thinking hard. 'Mrs Smart went into the drawing-room. I saw Johann in the hall, just for a moment. And someone told me later that Derek was out in the garden.'

Robin shook his head at her. He said it was no good reporting other people's words about anything.

'Only what you actually saw, dear,' he said.

He offered cigarettes politely to the two policemen, which they politely refused.

'I did see Giles go upstairs,' said Emma. 'At least, I think it was he. But I was in such a rage that I wasn't concentrating on anything else.'

The Superintendent had glanced at a page in Fisher's notebook, and he nodded.

'Yes, madam,' said he. 'Mr Warrington went up to his office, to check your contract. He says here that he wished to make sure of your rights before you committed yourself too deeply on the wardrobe problems.'

'Did he now!' Emma's eyes flashed sparks of gold. 'And what would he have done if my rights had been limited? Come down and snatched the phone from my hand, and told them to hire my gear from Simmond's?'

The Superintendent said he was sure he couldn't say. Emma gave a slight snort.

'Don't be tiresome, dear,' said Robin.

She looked instantly stricken. She said she was extremely sorry, and must be out of her mind.

'Imagine boring you with trivialities!' said she. 'When Lynn is . . . when she . . . .'

'Very natural,' soothed Stillman.

'No! It sounds so petty . . . and heartless . . . and I'm not really. . . .'

Emma turned her head aside against her husband's arm. He said no one was criticising her. The Sergeant gave her a long, measuring stare, only desisting in this when he realised Robin was giving him a long, measuring stare. Emma mopped her eyes fiercely and sniffed. Woolsey snapped his notebook open, and began making a list of names and places.

'Let's see,' he thought. 'Sir Robin was in his study, at the time of the young woman's death. Lady Randall was in her office downstairs, arguing with the B.B.C. Mr Warrington was in *his* office, checking the contract. Johann . . . what's his name? . . . Schulter seems to have been skulking on the landing. Mrs Smart was in the drawing-room, and there's a rumour that the other cook-chap was in the garden. According-ing,' thought the Sergeant, 'to these people here. But have they told the truth about anything?'

Hearing a quick, harsh intake of breath, he looked up.

Emma had put her hands to her mouth, and shut her eyes. Robin, looking very remote, was staring into the fire. Woolsey wondered what was the matter with them both. Then he heard what they had heard.

Muffled voices in the hall; a trampling of several pairs of feet over the floor; a thudding on the stairs. Woolsey was so used to these sounds, and the sad reason for them, that he had not been aware of the arrival of the ambulance and the stretcher team.

The Chief Superintendent had got to his feet. Now Woolsey rose quickly, shutting his notebook.

'Is that all you want to ask me?' whispered Emma.

'Oh, I think so. For the moment, madam. Unless there's anything you would like to add?'

Shakily, but with grim determination, Emma got up and came close to Stillman, to gaze into his face with her amazing golden eyes . . . now pink-rimmed and swollen. She said there was indeed something she would like to add.

'I want you to find out who did this to Lynn *quickly*. Not because I'm afraid he'll have another go at killing me . . . but because I liked her very much, and I want him punished.'

'We'll do our best, Lady Randall,' promised Stillman.

'Naturally!' snapped the Sergeant.

But he did not say it aloud.

Stillman was looking at the Randalls. They were an attractive pair, he considered, standing close together in that lovely room. But their eyes were haunted. The Superintendent gave a little apologetic cough, which made his junior wince.

'Forgive me, I've just thought of something else,' said Stillman. 'Why was Miss Sanderson in that bath, in the first place?'

If a pause followed, it was momentary.

'My wife gave her permission,' said Robin.

'Oh, dear God! How I wish I hadn't!' cried Emma.

'You couldn't guess what would happen.'

'But if only. . . .'

Emma pulled herself together with an effort, lowered her voice by half an octave, and said quite collectedly to the Superintendent that Lynn had asked permission to use the bathroom, just after she (Emma) had come downstairs that afternoon.

'She told me the lock was broken on the other bathroom door. It wouldn't shut properly. So I told her to use ours.'

'Didn't it strike you as an odd time to take a bath?'

'No, Mr Stillman, not for Lynn. She always chose teatime, if possible. It's all right, darling,' said Emma to her husband, 'I will sit down. Don't worry. I'm quite all right.'

She sank down in an armchair by the fire

'Lynn didn't take tea, ever,' she went on. 'It really was quite a sensible time for her to bath, before anyone else wanted to before dinner, or going out.'

'And which bathroom would she normally have used, madam?'

'The guests' one, just outside her room. The boys do tend to make a fearful mess of the staff bathroom,' said Emma. 'They leave soap about, and towels on the floor, and pools of water. And Lynn is . . . Lynn was a very tidy sort of person. And she said . . . .' Emma gave an unmirthful small laugh, '. . . . she said Derek's bath-salts have a smell that would turn the stomach of a skunk.'

Stillman said that she had made everything very clear. He thanked her. He wondered aloud why she had not thought it necessary to warn her husband that their private bathroom would be occupied that afternoon.

'It never occurred to me that he'd go in there,' said Emma, looking surprised. 'He prefers to use the guest one himself, actually, unless there are too many guests. And he certainly wouldn't start bathing at four-thirty.'

'I see.'

Reluctantly, the Sergeant was now forced to erase from his mind a vision that had been haunting it. A vision of Robin Randall sporting and splashing in all the Roman luxury, with a chaplet of roses on his dark head, and a couple of adoring slave-girls (who for instance?) standing by with the talcum powder. And yet, thought Woolsey, who could be sure of anyone's hidden desires, their secret lives? He put Robin back in the marble bathroom . . . if only occasionally.

'And, of course,' Emma was saying, 'there's another bathroom on the top floor, for when extra people are here. I think Giles stayed up there last night.'

'Fancy!' thought Stillman. 'A household where even the mistress isn't sure how many people are sleeping where! It'd never do for Ruthie.'

'Tell me,' he said to the Randalls, 'how did Miss Sanderson get on with the rest of the staff?'

'Very well indeed, as far as I know,' said Robin. 'I'm sure everybody liked her. She wasn't a quarrelsome girl. She was . . . kind. Friendly. *We* certainly liked her very much.'

He had raised his voice while he was speaking. But its deep tones were not enough to blot out the sounds from the staircase and hall. The kind and friendly girl was leaving the house where she had been so well liked.

'Oh . . . Lynn . . .' said Emma. 'I . . . I must go out and . . . and just . . .'

'I wouldn't, madam,' said the Superintendent. 'I really would not.'

'Don't, dear' said Robin. 'Believe me, please . . . Stay here, it's far better.'

Emma subsided in her chair again, and broke into a storm of quiet sobbing. She said if only Lynn had not put on that bath-cap.

'So unlike her, to do it without even asking!' she gulped. 'She was going to wash her hair . . . she must have done it before she bathed . . . and looked round for something to put on to keep the bath-oil from . . . oh, God! Why did she have to use mine! Why did I let her use the beastly bath. . . . !'

'Now, you shouldn't blame yourself, Lady Randall,' said Stillman, through Robin's calmative murmur. 'I'll get all this finger-printing business over as quickly as I can, so that you can have a bit of peace.' He turned to Robin. 'I'm told your doctor has already been here to see your wife.'

Robin said he had called Dr Simmons at the same time that he'd summoned the police.

'And he gave her some tablets to take when she goes to bed. And meanwhile,' said Robin, 'perhaps she can doze a little here, and we'll see if Derek can rustle up something to eat.'

'No! No, not for me!' said Emma.

'Perhaps later on. . . .'

Apologising for the ordeal of the interrogation, with what his Sergeant thought misplaced courtesy, the Superintendent made for the door. He paused for a moment on the way to say if, by any chance, he had need of further information. . . . ?

'Don't hesitate to come back to us,' Robin told him. 'We'll do all we can to help.'

'Most kind, sir.'

Stillman went out into the hall, where he found a small knot of men waiting to speak to him. The Sergeant began to follow him out. . . .

'Oh, God!' breathed Emma. 'I told him where everyone was, didn't I? Call him back, Robin. I'll invent something about you, and Giles, and Johann, and . . . I'll say you were all together in the hall, where I could see you, the whole time. . . .'

'Darling, do *not* start trying to confuse the police,' said Robin, with an edge to his voice. 'They've enough to worry about, without your assistance, besides, it would merely make them suspect you.'

'Me?'

'You might be trying to arrange an alibi for yourself, mightn't you? Do stay calm, my dear, and do your best to think before you speak. The Superintendent's a nice little man,' said Robin. 'He won't do anything rash.'

'I don't care if he brings in the rack and the Star Chamber!' snapped Emma. 'I want the bloody killer caught!'

Robin glanced away from her, and caught the interested eye of the

Sergeant who had been listening by the door. Woolsey gave him a forbidding stare, and left the room. He closed the door behind him with a heavy thud; muttered an apology to a couple of men who had been about to go into the drawing-room, with their apparatus for taking prints; caught a glimpse of his superior officer going in what he took to be the direction of the kitchens, and followed.

'And well, well, well!' he said to himself, as he went.

Then he wondered what was well about any of it.

*Chapter nine*

## SLOW ROAST

Having sent the local police photographer home, with thanks, and a request that the results of his labour should be handed over as soon as possible, and having dispatched the finger-print men to the drawing-room, Chief Superintendent Joseph Stillman went quietly under the curve of the staircase, and through the automatic doors into the kitchen. He had no intention of creeping up on anyone. But, being an unobtrusive-looking man with a habit of moving quietly, he often unwittingly startled people. It was luck rather than judgement that brought him unobserved into an interesting scene.

Mrs Smart, a steaming kettle in one hand, was making little shrill sounds. Derek was standing on a table, swiping wildly at Johann with a frying-pan that scattered hot fat in every direction as he whirled it. Johann, crouching like a huge lion, prodded at him with a stool. And Police Constable Dowling was clawing ineffectually at both of them, hampered by the fact that he had a lemon mousse spread evenly about his face and head. There was a lot of noise.

'I'm so sorry to interrupt . . .' began the Superintendent.

It was the last straw for his Sergeant, who had just come through the doors behind him.

With a yell of fury, Woolsey sailed into the arena. He roared orders at everyone. He flung the constable aside, and grabbed Johann. Dowling fell over a brush and pan, and crashed to the floor in a corner. Johann turned and struck untidily at the Sergeant, and Derek hit each of them with the frying-pan.

'That will do,' said Stillman.

In some curious way, his quiet voice pierced the uproar, and produced almost instant silence. Some irresolute mopping-up began.

'Now what are you all doing?' Stillman asked.

Derek descended warily from the table, and said that he personally was trying to get some supper for everybody. Single-handed, he added.

'And I,' said Johann, 'am merely trying to kill him.'

'You're under arrest,' said the Sergeant.

'Quite right,' approved Mrs Smart.

The constable had picked himself up by now, mopped his face sufficiently to see what was happening, and advanced. He took a deep breath, choked on a lump of mousse, and just managed to speak.

'Who are you men? What're you doing here?'

The Sergeant rounded on him. He told him bitingly exactly who they were and what they were doing there. The constable blanched under bits of yellow fluff. He mumbled how could he know? Woolsey said he should think before he spoke.

'Please,' said Stillman, 'let's all calm down a bit, shall we?'

'If to be arrested I am,' said Johann, dropping heavily on the stool he had been brandishing, 'I must the lawyer have, must I not?'

The Superintendent said he was not being arrested.

'He is! He punched me!' said Woolsey, with passion. 'That's obstructing the police . . . and so did *he* !' with a furious gesture towards Derek. 'Obstructed, I mean . . . and hit me!'

'Accidents, I'm sure,' soothed his senior. 'Neither of these young fellows had any idea that we were policemen when they . . . ah . . . obstructed you. Let's overlook the incident this once. But only as long as they do not repeat the performance.'

He then said that he took it he was addressing Mr Schulter and Mr Hawley. Adding that he had, of course, already made the acquaintance of Mrs Smart.

'She told us,' said Derek. 'Said she'd been assisting you with enquiries, silly old faggot! I'm Derek Hawley,' he said, 'in case you think I'm a great stupid German who hopes to get himself a work permit to be head chef at some ghastly skyscraper . . . . !'

'Thank you, sir,' said the Superintendent. 'I guessed you were Mr Hawley.'

He then glanced curiously at his Sergeant who was thinking through his teeth again.

'God have mercy on us!' went the thoughts. 'Now it's "sir" to the scullion!'

'And this big oaf is Johann Schulter,' Derek was rattling on, unsubdued. 'He's in a sort of frenzy at the moment, and not responsible for anything he says. And if you arrest him for murdering Lynn, I shall confess.'

'To what, sir?' said Stillman.

'The murder, of course.'

'Really?'

'Yes. Really.'

'And will your confession be genuine?'

91

'Ha, ha!' said Derek. 'That's where your powers of deduction come in, isn't it?'

'I see. Would you care to come to the library with me, sir, and make a statement?'

Derek said he couldn't possibly leave the kitchen.

'It's the food,' he explained. 'I'm right in the middle of getting it all ready. If I leave it to Johann, it'll be a shambles. I just haven't time to talk to you just now.'

The shocked Sergeant said he would damned well talk when and where the Chief Superintendent told him to.

'And what about the dinner?' said Derek.

Stillman hushed his junior at the start of a spirited description of what Derek could do about the dinner.

'Under these obviously trying circumstances,' Stillman went on, 'perhaps I can ask a few questions here, without being too much bother.'

'Carry on,' said Derek, 'I'll try to concentrate.'

'Thank you, sir.'

Stillman settled himself in a large wicker chair by one of the back windows, and put his notebook on a shelf beside him.

Woolsey, with an irritable sigh, sat on a stool by one of the long tables in the centre of the room. From its end, Johann lifted a tragic face and looked at him, then relapsed again with his hands over his eyes. Derek went to the Aga cooker, and sniffed delicately at a pot that was simmering there. Mrs Smart filled the kettle. The constable was drying his face on a roller towel on the rear door, having had a quick wash at the sink.

'Now, Mr Hawley,' said the Superintendent, 'Will you tell me what you know, if anything, about Miss Sanderson's death?'

'Just a moment, dear,' said Derek. 'I'm seasoning the stock.'

The Sergeant rose in a convulsive movement, but sank back at a gesture from his senior. The latter said perhaps Mr Schulter would care to contribute some information.

'You won't get much joy there,' commented Mrs Smart, with contempt. 'He can't hardly speak English!'

'Is better than yours,' said Johann, stung from his slough of despond.

'I *am* English,' said Mrs Smart, 'you cheeky wog!'

Sergeant Woolsey said would they just confine themselves to answering such questions as the Chief Superintendent cared to ask them. Mrs Smart said she was always ready to help anyone at any time. Johann said she was a rude, stupid, ignorant bitch. And Derek said 'hear,

92

hear'. The constable told them all to shut up.

'No no, not you, Sergeant,' he added, hastily.

Stillman wrote in his notebook:

'Mermaid . . . William Lobb . . . Roseraie de L'Hay . . . .'

Johann said passionately that if anyone thought he had killed Lynn they were crazed.

'For what would I do this thing?' he cried. 'There is nothing I have to kill her for. Is not I who should be tracked down by the law. I'm innocent! I know nothing of Lynn.'

'And that's not your fault, is it?' said Derek, wrapping fillets of sole round a mushroom mixture.

He then crushed a fillet against his mouth like a handkerchief, and said forget that remark.

'Come back everything! I didn't mean it!'

Mrs Smart said Johann was talking rubbish, anyway. Of course he knew Lynn. They both worked for Lady Randall, didn't they?

'One at a time, will you!' snapped Sergeant Woolsey.

'The kettle's boiling,' said the constable.

Stillman wrote: 'Must have Frensham.'

Johann asked why he should have murdered Lynn, seeing that he loved her.

'Cream pashernel,' offered Mrs Smart.

Derek said what the hell did she know about passion . . . or cream for that matter. He then marched to the back door. Constable Dowling, intercepting, asked where he thought he was going.

'To the bloody refrigerator,' said David. 'To get some bloody cream for the bloody fish. That bloody woman reminded me.'

'You watch your language!' said Dowling.

Stillman wrote: 'What about Sterling Silver and Africa Star?', and looked up.

'While Mr Hawley is dealing with the fish,' he said, 'perhaps you, madam, would tell me just where you were at the time Miss Sanderson was bathing. Then you can go home.'

'That's good,' said Mrs Smart, filling a tea-pot with boiling water. 'Then I can see to Henry's supper. Thank you, Mr Willman.'

'Stillman,' said the Sergeant.

'Is it correct,' said the Superintendent, patiently, 'that you stayed on here this afternoon because Lady Randall needed extra help? That she asked you to do so?'

Out of a welter of home-spun philosophy, it emerged that Lady Randall . . . stretched on her bed of pain, poor soul . . . had indeed requested the presence of one whom she trusted, one she knew would help her in every possible way, without counting the cost, and would never be so cruel and ungrateful as to try to kill her . . . .

'When?' said Stillman, into the flow. 'When did Lady Randall ask you to stay on?'

'When that Derek took her up a boiled egg for lunch,' said Mrs Smart. 'He come back and says in his cheeky way that madam wanted me to stop on for the afternoon.'

'And did she confirm this herself, later?'

'Oh, yes, sir. She thanked me ever so much for my trouble, when I was clearing the tea-things.'

Stillman jotted something in his book. And, this time, it had reference to his enquiries. He then heard, in some detail, the conversation that had taken place between Emma and Mrs Smart . . . including the fact that the latter had been given a free hand to take the cakes home.

'Henry will fancy them,' said Mrs Smart.

'And where were you before tea?'

'Clearing up madam's bedroom. You know, making the bed, and getting it all cosy for her when she wanted to get back. Very untidy it was, too. What with her turn-up last night, and the doctor there, and people in and out with trays . . .! But there! I made it look nice and welcoming, with fresh water in the flowers . . . .'

'When did the cat get on to the bed?'

'The cat?'

'The grey cat, Mrs Smart. It was on Lady Randall's bed a little while ago.'

'Oh, that beast!' said Mrs Smart, making a grimace. 'It's a real terror. I wouldn't stay in the same room. I never saw it there in madam's. I'd have shooed it out.'

Derek, who had come back, and was starting to butter some oven-proof pottery dishes, said she had never forgiven Chin-Chin for refusing to stay in the same room with her.

'He's got good taste,' he added. 'He only likes me, and Emma, and Robin, and Giles. He walks out on everyone else. Screams at them, too, when he feels like it.'

The Superintendent said cats were most interesting creatures. Then he asked Mrs Smart if she had been tidying the bathroom when Miss Sanderson had come in to have her bath.

'I didn't see her,' said the lady, very firmly.

'Did you, in fact, go into the bathroom at all?'

'Well, yes . . . just to clean and tidy. Like putting away madam's bath-oil, and laying clean towels on the hot-rail, and . . . .'

'And did you notice where Lady Randall's bath-cap was?'

'Not specially. It must have been on the towel-rail as usual. Lady Randall don't throw her things about,' said Mrs Smart. 'Not like some.'

'And then,' pursued the Superintendent, 'you came downstairs? What did you do then?'

She said she had gone to the kitchen, made herself some tea, and helped what she called 'these silly lads' to prepare the tea-trays for the drawing room.

'Helped?' ejaculated Derek. 'You just sat here, swilling tea and yapping, till you nearly got a jam-sponge wrapped round your silly face.'

Mrs Smart said if it wasn't for poor Lady Randall, she wouldn't stay one minute longer in a house where any twittering little skinny nancy-boy . . . .

Sergeant Woolsey said: 'Hey, just a moment!', and the constable said: 'Now then, missus!', at exactly the same instant. Derek said she'd have a thrombosis if she went all purple in the face like that; adding that the colour clashed with that of her dyed hair. Johann said he knew just how Mrs Smart felt. And the Superintendent waited until the uproar died down a bit, making a note in his book which read: 'Must leave room for a little lily-pond, somehow.'

At last his dry voice cut through all the others. He said:

'Apart from all that, you were here, Mrs Smart, in the kitchen when Miss Sanderson went upstairs? As far as you know, that is. Did anything at all unusual occur in here?'

'It all seemed about the same as ever,' said Mrs Smart. 'The lads quarrelling about the television stuff. Then that Derek crying and moaning because Johann says he hates him, and rushing off to sulk in the garden.'

'Who rushed?'

'I did,' said Derek. 'Who wouldn't?'

'He's forever at it,' Mrs Smart accused. 'Skimping his work to go and bawl in the summerhouse.'

'And that's a lie!' said Derek. 'I don't skimp. If I have to go out, for a bit of peace, I work twice as hard to make up for it. *And* I only go when I'm not up to me bloody ears in cooking. You've seen what it's like here, Mr Stillman. Could you stand the racket for long, without escaping for a few minutes to recover?'

'Recover what?' said Mrs Smart.

'My nerve, you silly cow!'

Johann produced an enormous snort, which surprised everyone. He said the day that Derek lost his iron nerve for one second, he (Johann) would be willing to believe that he (Derek) could cook. Derek said it was not a matter for belief or disbelief, but self-evident to anyone but a total moron. Stillman said could they get back to the subject . . . which was, he added quickly to avoid argument, Mrs Smart's statement.

'You just told me,' he encouraged the lady, 'that nothing unusual took place in here before tea. Now . . . Mr Hawley went into the garden. What did you do?'

Mrs Smart said she'd cleaned some silver, and told Johann he should be ashamed to argue and shout when poor Lady Randall had been so bad: she'd probably got a headache, and wouldn't want the house filled with noise.

'I'd have a headache myself,' she told the Superintendent, 'if I ever took much notice of all the yelling and shouting that goes on! I'd be as daft as the rest of them. I do me best to pour oil on the troubles, as any sensible person would, but other than that I just ignore it. Let's see, now. I had some tea, and then . . . oh, yes, I heard the phone ringing from madam's office. I started to go and answer it, in case no one had heard it in the . . . .'

'Do you normally answer the phone?' asked Stillman.

'If she can get her sticky hands on it, she does,' said Derek. 'She hopes she might get to speak to someone famous, so that she can tell all her addled friends at the pub . . . .'

'Wait your turn!' snapped the Sergeant.

'Please,' said the Superintendent, 'just leave this to me, sir.'

'All right, love,' said Derek.

Johann said he had stopped Mrs Smart from going to the telephone. He said she was an inquisitive long-nose.

'Is properly for Mr Warrington to answer the telephone,' said he. 'Or . . . Lynn . . . .'

His voice trailed off into a strangled groan.

'And did anyone answer this particular phone-call?' pursued the Superintendent.

Mrs Smart said Johann had shoved her aside, most rudely, and gone to the office across the hall. Then, a little later, she had heard Lady Randall speaking in there.

'And how long,' said Stillman, 'did you remain here in the kitchen, Mrs Smart, after Mr Schulter came back from calling Lady Randall to the phone?'

'He didn't come back,' said Mrs Smart, with a smirk, hopeful of sensation. She got it.

Johann sprang to his feet, shaking his fists and shouting that he had nothing done of wickedness. Derek accused her shrilly of being a racialist, and threw a wooden spoon at her. It missed, and landed on the Sergeant's bosom. Constable Dowling laughed.

The Superintendent said that was enough. Once again, his voice produced quiet. In which lull, Stillman said if there was any more skylarking he would send Derek and Johann out of the room . . . and then what would happen to the dinner!

'Well, I've warned you,' said Derek, retrieving the spoon, dabbing a blob of gravy from the Sergeant with a corner of his apron, and marching back to the Aga. 'If you try to pin anything on Johann . . . and that hag's doing her best to make you . . . I'll confess.'

'Thank you, sir,' said Stillman. 'I've made a note of it.'

The Sergeant, who had only restrained himself from violence by commendable will-power, glared at Derek, Johann, Mrs Smart and the constable, with equal loathing. It was this sort of people, he thought, that made you wish you'd joined the Navy. Then he wondered who did the cooking there? He winced at the vision of being mewed up on a boat, for weeks at a time, with creatures who screamed and flung things. At least this case could not go on forever . . . or could it!

He forced his mind back to reality, to hear Mrs Smart describing her activities in the drawing-room. Peeled of their constant references to her own virtues, it boiled down to the fact that she had collected things on trays, had a chat with Mr Warrington on the house-phone, gone to the terrace to get a book, and ministered to Lady Randall. In rapid succession.

'Dear thing,' said Mrs Smart, lovingly. 'All them nice cakes, to cheer Henry after the fish and chips.'

'I do hope so,' said Stillman, closing his notebook. 'Thank you very much for your help, madam, and very useful information. I think we can let you go home, now.'

'Oh. Are you sure I can't help any more?' Mrs Smart, in spite of her stated wish to return to her deprived husband, was loath to leave the scene of drama. 'I could stop on a bit, and make tea for everyone.'

Tactfully insistent, Stillman persuaded her to get her hat and coat from a cupboard in the back hall. He asked the constable to take her round to the front drive and instruct his own driver . . . Darling . . . to take her home. She departed, scattering tags of advice and moral axioms like confetti over everyone in the kitchen. She had already packed the cakes in her basket, and rejected Derek's suggestion that she should open it all up again, and show what else she was taking. Woolsey thought this was quite a good idea, and moved forward. But his senior waved him back, and wished the lady a kind good-night.

'She might be concealing evidence!' thought the Sergeant. 'Silly old fool!'

After the departure of Mrs Smart, Derek gave a gusty sigh of relief. He said now perhaps they could have a bit of sense.

'That is my constant hope, sir,' said the Superintendent.

'*I* really can't tell you anything that will assist your enquiries,' said Derek. 'As I was in the garden at the time . . . saw nothing, did I?'

The Sergeant reminded him that he was going to confess at some point, and Derek said he had not forgotten.

'I can always go back on everything I say. Now . . . I'm just going to get together a tray of supper for Robin and Emma . . . I mean, Sir Robin and Lady Randall to you, dear,' he told the Sergeant. 'And then . . .' he turned to Stillman, with a beaming smile, 'I'll give you and the pretty Mr Woolsey some food in the library. It won't be a feast, but we can't expect miracles under the circumstances, can we?'

Stillman said gravely that any food at all under the circumstances was a miracle. Derek invited him to come again when things were a bit calmer.

As he bustled about his preparations, the Superintendent looked at Johann. He said:

'Mr. Schulter . . . sir . . . .'

He got a dismal scowl from the German, and a grunt.

'You've heard Mrs Smart's statement. Will you be good enough to let me have your account of the afternoon's activities. Start here, in the kitchen, before tea,'

Johann went on scowling. But he confirmed what had been said. Yes, he had had a row with Derek. Yes, Derek had rushed off to the gazebo to sulk.

'Recoup,' said Derek, clattering some cutlery.

Johann said yes he had heard the telephone ringing from the office, and had prevented Mrs Smart from answering it.

'She try to chat with whoever call,' he told Stillman. 'Make them angry with foolish talk. She say who is it? And if some known name, she say "Oooh, fancy!" So I stop her, and go myself.'

'And who was calling?'

'Is the B.B.C. for madam.'

The Superintendent made two marks in his notebook. One was

against a statement by Mrs Smart. One was against an entry that read:
' "Cornelia" . . . is there room?'

'So?' he encouraged Johann.

'So I go to the drawing-room and tell Emma. She came fast.'

'And then?'

'Then I go upstairs.'

'Shut up, you fool!' said Derek. 'You should get a lawyer before you blab things like that.'

Johann looked sullen. He said he had no money for bribing policemen. So what use to look for fair treatment?

'Just what do you mean by all that?' said Stillman.

'Ach, I know of the English fuzz,' growled Johann. 'Often I hear Sir Robin's Harriet saying is best to offer big money, to escape wrongful arrest.'

'Sir Robin's Harriet is out of her mind!' snapped the seething Sergeant.

'Steady, George,' said Stillman.

He told the German, gently but firmly, that he had got hold of the wrong tale. He went on to say that if Johann wished to say no more without a lawyer present, that was his right.

'But, Mr Schulter, you'll make me think you have something to hide,' he concluded.

Johann looked stricken and confused. He said he had done nothing of wrong, but was resigned to arrest, being without means to buy his freedom. Derek told him to cut it out before he made enemies. The Sergeant told Derek to hold his tongue. Stillman asked if Mr Schulter would like to tell him why he had gone upstairs.

'To speak with Lynn,' said Johann.

George Woolsey held his breath so long that he nearly suffocated himself.

'This is it!' he thought. 'Answer to prayer! The end of the case. The poor old Super still in one piece . . . .'

'But,' said Johann, 'before I go up, I visit the library.'

'Why?' asked Stillman.

'It has books in it.'

The suffused Sergeant managed to breathe just in time.

'Before I speak to Lynn, I think it best to find out what she may mean when she tell me that she prays me leave.'

'That she tells you what?' the Superintendent sounded baffled.

'Look here, sir.'

Johann fumbled in a pocket, produced a crumpled bit of paper, and tossed it on the table in front of Stillman. He then sprang to retrieve it before it skidded to the ground, and handed it over with more care. The Superintendent pressed it out as flat as possible, adjusted his spectacles, and read aloud some neatly-penned lines.

'I pray thee leave, love me no more;
Call home the heart you gave me.'

There was no signature.

'The quote marks,' said the big German, 'make me think it is maybe something from a book. I go to find the dictionary of quotations by the Penguin . . . .'

'By the . . . .?'

'The publisher is the Penguin, sir.'

Derek giggled. Stillman said he was sorry to be so slow, and asked Johann to go on.

'I wish to know if Lynn is telling me to hand my notice to Emma, or if she is being poetic only.'

'Did you find the answer?'

'Very confusing, sir. Some person called Drayton writes the words to a lady. I think perhaps Lynn is mocking me. So I go upstairs to find her. To demand of her why she put this note in my pocket for me to find.'

'Did she tell you?'

'No,' said Johann. 'She is dead.'

The Sergeant took a pace towards him, but was halted by a small gesture from his superior. Derek stiffened but said nothing. Nor did Stillman speak, not wanting to break the tension of the moment.

'I do not, at the time, *know* she is dead,' went on Johann. 'I go and knock on the bathroom door, but it swings open, and she is not there. I see the bolt is loose. Then I tap on her bedroom door, but there is no word from Lynn. I wonder is she refusing to speak to me from un-kindness . . . I push her door a little, so that it is open. Then I whisper to her. First gently and pleading . . . saying I am sorry I annoyed her yesterday. Still no answer. So then I become angry. I say threatening things . . . .'

'Shut your big stupid face!' hissed Derek.

The other man seemed not to hear him. Nor did he notice how everyone was hanging on his words. The German plunged on, shaking his head from side to side as though he had a pain in his mind that tortured him.

'I talk violently,' he said, 'when I am in rage.'

Then he held out his clenched hands towards Stillman, in appeal.

100

'But I do not kill her,' he said. 'I love her. Never would I hurt her. I do not mean the things I say to her. Always I have thought she will turn to me one day. But not now.'

He rubbed both hands across his face, repeating the last words under his breath. Then he went hurriedly across to the back door of the kitchen, where he met the constable returning, and he swung round again to the Superintendent.

'Please allow me to go to my room,' he said. 'I wish not to weep before Derek. He always laugh at me.'

'No . . .' said Derek, under his breath.

'Very well, you go to your room,' said Stillman, 'if you wish. But don't leave the house, please. I might want to ask you a few more questions, and I know you must want to help me resolve this tragedy.'

'Maybe,' thought Woolsey, sceptically.

Johann muttered that he only wanted to be solitary.

'Shall I bring you some food?' asked Derek. 'Soup, or a boiled egg?'

'No!' croaked Johann. 'You poison it . . . as you did for Emma yesterday!'

He flung away into the back hall, and the narrow twist of stairway.

'Not himself, dear,' Derek told the Superintendent. 'Doesn't know what he's saying, poor lamb.'

He then suggested that Stillman and Woolsey should go back to the library, where he would bring them something to eat. He said he could not manage anything elaborate for the constables on duty in the house; but would give them home-baked brown bread, beer, and a tasty bit of farmhouse Cheddar. Dowling licked his lips.

'With my own pickles,' added Derek, lavishly.

The Sergeant licked his lips. Then he thought of something. He asked sternly what was in them. Derek, looking surprised, said just the usual . . . onions, garlic, sugar, salt, apples . . . and then he gave a snort of laughter.

'No poison,' he said. 'That was just Johann being dramatic. If anyone poisoned anything yesterday, it was that creepy Crawford, and his 'orrible 'erbs!'

He turned back to his simmering pots.

The Chief Superintendent said in winning tones:

'Now, Mr Hawley, please, sir . . . .'

'Me?' said Derek, without turning.

'You. Would you very kindly tell me just two things, sir . . . and please don't let me disturb the stirring . . . .'

'Cor!' said the Sergeant, and coughed artificially.

'Where were you, Mr Hawley, during the time Miss Sanderson was . . . .?'

'In the summerhouse,' said Derek. 'It's where I go to think, as I've told you. And I was thinking, right through teatime.'

'Thank you,' Stillman made a note in his book, and then added quietly: 'Who is Crawford?'

He got a libellous description of the Scotsman. When Derek ran low on scurrility, Stillman said apart from all that, was the man a competent gardener? With reluctance, Derek admitted that he was.

'Then why did you suggest he might mix toxic herbs with the kitchen stuff?' asked Stillman.

'Poet's licence,' said Derek. 'I mean, the man's a monster! Surly, sanctimonious, rude old bastard!'

'And a poisoner?'

'I bet he would be, given half a chance.'

'And who would he be likely to poison?'

'Me, I expect,' said Derek. 'He doesn't like me.'

The Sergeant began to say something, stopped abruptly, and choked. He got an arch glance from Derek.

'I'll have a chat with Mr Crawford,' said Stillman, hurriedly.

He was then told that the gardener finished work at five-thirty.

'At *exactly* five-thirty,' stated Derek, with a sneer. 'Catch that clown giving away one extra moment of his precious time!'

'Well, thank you very much indeed, Mr Hawley,' said Stillman. 'You carry on, sir, and we'll be in the library.'

He got up, and put his pen in his inside breast pocket.

'Will you stay here, constable?'

'Yes, sir.'

'And, Mr Hawley, please be good enough not to leave the house. And not to fight with the constable here.'

As he went with Woolsey at his heels towards the library, Stillman remembered something. He wondered whether the atmosphere of this house was atrophying his brain. Surely he had told that other young man to go and wait in the kitchen? Where had he gone, then? Had *he* left the house?

It was a relief to find Giles Warrington sitting quietly by the library fire.

## Chapter ten

## VARIED VEGETABLES

Sergeant Woolsey had remembered, too. He stared accusingly at Giles.

'Thought you said you were going to be in the kitchen, sir,' he said.

Giles had risen when they came in, rather slowly, as though the effort cost him something. Over his fair, good-natured face ran a weird assortment of expressions; self-reproach, deference, crestfallen recollection and guilt, jostled one another for position. Penitence finally won.

'Have you been looking for me? I'm sorry. I meant to go into the kitchen, but I couldn't face the shindy in there. I wanted to be on my own. I'm terribly sorry.'

The Superintendent made soothing noises; saying, not quite truthfully, that he knew Mr Warrington would be somewhere in the house.

'And if you'd spare me a few minutes of your time now, sir,' he ended, 'I'd be very glad of your help. You strike me, if you don't mind my saying so, as a responsible sort of person.'

'Unlike some others here?' said Giles, wryly.

He relaxed a little as the older man smiled, and dropped back into the great leather armchair. Stillman sat in the other, on the opposite side of the fireplace; and Woolsey settled himself in a wing-chair by the centre table.

'What can I tell you?' said Giles, rather helplessly looking from one to the other of the two policemen. 'I'm at a loss myself to understand anything that's happened.'

'Well, now . . . let's see. Start in the drawing-room this afternoon, when Miss Sanderson went off to have a bath. Were you there at that time, sir?'

'Yes – yes, I was. Emma – er – Lady Randall had just come down . . . you know she'd been ill?'

'So we've heard,' said Stillman.

'Yes. Lynn went off upstairs. And then the lads brought some tea. And – I poured out because Emma didn't feel up to it. Then the phone rang. There'd been hundreds of calls,' said Giles, 'all day long! Everyone wanting to know how Emma was feeling. People you'd think couldn't possibly know she'd been ill. Extraordinary!'

'A popular lady,' commented the Superintendent. 'Lots of friends, I expect.'

'Oh, yes. And there was everyone who'd been at the dinner-party last night, of course. And flowers arriving! God, it never stopped! It was bedlam. And that pest, Mrs Smart, always rushing to reach the telephone before anyone else, to get into the act. I'm sorry!' exclaimed Giles, abruptly. 'I shouldn't waste your time with all that!'

'You never know what small detail might help,' said Stillman. 'Now . . . you were having a quiet cup of tea, and the phone rang. You answered it?'

'No. I didn't. It was Johann. He got there just as I reached the door, and came to tell Emma it was the B.B.C. wanting to talk about clothes for this programme on Friday. She's got to be very particular about her appearance, of course. And she's wearing her own jewels, but all the rest is being . . . oh, lord! Here I go again! What does it matter a tinker's curse now what she wears for the show! What did it ever matter!'

'To Lady Randall, a good deal, I expect,' said Stillman, gravely.

Giles showed the glimmer of a smile. He said no truer word had ever been spoken.

'Of course it mattered,' he said. 'She was away like a wolf on its prey to get to grips with the wardrobe people about it. She forgot all about feeling weak. She couldn't wait to get at their throats.'

'And what did you do, Mr Warrington, while Lady Randall went to the phone?'

'Finished my tea,' said Giles, simply.

And then he told them how he'd remembered the parcel for Robin.

'From the National Gallery,' he said. 'I'd signed for it earlier, and, with all the worry about Lady Randall being ill, and people telephoning, I forgot it. I forgot to tell Robin. He was annoyed with me, I know. He's dotty about miniatures.'

He looked at the attentive face of the Superintendent, with the spectacles over the lined eyes reflecting the firelight; and he looked at the rapidly scribbling pen of Sergeant Woolsey. He said did they know that Sir Robin was an expert on some antiques? Stillman said they did.

'Well, these pictures were exactly his line,' said Giles. 'People send them to him from everywhere on earth. To have them identified, or valued. He's the senior partner of Randall and Clifford, and they're about the most famous. . . .'

His voice tailed off, and he went slightly red. He said he knew he was rambling and drivelling, insulting everyone's intelligence . . . being a pompous fool. . . .'

'Not at all,' said Stillman, kindly. 'You say what you like, sir, in your own way and time. We'll sort it all out.'

'Well – where was I? Oh, yes. Robin dashed off to his study to the parcel. And – let me think – Mrs Smart came in and began to tidy away the tea-things. I chatted with her a while. Then I heard Emma say something on the telephone . . . she was getting a bit steamed up, and her voice was carrying. I went to my office to have a look at the contract she'd signed with the B.B.C. To see where she stood, if they started being difficult. And, of course,' Giles added, 'to see where they stood if she was being awkward. She can be, sometimes.'

'So I've heard,' said Stillman.

He got a quick look from the young man.

'Don't pay too much attention to gossip, Superintendent,' said Giles. 'She's a public figure, after all. Of course, every exaggeration and idiocy gets printed! You can imagine! She can't move a foot, or say a thing, without people who ought to know better, twisting it into some rubbishy. . . .'

As Woolsey turned to a fresh page of his note-pad, Giles hesitated.

'I'm off again!' he said, apologetically.

Before Stillman could offer reassurance, there was a double tap on the door. The Sergeant went to open it.

'What do you . . . ?' he began. 'Oh – Sir Robin. Well, sir, I'm afraid the Chief Superintendent's rather busy at the moment.'

'Not at all. Do come in,' said Stillman.

But Robin only advanced a couple of paces.

'We were wondering,' said he, 'if you and your men would like something to eat, Mr Stillman. It'll be perfectly easy to arrange.'

The Superintendent thanked him, and said he thought the matter was already in hand.

'Derek, of course,' nodded Robin. 'Oh, well, that's all right, then. The boy has a firm conviction that life would grind to a halt, if food is neglected. And who,' he added, 'is to say he's wrong?'

Then he smiled faintly, and said he hoped they fully appreciated Derek. There was often a tendency at first to under-rate him.

'He pretends to be an idiot,' he explained, 'but he's not. My wife says he'll be a very great chef one day, unless someone takes an axe . . .' He stopped abruptly, and murmured: 'I nearly said something extremely tactless. Sorry.'

He apologised for disturbing them, pointed out a tray with bottles and glasses on a side table, hoped they would feel free to take whatever they fancied there, and departed. Giles went at once to the tray, deprecating his own remissness.

'I should have offered drinks long ago,' said he. 'But I suppose I had an idea that policemen never drink on duty.'

'We don't often,' said the Superintendent. 'And not at the moment, thank you, sir.'

He opened his notebook, and glanced through its pages.

'Let's go on,' he suggested. 'You were checking Lady Randall's contract. Yes?'

'Yes.' Giles brought a small whisky back with him to his chair. 'Forgive me for drinking alone. And – good luck.'

He took a few sips, thinking carefully. Then he said:

'I knew the contract, almost word for word, but I wanted to make sure. I couldn't stand the thought of having any more scenes with Emma! Then I phoned down to Mrs Smart in the drawing-room. She came in there before I left.'

'So she said.'

'Then you'll know I asked her to get a book for me, from the garden. I read the contract. She got me the number, and I rang it. I talked to Emma's agent. Then I heard Robin calling me. I went . . . and . . . and then I helped him to . . . but there wasn't anything we could do. I. . . .'

He drank the rest of his whisky at a gulp.

'It's a most distressing business,' said the Superintendent. 'And I'm sorry to have to make you go over it all again.'

He paused, and looked at Woolsey. The Sergeant had made a strangled grunting noise.

'Go on!' he was shouting, inside his own head. 'He's stalling! Press him, you old milk-sop! He knows more than he's telling. For the love of God, you doddering nitwit, make him talk!'

'Are you all right, George?' said his senior.

'Yes, thank you, sir,' husked Woolsey.

Then he said might he be allowed to put a question or two to Mr Warrington – if the Superintendent had quite finished.

'Why not?' said Stillman.

Rising to his full, burly height, the Sergeant bore down on Giles, and loomed over him. This was not as overpowering as it might have been. Giles was just as well-built as he. The two men looked measuringly at one another.

'Yes, Sergeant?' said Giles.

'What else happened?'

106

'Like what?'

'Oh, come *on*, sir! You've only given us bare outlines of what you did. Did you go to the lavatory, for instance, while you were upstairs?'

'Steady, Sergeant,' said the Superintendent, mildly.

'People do, sir.'

'Well, I didn't!' snapped Giles. 'I did exactly what I've told you. When Robin called me, I went and helped him – with Lynn. Then I came downstairs and stayed with Emma while he called the police. And that's the lot.'

'Was the door of your office open while you were in it?' said Woolsey.

'Yes, a bit.'

'Could you see across the upstairs landing, from where you were sitting?'

'Part of it. The front part. But I wasn't looking. . . .'

'Did you happen to notice Sir Robin going from his study into his bedroom?'

There was a slight pause. The Superintendent wrote carefully in his notebook. He wrote: 'Space for orchard? One apple?'

'Well, sir?' demanded Woolsey.

'I was busy,' said Giles. 'Doing the job I'm paid for! I thought I heard movement on the landing. I don't know whose. Then I heard footsteps on the stairs. And Robin came out and . . . he walked about . . . and then he called me. I've told you this!'

'If you saw nothing,' said Woolsey, 'how did you know when it was Sir Robin outside, and not anyone else?'

Giles's voice went suddenly cold and steady. He said:

'Haven't you noticed, Sergeant? Sir Robin is lame.'

'Oh, I see,' said Woolsey, slightly punctured.

'He doesn't show it very much, does he?' put in the Superintendent, whether in defence of his junior's powers of observation, or merely for something to say, was not obvious.

'He tries not to,' said Giles, simmering down. 'It was a car-smash. And Emma was driving. So he doesn't like to remind her too plainly that she nearly crippled him.'

He looked from one to the other of the two policemen, as though wondering if they understood human feelings, then he said:

'And another thing about Sir Robin . . . he's not showing how shocked he is about this frightful business. That doesn't mean he's being callous. He's very upset. I can tell, if you can't. Oh, I'm sorry,' he said. 'I didn't mean to. . . .'

'Never mind, sir. We understand,' said the Superintendent. 'He's had a most worrying time. With his wife's illness yesterday, and now this. . . .'

'Mr Stillman,' said Giles, in a tense voice, and screwing up his face as though in some distaste for what he was saying, 'you must by now have heard rumours that Emma was poisoned last night – whether by accident or on purpose. Have you looked into the question at all?'

No one had noticed the door opening, and now an excitable voice brought their heads round as one.

'If you're trying to shop me,' said Derek, 'you want to watch it, mate! I can tell these lovely people all about the raging and gnashing of teeth that went on between you and Emma yesterday! Sacked you, didn't she? Have you told them that? Tossed you out on your ear! Funny she should be poisoned, almost instantly. Eh?'

He held the door open with his elbow, and steered a laden food-trolley into the room. He brought himself and it to a halt by the big table, and looked at the three men with narrowed mouth, eyes, and nostrils. He said he despised them all, and was now going out to the gazebo, and please don't come looking for him there. The Superintendent said it would be bitterly cold outside at this time of night.

'And no one, Mr Hawley,' he went on, 'has accused you of anything at all, so far. No one has accused anyone of anything. I shall be the first to let you know should the situation arise.'

Derek sniffed disbelief.

The Sergeant moved into the act. He said sourly that anyone who made so much fuss about nothing, could easily be trying to hide his own guilt.

Derek leaned across the table, and glared into Woolsey's face.

'You're a very nasty man, really,' said Derek. 'With a mean, paltry mind. You're a bully, I do believe . . . and I bet you take bribes, like Johann said.'

The Sergeant bristled.

'No, no! Steady, George!' said Stillman. 'He doesn't, Mr Hawley. Take bribes, I mean. Mr Woolsey is a most honest and scrupulous officer.'

'I don't need to be defended against this babbling saphead!' said his Sergeant, hotly.

'Who does?' said Giles. 'And what a good description.'

Derek, with a ferocious scowl, said he considered Giles no better than a liar, a crook, and a probable killer.

'I've made a list,' said he, 'of all the things Emma called you, and I'll be

108

happy to show them to these clever sleuths. Make 'em think a bit, perhaps.'

'Stop playing the clown!' snapped the goaded Giles. 'You're always showing off by acting the stage queer! And, believe me, it's not necessary! Too obvious, anyway.'

'And you're a swine,' said Derek. 'Your act is being sensible and hearty. The one rational character in the house. Well, ha, ha! I could tell. What about the time you got Emma to open a bazaar at Brighton . . . only it should have been Bristol? What about the time you got her charities mixed, and she gave fifty pounds to a . . . ?'

'Oh, shut up!' said Giles, curtly.

'*And* what about the time . . . ?'

'Shut up, do!'

Stillman stirred, and both the young men looked at him uneasily. He smiled at them.

'Most interesting,' said he.

Giles could see a sort of rough plan he had been drawing across a page of his note-book. It looked unlike any part of the Monksend complex.

'I'm sorry, Superintendent,' said Giles. 'I shouldn't have said any of that. Sorry, Derek. I didn't mean . . . It's just that I'm feeling a bit raw. How can you keep up this squabbling and skirmishing, when . . . God, don't you feel anything about Lynn? Don't you . . . ?'

He turned on his heel, and went to the French windows at the front of the library, where he stood with his shoulders hunched rigidly.

'Yes,' said the Superintendent. 'I've noticed that people do tend to say more than they mean, when they get excited and nervous.'

He closed his notebook with a little sigh. He had almost got on the trail of an idea for combining a vegetable garden with a tiny orchard (James Grieve and Charles Ross to fertilise each other among the spinach) . . . but that would mean having no pool, which was unthinkable. If only, he thought sadly, a policeman's pension would run to just a few more square yards of garden. He dragged his mind back to the more immediate topic.

'I only listen to things that give me ideas,' he said, addressing Derek and the back of Giles impartially. 'I get easily confused, so I scribble to help me concentrate. You must forgive my apparent absent-mindedness.'

'We're off again!' grated the Sergeant, to himself. 'Making out to be a fool, now! So he is, of course, but it's not for him to say. Don't let him go falling on his knees to them, apologising for his existence!'

'I'm sorry, gentlemen, for all this questioning,' said Stillman. 'I expect you want your supper. I may not need to ask you any more tonight, but you'll have to bear with me. . . .'

'My God!' said Giles.

They all looked at him. He spun round to face them, looking distraught. His voice was shaking when he said he'd just seen the new moon.

'What?' said Stillman.

'Through glass! I moved the curtain a bit, and there it was. Brand new! That's it, then . . . disaster. I might have known this would happen, on top of everything else. I must go. . . .'

Giles went across the room like a colt that had just experienced its first horse-fly, and was out of the door before anyone could move or speak.

'Hey!' said the Sergeant.

He sped to the door, and then looked back at his senior.

'Gone upstairs,' he said, harshly. 'I'll see what he's up to!'

He also vanished into the hall.

The Superintendent sighed, and half-rose from the armchair.

'It's all right, Mr Stillman, love,' said Derek. 'He's only gone to look at the dog.'

'The . . . ? I didn't see a dog in the house. The cat, yes, but. . . .'

'It isn't real.'

Derek gave a suppressed giggle at the expression on the Superintendent's face. It seemed to restore his good nature. He went closer to the policeman, and said with some satisfaction:

'It's just as I told you. Giles pretends he's sane, but he's not. He's raving mad, like the rest of us. He goes for lucky signs and wonders. If he walks under a ladder, he mustn't speak till he sees a dog. Same with the new moon through glass, like now. You should have heard him when Emma bought an opal ring! She's never worn it, he scared her so. "Bad luck! . . . Might have been stolen by the dealer!" Gawd!'

'This dog?' said Stillman.

'He's got a toy one in his office. Floppy-eared affair, like a. . . .'

'Beagle. Yes, I did see that,' the Superintendent told him.

'*And* a bit of wood in his pocket for touching,' went on Derek. 'Mind you,' he added, 'I'm not above *that*, meself! There's times when it's the only. . . .'

Giles came back into the library. He was followed by a stunned-looking Woolsey.

'He found a toy, and patted it,' said the latter, glumly.

'Never mind,' said Derek. 'You come and sit down, duckie, and have some food.'

The Sergeant sat down, with a pleading look at his senior. Stillman nodded at him, reassuringly. And Derek said he'd done his best to provide a nourishing meal for the police because it would, in his opinion, assist their brains to function.

'It's not y'r actual feast,' he deplored, wheeling the trolley nearer. 'Mostly bits and pieces left over from the dinner yesterday. But it's not bad. Some real mushroom soup* . . . and you'd better get outside that fairly soon, or it'll be luke . . . hotplate or no. Then there's cold duck with orange salad. A couple of hot baked potatoes in that covered dish, and cream and chives to spread on them. Fruit and cheese. Home-made bread. A nice bottle of Riesling. And I'll fetch you some coffee when you're ready for it.'

Woolsey was stricken speechless. He feared he might start to dribble. And Stillman thanked Derek for them both. He got a stately bow in acknowledgement. Then Derek asked Giles where he would like to dine.

'In here, with the law? In the drawing-room with the nobs? Or in the kitchen with me and a lowly copper? There's the front hall with the other copper. Or there's the dining-room, all on your own. You've a wide choice. That is, if the Chief Superintendent . . . or am I stepping outside convention if I go on calling you Mr Stillman . . . ?'

'Please do,' said Stillman.

'Thank you, love. If Mr Stillman has finished asking you about your motives for murder,' he said to Giles. 'If any,' he added, as a sop to concord.

'Now, now, sir,' said the Superintendent.

He then said it would be best if both Mr Warrington and Mr Hawley went and found a quiet place to eat, as far from one another as possible. And Giles said he was going up to the room where he would be staying overnight, and wanted no food of any kind. As he left the library, Derek trotted after him, saying he'd only been joking about motives, and wouldn't he feel the better for a bowl of nice soup at least.

'Wait a moment,' said Stillman. 'No, you carry on, Mr Warrington. I'd just like one word with Mr Hawley.'

Giles cast a slightly anxious look at Derek, but left him with the police.

'He's all right, really,' said Derek, coming back.

Stillman had turned over a page or two in his notebook, and was looking thoughtfully at some scribbles. He said there was a point on which he would value Derek's opinion.

'Anything,' said Derek, expansively. 'Anything at all, dear. Just ask.'

'Then – from your personal knowledge, and as far as you could tell – how did Miss Sanderson get on with Lady Randall?'

'Oh,' Derek looked startled. 'I think they were good friends.'

'Thank you.'

'Is that all?'

'For the moment, sir.'

Derek pattered away.

The Sergeant was left staring bemusedly at his superior. He said blankly:

'But, sir – you don't think that Lady Randall and the dead woman . . . might have been . . . were actually . . . ?'

'What on earth are you suspecting now, George?' said Stillman, austerely. 'You heard what Mr Hawley said. The two ladies were just good friends. Drink your soup.'

*Chapter eleven*

## A RIGHT MOUSSE

The divided diners finished eating, in various parts of the house. Derek went round with trays of coffee. He also removed the trolleys, with the help of Constable Dowling who had been hypnotised or terrorised into kitchen service. Derek noted that all the police had made hearty meals, though Robin and Emma had apparently only stirred the food with forks.

'If you'd fancy a nice lick of brandy . . . ?' said Derek, coaxingly, to Stillman.

'No, thank you. I don't think so.'

'Damn you!' snapped the Sergeant. 'I was just going to accept.'

He did not, of course, say this aloud.

'You wouldn't want us to start feeling sleepy, now, would you?' Stillman was saying to Derek. 'Or, worse still, muddled. We've got work to do, remember.'

Through Derek's hasty denials of any ulterior motive, the Sergeant did a quick *volte face*.

'Sneaky bastard!' he thought. 'Make us drunk so we can't think straight, eh? Not that he'd catch me, I've a head like a horse . . . (do horses drink spirits?) . . . but old Stillman . . .! Hell, he's muddled enough already, without soaking himself in booze. Lucky he happened to think of it.'

Derek went away, and the two officers drank their coffee. Stillman had cream and sugar in his, but Woolsey took it strongly black. Someone must keep awake!

'And now, if you're ready,' said the Superintendent, 'I want one more word with them in the drawing-room. Young Mr Hawley said they've finished their dinner.'

He had spent the last half-hour, as well as eating, in poring over his notebook. To a tentative enquiry from the Sergeant, he said the most worrying point he had found was the matter of whether irises liked chalk or peat. This effectively shut Woolsey up, and his senior continued to brood in peace.

Now he closed his book, and ambled to the door and across the hall, with the Sergeant sighing at his heels. He tapped on the drawing-room door. . . .

'And why not fling it open!' thought Woolsey. 'Catch the suspects doing something suspicious, like burning evidence. . . .'

*What* evidence? Any evidence going. Going where? Woolsey stopped thinking.

'Do come in,' called Robin.

They were given comfortable seats, offered brandy . . . which both refused . . . and asked if they had come to any conclusion about Lynn's death.

'Not to say conclusion,' said Stillman. 'There are always ideas. But the question is, are they of any value? I wish I didn't have to trouble you again tonight. But I don't seem to know quite enough about the weapon. This statue-thing . . . what did you call it, sir? The Queen of the West? Yes. Now, where was it normally kept?'

'In my bedroom,' said Emma.

'Ah. On that white pedestal by the window? I noticed there was nothing standing on it, and wondered why not.'

'It looked lovely there,' said Emma. 'The light shone through the jade a little. And the pedestal is alabaster, so it was slightly transparent as well.'

'Very pretty,' commented the Superintendent. 'And the statue was always in that same place? I mean, everyone knew it was kept there?'

'Well . . .' Emma hesitated. 'It's a bit more complicated than that . . .'

She cast an odd glance at her husband, and bit her lip. Robin said there had been a certain amount of disagreement over the Queen of the West. Emma said surely they need not bother the Superintendent about all that silliness.

'Please, Lady Randall. It's no sort of bother. I'd like to know everything you can tell me about the statue. It had your fingerprints on it, and those of your husband, as you'd expect. Bit blurred, of course . . . smeared . . . but clear enough.'

Emma took a gasping breath, and a gulp of the coffee beside her. She said he would think Robin and herself perfect fools.

'Oh, yes you will,' she insisted, as Stillman demurred. 'We argued furiously about the jade. I loved it, it's so beautiful. I wanted it more than I've wanted anything for a long time. And Robin was terribly stubborn, and said I couldn't have it.'

'Just for the record,' said her husband, 'it didn't belong to me. It was bought by my firm, on my advice, and sold for a large sum immediately.

114

I only brought it home to show my wife because it really is lovely, and. . .'

'To tantalize me!' snapped Emma. 'You knew I'd go mad for it. That I'd pay your old firm twice what they'd been offered . . .'

'Not offered, dear. Paid. The thing was sold. I'd have given it to you willingly,' said Robin, 'but it wasn't mine to give. If I'd known *before* it was sold . . . I tried to buy it back, but Mr Ringston was determined to have it. Whether he wants it now . . .'

Emma flinched.

'How horrible!' she exclaimed. 'I'd forgotten . . . ! *I* don't want it now. Mr Stillman, I said you'd think badly of us, and now you really will!'

She got a politely worded denial, and plunged on:

'It was all completely petty, of course. I knew perfectly well that Robin couldn't let me have it. But I did like it, and I got bloody-minded. I went and bought that pedestal . . . oh, I was being impossible!' she stared wide-eyed at Stillman. 'If it hadn't been there, in my room, perhaps . . . oh God! Perhaps. . . .'

She gave a little moan.

Robin said even if the statue had not been there, plenty of other things were.

'Heavy glass vases,' he suggested. 'Ashtrays. That great marble bowl with the phone in it . . . weighs a ton! And the bathroom stool. . . .'

Emma said it would take giant strength to lift the bowl from the shelf, and Robin drawled that for all she knew it might have been a giant who did so. She said wouldn't someone have noticed a giant creeping round the house? They both turned to Stillman and apologised.

'You must be heartily sick of us!' said Emma.

Robin said they were not themselves, wasting time with silly bickering. Stillman said it was all most instructive.

'You never know what will come in useful.' he told them. 'I think I might even recognise a piece of jade, if I see another. Or alabaster, or marble. If I had a proper, docketing sort of brain, I could learn a lot in a house like this.'

He paused for a moment, and then asked Emma if she usually kept her bath-cap in the bathroom.

'Oh, yes. It hung on the end of the smaller towel-rail, where it could drip happily . . .'

She caught her breath, turned her head away from the men, and buried her face in a cushion. There was a short and awkward silence. They all visualised the drips. After a little while, Stillman said he would like permission to go upstairs to the scene of the crime again.

'What'll he do, if they refuse?' wondered the Sergeant, inside his mind. 'Walk out backwards bowing, and commit *hara-kiri* in the hall?'

'Need you ask?' said Robin.

For one moment, Woolsey panicked. But it was not to him that the words were addressed.

Suddenly a door-bell rang. There was the sound of deep-timbred voices of men in the hall. There was a tap on the door. With Robin's invitation to enter, a policeman put his head in, and said a Mr Sanderson was here. Emma gave a shiver and sat up, and Robin went quickly to the door, saying please come in.

He brought back a middle-aged, soldierly man, whose hair had faded to a sandy colour, with only a few bright streaks in it to show it had once been red. But he had undimmed green eyes, and so strong a likeness that Emma went straight to him and clutched his hand in both of hers.

'My dear . . . Mr Sanderson . . . .' she said. 'Oh, I'm so unhappy . . . .'

Robin introduced the two policemen, and Sanderson nodded to them. The Chief Superintendent said:

'This is a heart-breaking business, sir. I deeply sympathise with you in your loss.'

The father of Lynn thanked him, but he looked challengingly at Stillman, and asked to know exactly what had happened.

'I'm afraid I must tell you,' said the Superintendent, 'that all evidence indicates that your daughter has been murdered.'

Emma gave a small cry, and said he might have tried to break it more gently.

'I would rather hear the truth outright,' said Sanderson.

He was led towards an armchair by Emma, but did not sit down. Instead, he stood by the mantelshelf, and looked round at the others for a moment. Then he said to Robin:

'You told me, on the telephone, that there had been an accident. But I guessed by the tone of your voice, that it was more than that. May I now know just how, and why, my daughter has died? Superintendent?'

'Yes, sir,' said Stillman. 'But first, let me say that I think Sir Robin was right not to go into any details earlier. We are still very much in the dark, and going by guesswork.'

He then gave the stiff figure before him a clear and factual account of the finding of Lynn's body, and the apparent cause of her death.

'The motive, if any, is as yet unknown,' he concluded. 'I hope to find out, in due course, just why. . . .'

116

'If any?' echoed Sanderson.

Even hearing the dreadful details, his shoulders had not sagged; but he now sat down in the chair by the fire. He looked very straightly at Stillman.

'Thank you, sir,' he said. 'You've been very honest with me. I'm grateful. But . . . has no one any idea why Lynn should be killed? An enemy? I can't imagine it. She was a considerate girl, and very loyal to her friends.'

Emma said huskily that everyone had loved her.

'Tell me, Mr Sanderson,' said the Superintendent, 'did your daughter never give you any impression that she was in difficulty of some kind . . . either with a person, or some situation. . . . ?'

'No. Never,' said Lynn's father. 'This has come as a complete shock to me. We . . . I suppose my wife and I would be considered an old-fashioned pair. A bit dull, living very quietly. We were . . . well, worried when Lynn came to work here with Lady Randall. . . .'

He looked at Emma, and for a moment a slight relaxation of his hard mouth showed a trace of irony.

'Forgive me,' he said. 'It was not you whom we mistrusted, but the effect of so different a life from the simple one that Lynn was used to. She had always lived at home. Worked as a secretary to a solicitor in the town. This job might have . . . bewildered . . . her. Made her vulnerable. But, indeed, she seemed to take to it very easily. I know she was happy here, Lady Randall. So this made us happy.'

For a moment, no one spoke. Then:

'I believe she often came home to visit you,' said Stillman.

'Yes, she did.'

'Did she write to you?'

'Yes, often. Very cheerful letters, too. Describing the exciting things that went on here. News of television plans, and famous people who came to the house. She was good at writing letters, and we looked forward to them.'

'And recently, sir, did she mention anything unusual happening? Anything worrying?'

'Good Lord, no. Just general newsy chat . . .' Sanderson paused for a moment. 'Well . . . she did say . . . but it wasn't worrying or. . . .'

'Do you mind telling us what she said, Mr Sanderson?'

'Go on!' shrieked the brain of Sergeant Woolsey. 'Make him talk! This may be it . . . the vital clue! Under your silly nose . . . *now*! Use pressure! Put burning splinters under his fingernails. . . . !'

He stopped. Even he felt this might be going too far.

117

'A few weeks ago,' Sanderson was saying, thoughtfully, 'Lynn wrote to say she would not be able to come down for a while, or even to do much writing. She was going to be extremely busy, she said. There was something nice to tell us, that must wait until she had time to go into details. That's all,' he said. 'It doesn't add up to much, does it?'

'You never know,' said Stillman. 'Have you any idea what she might have meant, madam?'

'Emma,' said Robin, 'do you think she was referring to those pearls you gave her? She was very elated about them.'

'She said nothing about pearls,' said Lynn's father.

'That may have been it, then,' said Emma. 'Oh, it's a nightmare! That she can be dead now! So suddenly and horribly. . . . !'

'And uselessly,' said Stillman. 'Even perhaps to her murderer.'

Everyone looked at him. He said gravely that it was on the cards that the killer had not meant his blow for the girl. Emma nodded in bitter agreement.

'Are you saying . . . a mistake?' asked Sanderson, blankly.

'Possibly.'

It gave no one any satisfaction to see the stiff shoulders bent at last. The man folded forward, hands to his face. He muttered his daughter's name almost inaudibly, and then said:

'Could anyone kill . . . by mistake? Like . . . catching the wrong bus? Lynn. . . .'

Emma went to the Superintendent. She said softly that it might be better if she was left alone with Mr Sanderson for a while. 'We'll ask him to stay here with us tonight. . . .'

But Sanderson had already pulled himself together. He sat up, white-faced and stern, and said he would go back to his own home.

'My wife will have to be told,' he said. 'I'd prefer to do it myself, and as soon as possible. She is already deeply shocked at the news of Lynn's death. Our only . . .' he hesitated a moment, and then went on firmly. 'The manner of it will be an even greater blow. I'll stay here as long as you need me, Superintendent, of course. But then I must go home. It's two hours' drive to the coast.'

'You came as soon as Sir Robin telephoned?' asked Stillman.

'As soon as I had telephoned to our doctor, and waited for his arrival. My wife was . . . of course, I had to tell her that Lynn was dead. I came away as soon as I could leave her. She wanted to come with me, to find out . . . but the doctor thought it better that I came alone. I have a sister living near, and she came to stay with my wife.'

'Alibi!' Woolsey was thinking. 'The clever old devil has slipped us an alibi. Letting us know he was two hours' drive away . . . but we'll check on him!'

'Sergeant!' Stillman was saying. 'Sergeant Woolsey . . . I'm just explaining to Mr Sanderson that you'll be down tomorrow morning, early, to have a look round.'

'Oh . . . yes, sir.'

'We'll expect you, Sergeant,' said Sanderson, politely. 'And nothing of Lynn's will be touched, in her room . . . anywhere in the house . . . until you come.'

Woolsey muttered a courteous reply, and then listened with gritted teeth to his senior officer. Stillman was saying good-night to Emma, Robin, and Sanderson, with many regrets for inconvenience caused by the presence of police, and absurd references to his own shortcomings. It was a relief, at last, when he found himself alone in the hall with the Superintendent.

'At least he won't apologise to me for anything,' he thought.

'I'm sorry, George,' said Stillman. 'I just need a few more minutes here. Then we can get back to London and report. You must be getting tired.'

'Tired to death of you, you old idiotic muddler!' snarled Woolsey, behind his teeth, and in seething silence.

'Are you all right?'

'Perfectly, sir.'

Woolsey struggled to control the flush of rage that had flooded his face. He only made it worse, and for a moment thought he was going to faint. He managed to say something about the heat in the hall. . . .

'It just seems comfortable to me,' said his senior. 'Are you coming down with something?'

'I'm all right, sir!'

'We're just going into the kitchen. I'm afraid it'll be even hotter for you there. Better sit down, and have a glass of water.'

They found Derek playing 'Scrabble' with Constable Dowling, or rather arguing fiercely that there was no such word as 'braw'. Dowling was maintaining stoutly that there was, and that it meant nice in Scots. Derek said foreign languages didn't count. They then saw the newcomers. The constable sprang to his feet.

'Excuse me,' said the Superintendent, 'I hate interrupting your game, but Sergeant Woolsey isn't very well. Could he have a drink of water?'

Derek began to fuss round the fuming Sergeant with small cries of anxiety and sympathy. Woolsey found himself seated in the wicker

119

armchair, with a hessian cushion behind his head, and a glass of iced water in his hand. He was not pleased by any of it, and least of all by the faint gleam in Stillman's eyes.

'There,' said the latter, gently. 'You'll soon feel better.'

He then turned to Derek, and said would it be all right if he went upstairs?

'There's one in the passage over there,' said Derek. 'By the back door.'

Thanking him for the thought, the Superintendent said he really wanted to take a quick stroll through the bedrooms, bathrooms, study and office on the first floor.

'Just to refresh my memory,' said he, 'which really is getting a bit creaky, like the rest of me. I'd like to go away with a fairly clear picture in my mind.'

Derek said he understood, adding that his own brain creaked at times.

'And that's why you go into the garden, sir? To lubricate it, as it were?'

'Ha, ha!' said Derek. 'You wily thing, you're trying to trap me!'

'How do you make that out?'

'Because I told you I was going into the garden after supper. Oh, yes I did. And now you've gone all suspicious because I'm in here instead, playing "Scrabble". What have I been up to, eh? What false trails have I been laying? Well, you're up the wrong tree, Shylock . . . oh, I mean Sherlock! . . . terribly sorry!'

'That's all right, Mr Hawley. I don't mind my Jewish blood, if you don't.'

The Sergeant gulped down his iced water to the last drop, and was glad of it.

'You're a very dear, cosy thing,' Derek told the Superintendent, 'and I'll tell you why I came indoors. The gazebo was just too creepy. I took one look into the black, open doorway . . . and I asked myself how did I know what was lurking inside, ready to smash my head in! And I answered that I didn't know, and wasn't going in to find out. And back I came. Do you believe me?'

'Why not?' said Stillman.

'Thousands wouldn't,' said Woolsey.

By mistake, he said it aloud. He got a hurt look from Derek, and a mild tutting noise from his superior.

'And I wonder if you'd mind coming up with me, Mr Hawley?' said the latter.

Derek said he'd love to, adding that he reckoned he was safe with Mr Stillman.

'Being Scotland Yard,' he threw in, hastily, 'not because of your age!'

'I thought that would be what you meant, sir.'

Woolsey rose to follow them, but was gestured back to the chair.

'Don't you move till you're better,' said Stillman. 'I don't want you ill on my hands, just when we're going to be so busy. Keep an eye on him, Dowling. Give him some more water, if he looks odd. Do take that anxious look off your face, George. Mr Hawley will see that I don't get lost in the house . . . or start planting false evidence.'

'I'd prefer to come with you, sir.'

'And I forbid it.'

The Superintendent left the kitchen with Derek.

'A quick stroll round to refresh his memory!' fumed Woolsey, to the constable. 'More likely get himself murdered . . . or raped!'

Dowling looked worried, and said surely the Superintendent could yell for help.

'If he thinks of it in time.'

But indeed, it was not much more than ten minutes later that Stillman came back to them, with Derek at his heels.

'That bell over there rang,' Dowling told them. 'I answered, and it wanted some fresh coffee in the drawing-room. I said all right . . . but I didn't know where anything was, so I didn't make it.'

'Thank God for that!' said Derek. 'I wouldn't trust you to make a cup of cocoa.'

'All right, Dowling,' said the Superintendent, into the indignant statement by the young policeman that he could make a very good cocoa. 'I've finished here for the time being, so I'll be getting along. How do you feel, George?'

'None the better for your ribbing!' said Woolsey, adding aloud that he felt fine.

'Then come along, lad. Er . . . Dowling, you and the other chap in the hall are on night duty here, aren't you?'

'That's right sir. We'll stay here till someone turns up in the morning.'

'*I* shall turn up in the morning.'

'Yes, sir.'

'Bringing your relief,' said Stillman, kindly, 'Mr Hawley, I wonder if I could ask you to do something further?'

'Ask away,' said Derek, busy with the coffee-pot.

'Would you see that the constables are comfortable, if they want to rest? They won't sleep. Dowling can stay in here, with the big arm-chair. And see that the man in the front hall has a cosy chair, too. And, Mr Hawley, I'm sure you'll look after your employers . . . some hot milk, perhaps, before they retire. Johann Schulter too, if you can per-suade him. And have something yourself. You look a bit peaked,' said Stillman.

'Sweetie, I must look like the dustman's leavings!' said Derek. 'It's been a proper mess, hasn't it! No way to get decent food on the tables.'

Then he said he would do his best to get everybody comfortable and happy, adding that he didn't actually mean laughing-happy, if the Superintendent saw what he meant. Stillman said he saw exactly what he meant.

'And will you be here for breakfast tomorrow?' asked Derek. 'Just so's I know what to start cooking.'

'My men and I,' said Stillman, sounding vaguely royal, 'will arrive after breakfast. We'd all enjoy some coffee later, if we may have it. You make the best I've ever tasted.'

'Thank you, dear,' said Derek, charmed.

'Thank *you*, sir,' said the Superintendent, solemnly.

*Chapter twelve*

## HOT AND SWEET

The only reliable statement came the following morning from the Home Office. It informed Chief Superintendent Stillman that post-mortem examination of Lynn Sanderson showed she had died as the result of a blow on the head. This having been strongly suspected already by Stillman ... not to mention the entire population of Monksend and the surrounding district ... did little to further investigations. It merely eliminated an area of possible doubt.

Just before mid-day, Sergeant Woolsey drove back from Kent. He found his senior in the library, sorting through notes, statements, and horticultural catalogues.

'Drew a blank at the girl's home, sir.'

'Pity. Sit down, George. You look worried.'

'Me, sir? No, I'm not worried.'

'Yes, I am!' he told himself, fiercely. 'Look at the old zany! Willows, no less! One of those would flatten his damn bungalow in three years!'

Aloud, he asked sedately how Stillman's day had progressed.

'Nicely,' said the older man. 'It's been quiet and peaceful in here. And young Derek gave me a second breakfast. He wanted me to try his Scotch butteries.'

Licking his lips, the Sergeant asked if they were nice.

'Oh, very. But not for every day, no matter what the Scots think. Not for me. I do like my plain brown toast and marmalade.'

'I've not even had that,' said the Sergeant, morosely. 'I left London at seven, with only a cup of tea! No time for anything at all since.'

'Bad luck, my boy. Now, tell me . . . .'

'Yes. Well, Mr Sanderson was very helpful. His wife kept to her bed, and we didn't bother her. He let me search the house pretty thoroughly, but either the girl kept no private papers there, or she'd destroyed them. Or someone had. Have you thought seriously,' asked Woolsey, 'about the father?'

'Yes, indeed. He has my deepest sympathy.'

'I meant . . . well, anyway . . . he gave me the names of some of his daughter's friends. I made a list.'

123

Woolsey handed it to the Superintendent, and went on with his report.

'Seven. Three men, and four women,' said he. 'All of them known to the parents. And none, according to her father, of greater importance than the others. I went and saw the first three on that list, sir. They were the ones she was thickest with. There's a John Mayston . . . solicitor, well-known in the area . . . and his sister Mary Mayston. She works in the local public library. Both shocked by the death of their friend. Or so they said!' commented Woolsey, darkly. 'John seems to have spent all yesterday at Tunbridge Wells, working with a branch of his firm. And sister Mary didn't leave her library until late evening. Their stories are being checked, sir. Then I saw Mrs Edith Holt, who went to school with Lynn Sanderson. Married now, with an infant. And she cried like mad while I talked to her, and said she'd been shopping and having tea with her auntie yesterday.'

Woolsey then said he had left the local Kentish police rounding up and interviewing the other people on the list. Their reports would come to Stillman as soon as possible.

'I thought I'd better get back here quickly,' said the Sergeant, with conscious virtue. 'So I didn't stop for food or anything.'

'Look, why don't you go and captivate Derek?' said Stillman. 'Dazzle him into giving you a snack.'

'Are you mad!' said Woolsey. 'Sir,' he added.

'Not at all. I don't want you fainting with hunger. You're going to a sort of rehearsal of this television show this afternoon,' explained his senior. 'I can't go myself. There's things I need to do, here. So I'm sending you along with Lady Randall to this meeting at her club in London. A sort of rough briefing for the show, I gather. You're to sit in on it, George, and just keep your eyes open. In case of any sort of . . . incident. Now go on, do what I say. Chat up Derek, and he may give you some lunch. I'm getting some, he says.'

Woolsey nodded nervously, and went.

'Oh, la!' said Derek, in the kitchen. 'Eff off, love. We're busy.'

'Yes, I . . . I can see that . . . but . . . .'

'But what!'

Woolsey's brain seethed, working out some way of captivating Derek without committing himself.

The kitchen was full of bustle. Derek, Johann . . . and, suddenly, Emma. She came in through the back door, with an armful of roses, and gave a charming cry of pleasure when she saw Woolsey.

'Nice to see you, my dear boy!' she trilled, putting the flowers in the sink. 'At least, it isn't really, of course, but you know what I mean. Have you had luncheon? It's just about time we all had some. There's enough for Sergeant Woolsey, isn't there, boys?'

'*Wir sind sehr beschäftigt*,' said Johann, sourly. 'We busy are.'

'Oh, shut your face!' said Derek. 'There's lashings of food.'

'If either of you is speaking to me . . .' began Emma.

Her pupil-cooks assured her hurriedly that neither was.

'There then, Mr Woolsey,' said Emma, brightly, washing some scratches on her hands with disinfectant. 'You shall be fed. In the library with your nice boss, dear?'

'Or in here,' said Derek, leering hideously, 'with nice us?'

Fearing he had overdone the dazzle, Woolsey hastily said the library. The Chief he hinted, would be needing him there for consultation.

'I'll bet, flower,' said Derek.

The Sergeant bolted.

He nearly fell over Mrs Smart, coming through the hall dragging the long entrail-like appendages of the vacuum cleaner; he saw the front door being forced shut by Giles Warrington against what seemed an assault by the press; and he scuttled back into the library, like a crab that had fallen out of its second-hand whelk-shell, and wanted another . . . thicker . . . fast.

'Are you all right, son?' said his senior.

'Yes . . . I'm . . . yes, fine . . . .'

'You know what. You've been away from this house for some thirteen hours, and you've forgotten how to handle things here.'

'How to . . . .?'

'Like rape, George. If you can't avoid it, lie back and enjoy it.'

'Sir!'

Lunch came and went. And so did Woolsey, in a vintage Rolls driven by Emma, heading for her London club, where a private dining-room had been reserved for this first briefing of the well-known actors who were to be her 'guests' at the television banquet tomorrow. Woolsey was not happy during the drive. For one thing, Derek and Johann were sitting together in the back of the car, arguing fiercely the whole way. And, for another he felt the helpless terror of the expert driver who is being driven by another. He was quite cowed and silent when they pulled up outside a tall, Georgian house in a street behind the Haymarket. He padded after Emma and her cooks, to a large, comfortable dining-room, with settees round the walls, and an enormous table down the middle, set with chairs.

Mike Peel came forward to meet them. And cries of welcome went up from a group of about a dozen people clustered at one end of the room. Woolsey gasped when he recognised some of the faces. Famous actors and actresses, comedians, personalities. Not one was stand-offish or spiky. Words of sympathy were pouring from them now. And Emma's voice lifted clearly above them all in response.

'You must realise,' said she, 'that I'd rather eat a live caterpillar than do this show at all. After the ghastly tragedy . . . .'

Everyone assured her that they felt the same.

'Unless it's a fuzzy one,' said a plump actor called Harry. 'I think I'd rather do the show than eat one of those.'

'*But,*' said Emma, putting a tiny fraction of edge on her voice, 'Scotland Yard wishes us to continue as arranged. That handsome young man lurking in the corner is Detective Sergeant George Woolsey, and he's very clever. He's going to stay here with us while we're talking, and generally keep an eye on us all.'

'Poor soul!' said a very famous actor, tall and balding, with a face like a gentle hawk, and a voice of warm honey and bells. 'He'll see a seamier side of life than he expects.'

'On a long hook!' said Woolsey.

Aloud, he just told them to ignore him. A dark actress with a cleft chin and a suede trouser-suit told him to be less beautiful or be less brief. He blushed, and effaced himself in a dimmish corner.

'Stop teasing the fuzz, Wanda!' said Mike, sternly. 'We've got work to do.'

He counted heads, found everyone present, and introduced his assistant. A long, thin, young man with the pointed ears and pointed face of an elf or Martian. His name was Kay Stangrove, and he had hair-coloured hair, eye-coloured eyes, and a sudden flashing smile. He wore a thick yellow jersey, thick tweed slacks, and thick round spectacles. In a year or two, he would be the finest director in television . . . if jealousy had not sacked him long before. Films would claim him ultimately, and he would be world-famous. Meanwhile, Mike Peel relied implicitly on his competence and good humour. The only two things ever seen to disturb Mr Stangrove were (a) to be asked, on introduction, what the 'Kay' in his name stood for . . . and (b) the fact that Kay was sometimes misguidedly used as a girl's name, being properly male. Emma had won his heart by pointing out the equal stupidity of using 'Jocelyn', 'Esmé' or 'Robin' for women's names, presumably by people who liked causing irritation and confusion.

The actors eyed Kay speculatively. The whole show depended so much on him, once Mike was shut far away from them in the control room, his only link with them would be by telephone through this tall creature with the smile.

Also presented to them was a plump young woman whose only name seemed to be Jujube. She was Mike's secretary, and clung like a possessive foster-mother to his script and his notes, in which he had already plotted every move, camera-shot, every microphone position, the timing of Emma's dialogue, and a thousand other vital matters connected with the present programme. Jujube never left his elbow, and seemed to regard him and his script with equal and passionate devotion. He constantly referred to her and to the notes as if they were extensions of his own brain. In a way, they were.

'Now settle comfortably, loves,' he said. 'I'll position you roughly at the table. John, you here at the head ... now you, darling, on his right ....'

He placed his cast. And hurriedly reassured those who found themselves with their backs to where the cameras would be.

'I've a special one, just for you happy few,' said he. 'Concealed with incredible skill and cunning, in the back wall of the set. You won't be ignored, my treasures.'

And now Emma went to her end of the table, and smiled down its length at the 'Guests'.

'Behind Emma,' said Mike, 'will be the doorway through to the other set. The kitchen, with stoves and fridges, where Derek and Johann will be getting food out ready for ....'

'We'll be bringing it through ourselves, sometimes?' said Derek, anxiously.

'Oh, yes! Your millions of fans won't be disappointed! You'll be on view,' Mike told him. 'Anyway, some of the action will be happening *in* the kitchen set.'

'If so,' put in Johann, acidly, 'is better keep all cameras off Derek. He show off, and muck the lot!'

'Shut up!' yelled Emma and Derek, in unison.

It was fairly chaotic at Monksend, too.

For instance, the Press. Giles was being run off his feet, and had been since early morning. Cracks were beginning to appear in his tactful courtesy. It was not only the endless phone calls, but the stream of people at the front door demanding interviews, chats, certain that he could easily spare a few minutes of his time ....

He had written a carefully-worded hand-out, and made hundreds of roneoed copies, bitterly lamenting the absence of Lynn, who would

127

have helped with them. Robin, to whom he made this comment, said he lamented the loss of Lynn for less prosaic reasons. Giles muttered that he had not meant it the way it sounded. He then ran through some of his more kaleidoscopic expressions, settling finally on despair. He said none of this would be so frightful if only Lynn were here.

'None of this would be happening, if she were,' pointed out Robin. 'Don't be stupid. Listen, Giles. If you really do get out of your depth, and can't cope with these people, give me a shout. I'll be in the study, proof-reading Professor Grey's elegy on Isaac and Peter Oliver. Did you know he compares the father quite unfavourably with the son?'

'Does he really?' said Giles.

Robin laughed. Then he sobered immediately, and said:

'Warn your journalist chums that if one of them puts a toe into my house, without actual invitation, I shall be only too glad to toss him or her out on his or her ear.'

He went away upstairs, and closed his study door firmly.

Giles cast a sad look after him. He took a small, crumpled sprig of green leaves from his pocket, and patted it. Then he gave a start, and hurried downstairs to intervene in the melee that had suddenly broken out at the front door.

It seemed that Mrs Smart had managed to get among the pressmen, probably by creeping round the side of the house, and was inviting them all into the hall; ignoring the angry protests of the constable on duty there.

'But where's the harm,' Mrs Smart was shrilling. 'World news, isn't it? Lady Randall, dear thing . . .' she smirked at a photographer, who did not notice, '. . . well, everyone wants to know all about her, don't they? And I can tell a thing or two! None of your nasty tittle-tattle, neither, but true-to-life stuff . . . with a bit of ginger . . . .'

Giles went into furious action. He dispatched Mrs Smart to the kitchen, saying, quite untruthfully, that Superintendent Stillman was demanding her presence there. She tossed her head and flounced away, telling the Press across her shoulder that some people knew a key witness when they saw one.

The Press closed round Giles. Exactly as a pack of hounds, its worst instincts encouraged, closes on the helpless and exhausted prey. It is never a pretty sight, and makes the onlooker, if human, ashamed. No one was blushing for the running-down of Giles, for the pressmen and women were not, at this moment, members of humanity. The sudden arrival of Betsie Bloot, bursting through the throng like a firecracker, and demanding attention on the grounds of friendship, did little to improve the situation.

In the kitchen, where Stillman actually happened to be, Mrs Smart complained loudly.

'Shoving me off as if I was a servant or something!' she snorted. 'What's he, then, but hired help! And what's he so scared I'll tell the papers about?'

'I really couldn't say, Mrs Smart.'

'Anyway, I'm too busy to bother with them newspaper chaps. Or the police, come to that. Madam will be back soon, expecting everything clean and nice . . . and there's that sink full of washing-up, and no tea-tray set out for her . . . .'

'When are you expecting her?'

'And me all on me own,' went on Mrs. Smart, bustling round the kitchen. 'So, if you'll excuse me, sir, you'll have to get out of me way . . . .'

She fell over Chin-Chin, who was sitting by a table-leg.

'Get out from under, you saucy minikin!' screamed Mrs Smart. 'Go on out! Half a chicken you had for your lunch. I saw you. You'll get nothing more, till them lads comes back. Spoiling you rotten . . . !'

Chin-Chin struck at her leg, with a maniacal shriek. He missed, and stalked furiously to the automatic doors of the kitchen. He knew how they worked, and had spent a lot of his valuable time trying to make them do it. He couldn't believe that his weight was not enough to activate the mechanism. Now he sat there, bawling. Stillman went and stood beside him. The doors slid open. The cat shot into the hall, and Stillman bowed to his departing tail.

Mrs Smart, now fearing that the Superintendent was leaving the room also, demanded to know why he had sent for her. Mr Warrington had said it was an urgent matter. It was the first Stillman had heard of it, but he guessed the reasons behind Giles's statement and did not betray him.

'Ah . . . yes . . .' he said. 'There is something I'd like to ask.'

'It's me bounden duty to help the law,' said the woman at the sink, dipping plates in clean water, after their wash in foaming detergent.

'Well, when you went into the garden yesterday, to get Mr Warrington's book, did you see the gardener, Mr Crawford, anywhere about?'

'Him!' hissed Mrs Smart. 'That hairy ape!'

'Mr Crawford, yes.'

'I wouldn't care if I never set eyes on him again in me life!'

'Did you, in fact, set eyes on him yesterday, when you went out . . . .?'

'Not a glimpse. Probably sitting somewhere on his backside, well out of sight, smoking that stinking pipe of his, and eating all our fruit!'

She went on in a flowing spate of angry words, to say that there was never much good fruit to spare . . . out of this great garden, with its orchard and hot-houses, and frames . . . because that horrible rude monster ate it. Lady Randall, said she, had told her to take whatever she wanted, any time, but Crawford had forbidden her to touch anything but the smaller, poorer stuff. When she finally ended her complaint, Stillman paused in the list of soft fruits he was writing, and asked how far into the garden she had gone at teatime yesterday.

'Just to one of the seats under the terrace, sir. I rushed the book back to the drawing-room, and upstairs with it. I never grudges my time. Offering is for giving, eh?'

'Yes, indeed, Mrs Smart.'

'Nearly got bowled over by that hulking German chap at the top of the stairs, too,' she remembered, indignantly. 'And Mr Warrington was phoning, so I put the book on his desk and slipped away. Some folks you don't mind obliging any time. And others . . . .!'

'You're sure you didn't catch sight of Crawford? He told me this morning that he was working on the terrace at teatime yesterday.'

Mrs Smart said if the Superintendent believed one word that creature said, he'd be ready to fall in love with a crocodile. Stillman sighed. He thanked her for her help, declined a fresh cup of tea, and went out to the garden by the back door.

When he had gone, Mrs Smart hurried cautiously into the main hall. She peeked from the shelter of the staircase, but only saw that the front door was firmly shut, with the constable stationed squarely in front of it. The door bell rang several times, but someone had muffled it, and it only made an angry vibrating noise. No one made any attempt to answer it.

Then Giles came from the drawing-room with Betsie Bloot. They were talking quietly, and the man was telling her to be discreet in what she wrote. Mrs Smart ducked back into the shadows before they could glimpse her lurking there.

'That's all I know,' Giles said. 'Honestly, love. I tell you, those bloody people out there are like wolves! I lost my bit of lucky Mercury scuffling with them . . . and I've no time to go and look at my dog . . . just when we need all the good luck going!'

They went into Emma's little office. Mrs Smart retired stealthily to the kitchen.

Meanwhile, Stillman stood outside the back door, and looked about him. He faced a long building, green-pantiled, which proved to house the deep freezers. Adjoining was a fuel store. He turned right, and went along a wide concrete path to the back of the house. He stopped there. But the path went on for some way, past neat vegetable beds on its left, to a high brick wall with a door in it. This looked to be a walled garden. Beyond it could be seen the tops of orchard trees. A path between the vegetables led to them, past three enormous greenhouses, in the background of the sweet corn and late green beans.

Stillman went through an iron archway on his right, wound about with clematis and roses, and found himself beside the raised, stone-balustraded terrace that ran the rear length of Monksend. It was broken in two places by shallow stone steps curving outwards down to the lawn. There were marble vases on the upper and lower baluster-ends, in which pale-blue hanging campanulas and double petunias still flowered. Near the centre of the terrace, a huge rose was spread along the house walls, firmly tethered.

' "Albertine" ', thought the Superintendent, looking admiringly at the thorns.

To the left and the right of the rose, the walls supported an ancient wisteria and some mixed honeysuckles and clematis. On the stone flags near the house, were more vases with cottage carnations and honied alyssum in full flower.

The man heaved an appreciative sigh. But not of envy. This sort of thing was not quite what he had in mind for his new garden. Nice, though. He walked across the grass in front of the terrace to a cast-iron seat, all grapes and tendrils painted white; he looked at the great clump of lilies behind it, and wondered what colour they had been. Then he walked slowly on, past the two flights of steps, to another, identical, garden seat. Another clump of lilies grew behind this one. And a pale-grey elegance stepped out from their sword-like leaves, gave a faint wail of welcome, and leaned heavily against the Superintendent's ankle.

'Hallo,' said the man. 'How did you get round here so quickly, then? Found yourself an open window . . . or a slave to open one? It must be a bit noisy for you in the house, and a garden is a very nice refuge, isn't it?'

This reminded him of Derek. He smiled faintly, stooped to stroke Chin-Chin, and then straightened, and gazed admiringly down the vista of the great lawn.

He judged that it must be at least an acre in extent. And beautifully kept. Its expanse was broken here and there by strands of silver birch, flaming maples, and trees that would flower in the spring or the sum-

131

mer. Down the left side of the lawn, hiding the path to the walled garden, was a high rose hedge. Because of the clement weather, it had plenty of blossom.

' "Chinatown" . . . "Iceberg" . . . "Kathleen Harrop" . . .' breathed Stillman. ' "Ballerina" . . .'

At the far end of the spectacular sweep of lawn was a similar rose-hedge. Arched openings hinted at a formal rose-garden beyond. Stillman made his way there, heading straight down the middle of the long lawn, towards a statue. Having got to it, he paused. It was beautiful. A life-sized garden god, with a marble bird on his hand, and a real one on his head. The latter looked at Stillman with its beady eyes and stayed still. Then it saw the cat, and took off with a shrill squeal. Round the plinth of the statue and most of his lower limbs, a white rose was festooned. A pool at his feet was set round with decorative reeds and grasses, and water trickled into it from a slightly higher basin where birds obviously landed to drink and bathe.

Stillman nodded politely to the laughing faun, and went past him to the rose-garden. Chin-Chin strolled a pace or two ahead, as though he was conducting a tour. He liked going for walks with people he fancied. And he was quite patient, waiting kindly when the man stopped from time to time to look longingly at some of the roses. The bushes, the standards, the pillars. They came to another arched opening, with 'Handel' climbing over it. And there, a little way to their right. . . .

'Well!' said Stillman, aloud. 'Now that *is* pretty. I wish. . . .'

He pulled himself together. There was no point in being ridiculous. And yet . . . a tiny summerhouse? A very tiny summerhouse? Where he could go to read the paper on a fine Sunday morning, and Ruthie could bring her knitting. A house made of trellis, with a plastic roof? Just room inside for two deckchairs. One thing he knew for sure. It would be nothing like the one he was looking at now.

The gazebo was circular, and about twenty feet in diameter. It was made of wood and iron, painted white. There was a slight touch of the Greek temple about it, and more than a touch of fantasy. It had a white, domed roof, windows on all sides, with slender columns between them; and a continuous run of three-tread steps to a platform round the little house. Its double doors faced slantwise across the lawn towards the west. They were the sort that could swing in on themselves and fold flat inside like shutters. One of them stood ajar.

The Superintendent went up the steps towards it. He felt the whole building quiver a little, and realised that, large as it was, the entire place could be rotated on the turntable to which it was fixed. He pushed the door further open, and the cat flowed between his feet into the shadowy interior. It then gave one of its unnerving yells, and shot out again. It almost brought the man down. It vanished into a nearby clump of auburn leaved peonies. Perhaps, thought Stillman, it disliked the sudden chill of the gazebo.

It seemed dim and gloomy there, in spite of the many windows and the opened door, contrasting with the sunshine outside. Stillman moved forward cautiously, letting his eyes grow acclimatised. He tripped on something that crunched. For a ghastly moment he thought Chin-Chin had returned. Then he found he had stepped on a large cauliflower which now lay in some scattered lumps on the floor. Muttering Derek's name with acrimony, the Superintendent began to explore the room.

It was comfortably furnished. Round the walls, wide benches with foam-rubber seats and backs were gay with floral waterproof material. A big, round table in the centre had upright and lounging-chairs set about it, and on its white-painted surface were ashtrays (some overflowing with stubs), scattered books, a pair of secateurs, a roll of rose-wire, gardening gloves, and a wooden trug.

Heeling aside the remains of the cauliflower, Stillman crossed to glance at the book titles. *Hell-Hunters from Space 90*, *The Flaming Deeps of Pluto*, *Ape-Brides in Orbit*. He chuckled. It was one way, he supposed, of soothing the spirit and calming the mind. He prowled on, round the gazebo. He saw croquet mallets leaning against a bench on which lay the box of heavy wooden balls, and the white hoops. He saw a pair of small silver sandals tossed carelessly under a chair, and wondered who had gone back to the house barefooted . . . or had she changed into gum-boots? The Superintendent went to the door, crunching bits of cauliflower underfoot again.

'Tantrums,' he murmured. 'Better out than in, I suppose.'

At the foot of the steps he looked round for the cat, but there was no sign of him. More tantrums? Stillman considered what to do next. From where he was now standing, with his back to Monksend, a brick path ran away to his left towards the walled garden. The hedge of the rose-garden was on one side, and, on the other, a magnificent yew hedge. Seven feet high at least, three feet thick, and clipped so well that it looked like a putting-green standing on end. Just beside the gazebo was an arched opening in it. The Superintendent went through, and found himself beside a swimming-pool. He realised that the gazebo could be revolved until its doors faced this, and so could be used as a changing-room when required.

133

The pool was oblong, forty feet by twenty of glittering water. Leaves drifting on its surface had fallen from a stand of great willows beyond the far line of the surrounding yew hedge. All round the pool was a pale-green marble pavement, with pale-green marble benches on each of the four sides. At the left-hand end of the pool from where Stillman was standing, was a graceful cluster of stone nymphs. One, with outstretched hand, seemed offering to hold someone's towel.

'Ruthie and I can dabble our feet in a washing-up bowl of water, while we laze in our deckchairs,' thought the policeman, with mild amusement.

He walked slowly round the pool, until he came back to the gazebo. He went through the archway, and took the brick path to a wooden door into the walled garden. Pushing it open, he went in.

Crawford, from a crouching position, lurched to his feet and cried to God to have mercy on him. He then demanded to know why a body could not get on with his work, without being spied upon by fellows with evil suspicious minds.

'Well, I'm sorry if I startled you,' said the Superintendent.

Crawford said that to be startled was not a sign of guilt, and Stillman hastened to agree with him. He then asked if the man had time for a few words.

'Ye've got eyes!' barked the gardener. 'Look at they weeds, man! If I let 'em run, they'll choke madam's laxatives.'

'Bless my soul,' said Stillman, 'will they really?'

He peered with interest at the nearest bed. A number of herbs was instantly recognisable; sage, tarragon, fennel, and a line of chives. But others were unfamiliar, and he pointed to one of them.

'What's that feathery-looking . . . ?'

'Southernwood. Supposed to keep fleas from your clothing, if ye stuff it into your wardrobes and chests,' said Crawford, breaking off a twig and handing it to the other man.

'An odd smell. I suppose you could come to like it.'

'I do like it. But then, I'm no' a flea!'

'Quite. And the . . . laxatives, did you say?'

Crawford grinned. For a moment his weather-beaten, grimy old face looked almost pleasantly human. He said he had no personal experience of these plants. He preferred straight Syrup of Figs, if it was called for.

'But Lady Emma, she goes by the word of some mad body called Gerard,' said the Scot. 'She read me some bits from his book, once. But, to tell ye the truth, I was no' listening . . . not after the fellow saying most of the herbs were for the curing of scorpions' stings and mad-dog bites! I've seen neither of the beasties in this garden, nor look to. But on the other hand,' said Crawford, fair-mindedly, 'I don't mind growing her face-lotion stuff, and cough herbs, and the ones for hair-wash, and liniment, and for making her bath-water smell.'

His lordly gesture took in the whole big herb department of the garden.

'Just suppose,' said Stillman, 'that you wanted to make someone very sick, even to kill them, could you find the stuff you needed here?'

He got a look of startled anger. Then Crawford turned away towards a barrow piled high with weeds.

'To hell!' said the gardener. 'I've no' poisoned anyone!'

Stillman went after him, with hurried words of reassurance. No one, said he, was making any sort of accusation, or laying blame on Crawford. After all, anyone could walk into the walled garden, at any time . . . during the night, for instance. . . .

'Aye, if it's a maniac ye mean, there's stuff here would corrode you cross-eyed if he gave it to you! If he knew what to seek . . . look there. . . .'

He pointed to some tall plants growing in a clump at the back of the bed. They had thick stems, like pink glass, and pink-and-white flowers that seemed a cross between orchids and snapdragons. Their roots spread like fat pink toes all round them.

'Jewelweed,' said Crawford with distaste. '*Impatiens Roylei.* Spreading its seeds like a lunatic, wishfu' to take over the whole district! I hate the stuff. And I'd hate worse to eat it. But madam says it makes an ointment, an' for all I know she's right.'

'It looks extremely sinister. And over there, surely, is thorn-apple? People used to be warned against that,' said Stillman, 'when it grew on bomb sites in London, before the re-building began that's destroyed the place.'

'Aye, thorn-apple. *Datura stramonium,* and packing a nasty poison whatever its medicinal virtues.'

Crawford wheeled his barrow towards a great pile of rubbish at the end of the path. The Superintendent followed, looking thoughtfully at the herb-clumps they passed. The old gardener noticed, for he suddenly said if the police were seeking the killer of Miss Sanderson, there was no point in wasting time on these plants.

'It was no wee green leaf or seed that murdered her,' said he. 'But, as I heard it, a great ding wi' a pagan statue. Like enough she asked for it, poor hussy.'

'What did you say?'

'Ah, speak no evil! That's the rule, is it no'? But what about truth? Man, the truth must be spoke. The lass was too free. I've seen her myself,' and Crawford dropped the handles of the wheelbarrow so abruptly that some weeds spilled over a lavender bush. 'By the pool over yonder I've seen her, wi' scarce enough on to hide her nakedness from the birds o' the air!'

Stillman wondered aloud if the birds of the air would be likely to object.

'*I* objected!' said the other man. 'The world is too full of things that are out of one's reach. And she was no' a fit sight for a hard-working poor old man.'

'Where were you, Mr Crawford, when you saw this – sight?'

'By the yew hedge, where else? And *outside* it. No' gawping by the entrance.'

'But it's such a fine hedge. Surely too thick to see through?'

'Aye, sir. But there's places where ye can pull the twigs aside a wee bit. . . .'

The gruff voice tailed off into silence. After a few moments, the gardener said he wished to get on with his work, and be left in peace, not tricked into foolish speech.

'By all means,' said Stillman. 'If you'd just spare a few more minutes, to come and show me where you were working at about teatime yesterday. It would be such a help.'

Seeming slightly subdued, the old man stumped off down the path towards the doorway nearest the house, leaving the policeman to follow. Between beds of strawberries, rows of raspberry canes and gooseberries all in neat cages, they went. Stillman looked admiringly at fan-shaped peach-trees spread on the walls, apricots, nectarines; the vines, with small bunches of grapes still hanging in their polythene bags; the cold-frames, with melons on little beds of straw. He gave a longing look back, as he left the scented walled garden.

And in London, Emma finally lost her temper with her assistants.

'God Almighty, it's like Zoo Time!' said she. 'We can't go on. If these two fools are going to trample one another underfoot and scream, in the rush to get their stupid faces in front of a camera, I shall bloody well walk off the floor, and leave them to do the show on their own.'

Through the outraged cries from Derek and Johann, Mike said he was inclined to agree with Emma.

'We'd better try to do without one of them, at least,' he said. 'We discussed it, if you remember, while we were planning the show. . . .'

'And they've been like madmen ever since they got wind of it,' said Emma.

'I can't help their troubles,' Mike said. 'I've enough of my own. It's just hopeless with the pair of them behaving like amateurs. Which one shall we dispense with? They're your wonder-boys, darling.'

Sergeant Woolsey, in his quiet corner, held his breath. He knew what would come. It came.

When Emma could make herself heard again, she shrieked that both Johann and Derek could be dispensed with utterly. They were sacked here and now. They could go back at once to Monksend, by train and station taxi, collect their belongings, and depart forever. She had no wish to look on either of their hideous faces again. And it was useless to ask her for references.

'Anything I said about you two would keep you permanently unemployed!'

They tried to argue. She told them to collect their cards from Giles. They spoke with passion of contracts. Some of the actors began to join in the discussion. And Mike Peel ran both hands through his short, black hair. Quite suddenly, his stumpy figure was invested with power and authority. He demanded instant silence, and got it.

'You two had better go,' he told the stricken trainee-cooks. 'We'll work something out about the show, and let you know what's decided. Today is a bit fraught, so don't panic or despair. Just go away, there's dear good sweetie-pies, and let's have no more arguments and distractions. I do promise you, boys, that if you don't take yourselves off right this minute, you will get the ultimate sack! Now, I've warned you.'

Derek's pale eyes brimmed with tears, and Johann stuck out his jaw belligerently. But the pair said nothing more. It left, in a depth of dudgeon rarely before achieved.

'Now, where were we . . . ?' said Mike.

*Chapter thirteen*

# COLD AND SWEET

Just below the terrace, Crawford stopped. He pointed grimly to the great rose that spread to the upper windows in the centre. He said he had spent nearly two hours nailing 'Albertine' to the wall yesterday. Up a ladder? Of course. How else could he . . . ?

'Was it possible for you, on that ladder, to see into the bathroom?' said the Superintendent. 'I'm not suggesting you would look in deliberately, of course.'

Crawford said in any case the curtains were of thick net, and the windows had been shut all the time he was anywhere near. He also stated that he had gone to have his own tea in the kitchen when the skinny lad, Derek, had called him in. The gardener was staring at the rose while he spoke, and now he said it was a mystery how she had broken her moorings.

'I thought I had her secure,' said he. 'But there she was, wi' her long branches waving free, wicked enough to take the eyes from your head if you passed under thoughtlessly, wi' thorns two inches long. See that?'

He held out his hands, palm down. The Superintendent had already noticed the deep scratches and weals on the hairy backs of them. He murmured words of sympathy, and asked what Crawford had done with the ladder when he finished tying 'Albertine'.

'I put it back in the shed beyond the fuel store yonder. It's where we keep the garden stuff. And can I get back to me work the noo?'

'Yes. Yes, of course. Thank you for your help and patience. It's not easy to work things out when you don't know how a place is run. You've a big job here, Mr Crawford.'

Placated, the gardener said it was indeed heavy work. But he had two lads in to help when necessary. And, he said, in summer, the cook-boys helped to cut the grass.

'Talking of which,' said Stillman, casually. 'Did you see Derek Hawley in the garden anywhere, while you were up that ladder? He says he went out to the gazebo at about four o'clock. Would that be after he gave you your cup of tea?'

Crawford said he could not be sure of the time he had tea to within ten minutes. But was certain he had seen nothing of Derek afterwards.

'I never saw him go down the garden. Even if I did, why would I bother to give an alibi to the likes of him?' said he.

'It might give you an alibi, too,' Stillman told him, gently.

He left the gardener staring after him, and went along the foot of the terrace to the side of the house. He almost collided with Johann on the back doorstep.

The big German looked distraught. He was flushed and wild-eyed, and his hair hung in tangled snarls all over his forehead. He started when he saw the Superintendent, and made a praiseworthy attempt to assume a calmer look. He straightened his shoulders, and said he had just come back from London. A dreary, tiring journey, he added. And then he said that if to be arrested he was, he did not the tinker's damn give.

'I am not arresting anyone, at the moment,' said Stillman.

'Care I not, if you to hang the lot proceed! Where is Mr Warrington?'

'Talking to Mrs Bloot, the last time I saw him. She was just leaving.'

'Now it is talking to me he shall do. There must be justice for me. Or I also,' said the trainee-cook, 'have that to tell the Press which will the red-hot wires make buzz!'

'They'll like that,' said Stillman. 'I suppose,' he added, 'you wouldn't like to tell me anything, before you start the wires buzzing?'

'Police!' snarled Johann, glaring down at the Superintendent. 'I know that you would like well to put the blame for all on a penniless and innocent foreigner. . . .'

'No, no,' said Stillman, mildly. 'If you're innocent you have nothing to fear.'

'On the long hook!'

The young man shouldered past Stillman, snarling back over his shoulder that when he had consulted Giles about his rights, and his contract, he would the world tell many things concerning this house and its inhabitants. He vanished into the deep-freezer store. Whether to get away from the Superintendent, or because he thought to find Giles inside, there was no way of guessing.

Stillman went on into the kitchen.

'Cup of tea, dear?' said Mrs Smart.

'Not at the moment, thank you. Oh . . . Mr Hawley?'

A snivelling heap in the big wicker chair lifted a ravaged face from its knees, and said its life was at an end.

'That *cow*!' it sniffed. 'That wicked, horrible, hateful monster! That hell-kite!'

'Are we speaking of Mr Johann Schulter?' said Stillman, cautiously.

'No!' wept Derek. 'That harpy, Emma. I'd like to cut her throat! I'd like to slit her liver in four pieces! I'd like to burn her ears slowly down to the drums! I'd . . .'

'Now, now! There's a nasty way to talk,' said Mrs Smart. 'Have a cup of tea, and show some sense, do.'

'Go to hell!' said Derek.

'Yesterday,' said the Superintendent, 'did you give Mr Crawford his tea in here, Mr Hawley?'

'That dirty old bastard! I sent him to the shed with it . . . who wants blood dripping on the table!'

'Thank you, sir.'

Stillman had reached the swing doors of the kitchen, when Derek shouted after him:

'If you see Giles Warrington anywhere, tell him to get out my contract! No bloody, jealous hag can smash it up whenever she fancies! I'll show her! Tell Giles I'll sue!'

Stillman found the empty hall rather soothing.

He went into the library, and sat down to collate his notes. Also to cross out several items he had noted while in the garden. Most of them were too big for his plans, and some were ludicrous. But they did at least serve to remind him that Ruthie wanted some parsley and a clump of chives, a bush of sage, and one of thyme . . . and who could live without rosemary? The Superintendent gave himself a mental rap on the wrist, and tried to concentrate on the more immediate problems. He concentrated so well that it gave him a slight shock to hear a soft noise from the door behind him.

He looked round to see the tall, slim figures of Harriet and Thumper lurking shyly there. Stillman rose politely, and asked if they would care to join him, and tell him who they were. They said they were Harriet and Thumper. He said how did they do. They said very well, thank you.

'I'm Robin Randall's niece,' said the one with slightly longer hair.

'And I'm Thumper.'

'I'm Detective Chief Superintendent Joseph Stillman.'

'Cor!' said Thumper.

The newcomers perched themselves on the arms of chairs, and regarded the law with interest. The law was equally interested in them. He had not met the weirder samples of teen-age fashion at such close quarters before now.

'We've been upstairs, talking to my uncle,' said Harriet. 'We came to ask how Emma is. We'd no idea what had happened since we were

140

here last night. We've been on a little boat at Windsor. It sank, and we. . . .'

'Tuesday night, miss,' said the Superintendent. 'Yes, you were both here. What can you tell me about last night?'

He got a rapid account of the dinner-party, and of the early departure of these two participants. They said it had become a bit dull towards the end. And, they added, if there was anything they detested more than police . . . oh, sorry! . . . it was dullness. So they had slipped away and gone home.

'Well, not straight home,' said Thumper. 'We stayed in the garden here for a while. We thought of having a swim, but. . . .'

'Then we decided not to. So we sort of hung about, talking,' said Harriet, 'and *then* we went home.'

'May I have your addresses?'

Actually, the Chief Superintendent already had them, together with those of everyone who had been at Tuesday's party. He was just making conversation.

'Ah, thank you,' said he, making notes of what the young people told him. 'And you, miss, are the daughter of Sir James Randall, of Broomes Court. . . .'

'Don't!' said the girl, dragging her hair further over her face, as if to mask her expression. 'It's mean to laugh at me because of Daddy's silly title! Thumper's father is a Shop Steward,' she said, with admiration. 'What about that!'

'Very grand, miss. Now, would you tell me – both of you – what you thought of Miss Sanderson? Just your personal impressions of the young lady, if you'd be so good.'

There was a pause. Stillman wondered if they were marshalling their memories of Lynn, or pretending to be dead. It was impossible to tell from their faces, which were entirely hidden by their hair. At last Harriet said that people with conventional backgrounds were fairly unpredictable, weren't they.

'I mean,' she amplified, 'she wasn't obvious. Not secretive, I don't mean that. But – well, not obvious. Like us, a bit. We're not obvious, either.'

'She was a nice human,' said Thumper.

'I liked her,' said Harriet.

A sudden uproar in the hall rose and fell in confused hubbub for a few moments, and then became the clear voice of Emma calling for tea. The other noises died away in various directions.

The Superintendent excused himself to Harriet and Thumper, and went out to the hall. But it was empty by the time he got there. So was the library, when he returned. A slight draught from the french window showed where his recent visitors had gone.

Stillman went back to his notebook, and did not look up even when Sergeant Woolsey came into the room. He just bade him sit down.

'I know you've had an exciting day,' he told him. 'And I'll be glad to hear about it all, later on. But just be quiet for a few minutes, like a good lad, while I jot down a thing or two. I might forget, otherwise.'

Woolsey stayed quiet, though with an obvious effort.

'Ssh!' he hissed at Mrs Smart, when she bustled in with two large mugs of tea and a plate of digestive biscuits.

'Ssh, yourself!' she said, dumping her load, and sweeping out haughtily.

The Chief Superintendent sighed. He stopped writing, and stared into space.

'Sir?' said Woolsey, eagerly. 'Have you found out anything?'

'Lots,' said Stillman. 'Whether any of it matters. . . .'

'I've been thinking, sir.'

'Good.'

'And I think we should pay more attention to that German chap.'

'Why, George?'

Woolsey leaned across the table towards his senior. He looked tense, but Stillman attributed this to the fact that he had spent some hours watching Emma's rehearsal. The Superintendent had once watched a rehearsal when he was only a constable, and had never forgotten it.

'Let's take things calmly,' he suggested.

'You fool, no!' snapped Woolsey. 'Pick up your feet, and jump to it! It's no good slumping here, doing nothing!'

'Well, sir,' he said, aloud, 'this Johann Schulter. He was in love with the dead girl, wasn't he?'

'So we hear.'

'And she was playing hard to get.'

'It's possible.'

'And he wrote letters to her . . . love-letters . . . and poetry, so Derek says. . . .'

'Derek?'

'Mr Hawley. So Mr Hawley says. And we've found no letters or poems among the dead woman's effects, either here or at her home. If Schulter went and got them, after she was killed, to stop us suspecting him . . . it makes sense, sir.'

'Oh yes, George. It makes sense.'

142

'I think you should pull in Schulter on suspicion of murder, sir,' said the Sergeant, adding under his breath: 'And get this ghastly mess cleared up before you get hauled off it for the decrepit failure you are!'

'And I think you're a very bright young man,' said Stillman, 'and will go far. But don't let's do anything in too much of a hurry. I'm not quite satisfied that it's as clear sailing as you think. Johann may not be all that important. . . .'

But Johann was.

The library door crashed open, so that it slammed against the panelled wall. Mrs Smart stood in the doorway, quivering.

'You want the tea-cups . . . ?' began the Superintendent.

'Sir – you must come! It's Johann, sir. He's dead. In the swimming-pool, with his face all smashed!'

*Chapter fourteen*

## ON TOAST

The old house had seen many disturbances in its time, but nothing probably to what it saw now.

Police seemed everywhere. Photographers, finger-print experts, local worthies such as Superintendent Fisher and the thunder-throated little doctor. Stillman had summoned them to the new catastrophe at Monksend. The Chief Constable had also been called, of course. After due consultation with his Deputy, and with the head of the Murder Squad at Scotland Yard, he had confirmed Stillman's authority to continue investigations.

This decision may have saved the reason of Sergeant George Woolsey. He had half split his mind asunder, with two equal but divergent wishes. One, to see his senior relieved of the impossible burden . . . 'poor old dotard, best out of it before he totters further up the garden path!' . . . and two, bemusedly praying that the Yard would not humiliate its ancient representative . . . 'God knows they be as daft as he is, not to recall him! But not a public disgrace! Oh please! Let me come up with some solution! Let me get him off the hook! . . .'

And now, Stillman was again standing by the gazebo, inside the yew hedge, looking at the swimming-pool. The gazebo had been turned on its revolving base, so that its doors now faced the water. Whoever had done this had (most probably) done worse. The Superintendent glanced sadly at the wet heap sprawling nearby. Water dripped from its clothes, and stained water from its head, over the marble on which it lay. With aversion, he saw the big red croquet-ball bobbing on the surface of the pool, where it had been left for his inspection. He wondered if it had been chosen deliberately in preference to the yellow, blue, or black balls. A macabre and silly idea, he reproved himself. People had no time for such refinements during the act of murder.

Curiously, and in spite of what the heavy wooden ball had done to his face, Johann looked peaceful. At least he had escaped from heartache. And when the ambulance came with stretcher and blanket, the young man who had loved Lynn went to join her in a morgue.

Now the weapon was taken carefully from the water, photographed, and removed in polythene wrappings for laboratory testing. The Chief

Constable and the doctor departed. The tumult and the shouting died. Joseph Stillman and his team remained.

'Mr Crawford,' said the Superintendent, once more seated by the table in the library, 'will you be kind enough to tell me exactly how you came to find Mr Schulter? It's distressing, I know, to have to go through it all again. I'd rather spare you. . . . .'

'Why!' shrieked Woolsey, in his impatient brain.

'. . . details. But you never know what might help me,' finished Stillman.

The old Scotsman sat, opening and shutting his hands as though they felt strange lacking tools in them, and peered at the Superintendent. His eyes were faded and acute under the craggy brows. He said he had finished weeding the bed in the walled garden. . . .

'The job ye interrupted,' he reminded the policeman. 'And then I went to pick some pears.'

'Still inside the walled garden?'

'Och, aye. An espaliered tree on the west wall. Madam wanted the fruit to prepare for this television orgy tomorrow. They had to be picked this afternoon. None but the big, well-shapen ones.'

The gardener stared at his hands, and then at the Superintendent. He said it was a terrible thing to have happened.

'Mind ye,' said he, 'I've little use for foreigners – which includes the English – and I may have said so a few times to the German lad. But it's no' pleasant to find him floating in the pool, and his face all broken. . . .'

'Not at all pleasant,' agreed Stillman. 'Why did you go near the pool, when you were busy picking the fruit? It's some way away.'

The big man half rose.

'You're not suspecting that I . . . ?'

'I require,' said the Superintendent, 'a good deal more to go on. Sit down, Mr Crawford. You've no reason for alarm.'

'Haven't you just, you – you foreign swine!' snarled the Sergeant, silently.

Crawford said it was Sir Robin. Stillman said *what* was Sir Robin? And the gardener gulped until his Adam's-apple bobbed in his knotted throat.

'He came and told me to leave the pears,' said he. 'I must go with him and get the cat down from a tree by the gazebo.'

'I don't believe it!' said Woolsey, aloud by mistake.

'Sergeant, please.'

'Sorry, sir.'

Crawford, his Lowland accent thickening even more with indignation, said he had never told a lie in his life. His mither, he said, would not have permitted such wickedness. Sir Robin had said exactly what he had just reported.

'He said the cat had run from him, and gone up the tree. And there's a curious wee beastie, with a devil in it,' said the Scot. 'But it's gey fond of me. And, mind you, it's usually fair besotted with Sir Robin. Yet today – he said because he'd pushed it from a chair, or the like – it canna abide him. And there it was,' he said, 'when I went with the master – right up at the top of one of yon smelly poplars. . . .'

'Trichocarpa,' murmured Stillman.

'Eh?' said Woolsey.

'Ye have it, sir,' said the gardener. 'Exact. The leaves and buds smell very strong in the spring and after rain. Verra pleasant! And there was this mad wee creature, on a high branch, hissing like a viper whenever Sir Robin spoke to it. So I called, and it came and let me lift it down. It bolted for the house when I set it on the grass.'

'And then?'

'Then Sir Robin went away after it, and I went back to the pears.'

'Ah – by the path beside the yew hedge?'

'Aye, sir. I noticed yon garden-room was spun round to face towards the pool, and I glanced through the archway in the hedge – just from habit, ye understand. . . .'

'Perfectly,' said Stillman.

'And I saw something floating there in the water,' finished Crawford.

He had then gone to see what it was. He told them how he had jumped in, and dragged the body of Johann to the side.

'I thought he'd fallen in, and maybe was alive. . . .'

But then the gardener had seen the face.

'I kenned fine he was deid. I left the poor lad, and went for help. There was no one in the kitchen, so I ran into the hall. . . .'

'Dripping wet?' demanded the Sergeant.

'Aye, so. What would you have me do? I found Mr Warrington in the hall, and called him to come. We ran to the pool, and got the German laddie up on to the pavement. There was nought else we could do for him. What a fearful business,' said Crawford.

'When did you change your clothes? And what into?' said Woolsey, doggedly.

The gardener said he kept other clothes in his shed. And washing things by the hand-basin there. He never went home dirty, or in his working duds, he said with hauteur. He had got himself into dry things as soon as he'd come back from the house.

'While Mr Warrington went to tell his employers,' he said. 'And sent to inform you.'

'Will you read over your statement, that Sergeant Woolsey has taken down?' said the Superintendent. 'Sign it, if you'll be so kind. And then you can go home, sir. You've had a nasty experience, and I'm more than grateful for your patience and tolerance.'

As soon as they were alone, Woolsey said what about arresting Crawford instead of sending him home with grateful thanks? Stillman said it was too soon to do anything so conclusive. He got up and wandered round the room a little. He said he wondered where Derek Hawley had been when Crawford was dripping backwards and forwards through the kitchen? He said he would like a word with Sir Robin, just to clear his mind.

'Good God!' said the Sergeant. 'It's been years since your mind was clear enough to tell the difference between butter and margarine!'

Aloud, he said what a good idea.

It took a while to find Robin. But at last, drawn there by raised voices, they came upon him in Giles's study. He was, apparently, assaulting the younger man. At any rate, he was clutching him by one shoulder and shaking him.

'You won't make me do it!' Giles was stuttering. 'Leave me alone, Robin, for God's sake!'

'Now, now . . .' said the Superintendent, as Woolsey hurried to intervene.

But it turned out to be no matter of life and death. Robin stood back instantly.

'Ah – Mr Stillman,' said he, 'could you impress on this idiot the importance of keeping his head? I don't seem able to get through.'

'Robin, how can I just sit here!' exploded Giles, jumping up. 'As if nothing was wrong! Taking phone calls . . . the Press . . . the B.B.C . . . the. . . .'

'You must,' said Robin, in level tones. 'Who else is there to do it? You know the people, and how to deal with them.'

'But – at a time like this. . . .'

'It's the moment of truth, dear boy. God will know his own,' said Robin, obscurely.

Stillman took over. He said he knew it was a lot to ask, but everyone would be grateful to Giles if he would just stay quietly here and cope with the telephone.

'I don't know that I can.'

'You're feeling the strain, sir, of course. If one of my men could be of

147

any help,' suggested the Superintendent, 'I'll send a constable up to take messages, or run errands for you.'

'Thank you,' said Giles. 'That might come in handy. All right, I'll carry on here.'

'That will put us all in your debt, Mr Warrington,' said Stillman.

'But, if anything else goes wrong . . .' Giles looked despairingly at him. 'Oh, how can it! Surely we've had all the bad luck going. . . .'

He stopped abruptly, and slapped the wooden side of his desk with one hand, while leaning forward to pat the woolly dog with the other.

'Touch wood! Touch wood! Touch wood!' he said, as the telephone began to ring.

The others left him giving a guarded but fairly lucid description of the latest tragedy to some eager enquirer.

On the landing, Robin thanked Stillman for his intervention.

'Giles was all for going up to Emma's bedroom, and handing her his resignation,' he said. 'And, if he had, I think she'd have gone mad. She's in a poor way, as it is. Her doctor's with her.' Then he looked darkly at the two policemen. 'I hear this show is to go on, as though nothing's happened. Is that correct?'

Stillman said it was. The Yard had decided to let the television banquet take place exactly as planned.

'Your decision, Mr Stillman?'

'Yes, sir, actually.'

'May I ask why? Come into my study for a moment, will you?'

'Thank you. In my opinion, Sir Robin, it's best this way. There's every chance of losing the threads of the whole unhappy business, if we get into a muddle of altered plans. If we just carry on, we'll know where everyone's supposed to be during the next twenty-four hours or so. We can keep an eye,' said Stillman, 'on the lot. Now I know it won't be easy for any of us, and least of all for Lady Randall. But she says she's willing. . . .'

'Lady Randall,' said Robin, 'is like a puma robbed of its young! She'd push an acorn up the side of the Post Office tower with her nose, if it would help to catch the killer!'

'That, sir, is my own estimation of her. Now, would you be kind enough to tell me about your cat going up the poplar?'

Looking surprised, Robin told him. The account tallied with Crawford's, allowing for variations of accent and phraseology. Then the Superintendent wanted to know where Robin had been just after his wife returned from her club.

'Before you became involved with the cat, sir.'

'Oh, Lord, what did I do? I heard Emma's arrival, and – yes, I know! She went to her room, demanding tea. And I went out to get cigarettes.'

Robin was standing by the window of his study, frowning down at the police and press cars on the drive below. Perhaps the havoc they were wreaking on the once-smooth gravel irritated him.

'I drove into the village,' said he. 'Everyone's been smoking too much, of course. I couldn't find any cigarettes, and I thought a shortage might prove the last straw. And half-way there, I remembered a secret cache I made, months ago. For emergencies. Four cartons of a hundred, in a sealed tin in the cellar. So I made an illegal U-turn, and came home again. That's all, Superintendent.'

'After that you went into the garden?'

'For peace, like Derek,' said Robin. 'And for a smoke.'

'And the cat . . . happened?'

Robin nodded. He said Chin-Chin had emerged from a bush, seen him nearby and gone mad. Had screamed like a banshee, raced over the lawn, and straight up the tree, where he had sat at the top wailing.

'I couldn't just leave the fool there. I went and got Crawford. He likes Crawford.'

Stillman thanked him for the information, and crossed to the door.

'I'll be here,' said Robin, 'or with my wife, if you need me again.'

And he lifted one of the National Gallery miniatures, and looked at it as though he found it soothing.

As they reached the top of the stairs on the landing outside, the Sergeant asked Stillman, in a breathless whisper, whether they should not arrest Robin.

'For any particular reason?' said Stillman.

'He's got no alibi!'

'Well, nor have you, George, come to that.'

'But who'd go out to buy cigarettes, when he's got thousands stashed away in the cellar?'

'Apparently Sir Robin would. Do calm down, lad. You can't go round arresting people just for fun, you know.'

'Fun!' said Woolsey, and choked.

He recovered a little, and asked where they were going now, in a voice that sounded almost normal.

'I thought we'd just wander into the kitchen, and see if Mr Hawley has anything to tell us.'

They found Mrs Smart ministering to Derek. At least, that is what she told them she was doing. Derek seemed to have other views. He said she was a nosy busybody, a degraded and dishonest slob, and that the tea she was trying to make him drink was probably poisoned. With the same stuff, he added, that she had somehow managed to give Emma before the dinner-party. Mrs Smart said he was not himself. He said it was hard lines on her that she *was* herself. She told him she knew just how he must be feeling at the moment.

'That poor boy,' she said, shaking her head. 'That nice, handsome Johann. You liked him ever so much, didn't you? Too much, for some tastes! It's no wonder you're feeling so miserable and guilty.'

'Guilty?' the Sergeant pounced on the word.

'Guilty!' shrieked Derek.

He had been weeping. His eyes were swollen and red, and his whole face was shiny, blotched, and streaked with salmon-pink and white. He looked awful.

'I'm not blind!' rapped Mrs Smart. 'I know you was chasing him something terrible. He often told me he couldn't be doing with that sort of thing. Said you'd drive yourself dotty with your goings-on, and do something you'd be sorry for. . . .'

'You lying cow!'

'Now, now, sir,' interposed Stillman. 'Let's all try to stay civil, shall we? Mrs Smart, I wonder if you could manage another cup of tea for my Sergeant and myself? Of course, if it's too much trouble. . . .'

This got the expected result. Mrs Smart abandoned Derek, and scurried about getting mugs and spoons to set on the table, beside the big blue teapot. While she poured the tea, she interrupted her monologue on the virtues of willing service to dole out a couple of Osborne biscuits to each officer.

In an effort not to roar with rage, not to glare too fiercely at his superior, and to swallow a great gulp of scalding tea, Woolsey nearly choked himself again.

'It's a nightmare!' he fumed inside. 'The woman's handing out free information – and making Hawley so mad that he's about ready to give himself away! Might all be wrapped up here and now . . . but he puts a stop to it, for more bloody tea and biscuits.'

He bit savagely into his Osborne, and it crumbled and scattered on the floor.

'Manners, George,' said the Superintendent. 'You're encouraging mice.'

'I know what you've come to say,' said Derek, looking wily. 'You want to know what I did after I got back here from Emma's club. Well, I'll tell you – and then you can piss off and leave me alone! I came in here. And I spent the rest of the time packing all me bits and bobs into that

150

cardboard box. Go and look. Paw through my effects. You'll find nothing wrong there. I've been sacked, you know. *And* I'm going to sue, for breach of contract. But I'm getting out – oh, yes, I am! I'm not staying a minute more than I have to. It was just . . . well, I couldn't go on packing . . . when they . . . when they came and told me he was dead. . . .'

'Take your time, sir,' said Stillman, gently.

'I'd have gone by now,' said Derek. 'I'd never set foot in this house again, after the way she treated me. Like a dog! Worse! I bet she'd be quite nice to a dog – if it was doing its best. She gives away millions to animal charities. If I'd been a performing ape, she'd have patted my head. But me! She talked to me as if I were a knout – I mean serf – and I've worked so hard. . . .'

He put his head down on his arms, and wept. Mrs Smart hurried round the table to put a hand on his shoulder.

'Now don't take on,' said she. 'Remember she's upset today. We all are. Because of poor Miss Sanderson. And now. . . .'

'Mr Hawley,' said the Superintendent, 'you said that someone told you Johann Schulter was dead. Was that the first you knew about it?'

Derek was understood to say yes.

'And who told you?'

'What?'

'Who told you of Schulter's death?'

Derek lifted a face that looked worse than ever, and said Giles had told him.

'What exactly did he say, sir?'

'Let's see. That Crawford had found . . . found Johann dead. That he – Giles – had been helping to get him out of the pool. His sleeves, and the front of his jacket, were all sopping wet. . . . Giles's, I mean.'

'Mrs Smart,' said Stillman, 'when did you hear about it?'

'Mr Warrington come and tell me, when he got back from the pool. He was proper wet like Derek says. He came to the front porch. . . .'

'And there you were,' snapped Derek, 'talking to the Press again. Trying to get your picture in the news by telling a load of lies. . . .'

'I was giving 'em the bits of paper Mr Warrington had left in the hall for them,' said the lady, with dignity. 'Telling them about Miss Sanderson. And Mr Giles he came and said to go and tell the coppers – er – the policemen in the library that Johann was dead, too. He said he was going to change, not go rushing about dripping, and he had to tell Sir Robin and all.'

She then turned on Derek, and demanded to know where he had

been, while people were getting drowned in ponds.

'Not *drowned,* you old fool!' snarled Derek. 'And I've been here all the time, like I said.'

'*All* the time, sir? You never left this room at all? But,' said Stillman, quietly, 'you didn't notice Crawford come through, the first time? Or when he went out again, with Mr Warrington.'

Derek sniffed violently. He said he had spent quite a lot of time in the lavatory by the back door. Being sick, as if anyone cared.

'Ah, I see,' said the Superintendent. 'Well, thank you for the tea, Mrs Smart. Most welcome. Come along, Sergeant. Don't just sit there, lad. We've work to do.'

'God Almighty!' said the Sergeant, aloud.

'Oooh, language!' said Mrs Smart.

The two officers tramped upstairs again. They found Giles in the office, putting down the telephone. He gazed at them with glazed eyes.

'Sixty calls,' he said, 'in one hour flat. That's one a minute.'

'So it is. Just one question, sir. When did you first know of Mr Schulter's death?'

'Er – Crawford – yes, the gardener came and told me,' said Giles, looking cheerless, woolly-minded and plodding. 'He came from the kitchen, all wet, and saw me in Lady Randall's office. I thought at first he was drunk. But he took me – and showed me . . .' He coughed and frowned. 'Even then,' he said, 'I couldn't believe it. I. . . .'

The telephone bell rang. Giles ignored it. He went on talking in a colourless voice.

'Right in the middle of all the arrangements for tomorrow's rehearsal, and the show. You wouldn't think anything else *could* happen! Oh, God!'

He snatched up the phone. And Thumper put his extraordinary head into the room and said the apple-picking party had arrived, and what should be done about them?

'*Who?*' snapped Giles. 'What are you talking about? No, no, not you. What? B.L.? Yes, of course, put him through. Get out, Thumper, for the love of . . . ! No, not you, B.L. Yes, she's all right. Worried sick, and terribly upset . . . yes, there *has* been more trouble. You'll hear about it, soon enough. Yes, she will be there tomorrow, as arranged. Tell Harriet to send them away, Thumper! Don't be so dim, boy! No, not you, B.L. . . . .'

The Superintendent gestured the Sergeant and Thumper out of the room.

An uneasy knot of ladies, huddled in the hall below, turned out to be a group that made a kindly habit of cooking and bottling jams, jellies and chutneys, for such local old-age pensioners as liked but lacked these dainties. Emma and Robin invited the group yearly to pick fruit from a particular pair of trees in the orchard that ripened early. Now they explained eagerly to the Superintendent that they had indeed heard of terrible happenings at Monksend – oh, dear, that *nice* Miss Sanderson! – and had telephoned today to know if it was still all right for them to come. A Mrs Smart had said yes, do come, and she would be happy to tell them the whole sad story. It was clear that they knew nothing of the latest disaster. They clustered round the Superintendent, twittering.

Stillman said they had better go ahead and get their apples.

'Shall I take you into the garden? This way,' said Harriet, materialising at the drawing-room door.

'No, darling,' said a clear voice from the staircase. 'Let's be informal, shall we, and go through the kitchen. You won't mind, ladies, I'm sure.'

Emma, alone and palely loitering, looked down at her visitors, one hand clenched on the curve of the banisters. She said they were all very deeply beholden to the Chief Superintendent for his kind permission.

'I'm sure none of you will trample on any clues,' she told them. 'Mr Stillman will play safe by sending a man to escort the ladies to the orchard. I would go myself, but I . . . I. . . .'

Everyone said she must not think of disturbing herself. She smiled faintly. Perhaps it was amusing to think she *could* be further disturbed.

'Harriet, dear,' she said. 'Will you lead the way? You know where James Grieve and the Rev. W. Wilkes are.'

Stillman put in a word. He asked the ladies to stay together, and go only to the orchard and back, by the path the constable deputed to the task would show them. And the ladies, bright-eyed with excitement at finding themselves (so unexpectedly?) in the midst of Drama, nodded their neatly-hatted heads. Harriet led them away, through the kitchen. Stillman wondered what they made of Harriet, and of Thumper hovering on the flank of the party, and, most of all, of Derek – if he was still sobbing on the table.

In fact, Derek erupted into the hall, as soon as the group of women had left. He said that a gang of lunatics had just rushed, whispering, through the house. He then saw Emma on the stairs.

'Derek, darling . . .' said she.

After a swift glance behind him, to see if someone else called Derek was lurking there, he backed to the wall, looking goggle-eyed. His late employer smiled forlornly.

'Derek, I'm so sorry,' said she. 'That was all a nonsense at the club. I always meant you – and poor Johann – to help with the banquet tomorrow. You must believe me. I was worn out. I went to bits. Derek, please . . . I didn't mean any of the beastly things I've said to you . . . ! Derek, I've said I'm sorry.'

'Er . . .' said Derek, weakly.

'I can't bear it!' Emma's golden eyes were full of tears, and she took another faltering step down. 'We're all so miserable now,' she whispered, 'we can't stand much more. I don't know what else to say. . . .'

Derek went up the stairs to her. He put a hand under her elbow, and gave her his support as she turned and went back to the upper landing. She cast a watery smile back at Stillman, as she went with Derek to her room.

'There, George,' said the Superintendent. 'They've both got nice natures, really.'

*Chapter fifteen*

## DESSERTS

'I'm dying!' screamed Emma. 'God, I'm going!'

'Cut!' barked Mike Peel, up in the control room, almost crossing his eyes to watch all the television screens banked before him, in order to see which camera had picked up what disaster.

'Cut!' said Kay Stangrove, on the studio floor.

'*Now* what's the trouble?' said his director, in electronic communication with him. 'What's the perishing woman on about!'

'What's the trouble, darling?' relayed the assistant director, tactfully.

'It's the heat,' said Emma. 'I feel . . . dizzy.'

She moved to the nearest chair, and leaned on the back of it.

'Give them half a minute, Kay,' said Mike, into his mouthpiece.

'Half a minute, everyone,' said Kay.

'And not a second more,' Mike told him. 'There isn't time.'

But Emma really did look strained and pale under her make-up, and she closed her eyes against the glare of lights in the huge studio.

Two widely differing scenes were set alongside each other, facing the intricate array of cameras, overhead monitors, lights and cables, and the small army of technical experts responsible for transmitting the show, at present on its final rehearsal run.

One set represented a large kitchen. Its back wall, and sides, were pastel-coloured and matt-finished to reflect no light. There were carefully placed gas-stoves, refrigerators, cupboards (all painted off-white and matt) and a big table, where Emma and her assistant could move easily, never out of range of cameras, lights, and mikes. Pots were simmering very gently. They had only water in them for the rehearsal. Dishes were heating. On the scrubbed wooden table lay spoons, knives, bowls, chopping-boards, covered dishes, jars of herbs, pepper-mills, a bowl of Essex salt-crystals, and a bowl of parsley.

On the left side of this set – 'stage left', meaning to the left of anyone standing on the set and looking towards the audience (cameras being the audience, in this case) – was a wide doorway leading straight through to the other set.

Here was a long dining-table, with elegant pseudo-Georgian candelabra, imitation crystal glasses and bowls, and prettily arranged sprays of artificial flowers. The chairs were set about it in an unusual fashion. At the back, near the cream-painted linen-fold panelling, they were side by side in a normal way; but on the near side, with their backs to the panoply of cameras, they were spaced very widely to allow for angles of shooting. As Mike had promised, he had one camera concealed in the back wall of the set to cover the actors occupying these chairs. No one wanted to appear in a show as just the back of a head.

Emma's own chair was set at the right end of the table (stage right). At the opposite end sat the most famous actor. He now said in his often imitated but never equalled voice that it was indeed warm in the studio, and that he was looking forward to the ice-pudding they had been promised for the evening performance.

'Get them moving, love,' said Mike, through his speaker to Kay. 'Fast! We've only another twenty minutes.'

'How do you feel, Emma?' said Kay. 'Shall we go on?'

Emma gave the young man a brave smile, straightened her back, and said ringingly:

' "Awake, my little ones, and fill the Cup,
Before Life's Liquor in its Cup be dry!" '

'Goodie-gumdrop!' said the plump actor called Harry. 'Are we getting real booze?'

'You are tonight,' said Kay, 'so watch it. Come on, everyone. We're running late.'

There was a quick indrawn breath from quite a number of people, showing the tension and excitement always felt before a performance of any kind.

Emma proceeded with her carefully-timed exposition. Derek came through the door behind her, in a white apron and cap, carrying a huge dully-silvered tray with a boar's head on it. There was a slight giggle through the studio. It was so obviously made of papier-maché, and for the rehearsal only.

In an unobtrusive corner, well behind all the activity on the floor of the studio, the cameras, and their swathes of cables, and the concentrated men, Sergeant Woolsey watched it all. Beside him sat a robust young man, who was so manifestly a policeman in plain clothes that it seemed a waste of time to make him don them.

'I say, Sergeant,' whispered the latter, hoarsely, 'surely that woman with the big – with the fine figure there, is the one who played the tart in that film . . . ?'

'Ssh!' breathed Woolsey.

'Ssh!' breathed a nearby cameraman.

The constable wilted.

Emma was by now standing behind the table, centre. Her hair looked like a slightly ruffled metal helmet; her eyes caught the lights as though they, too, were made of metal. She wore a long, pale-grey, many-pleated gown. Her earrings were sapphires, and so was the great ring on her right hand. She would have preferred opals, but Giles had frightened her off them with superstitious legends. The imitation sable cloak was draped carelessly over the back of her chair. On her feet, a pair of high-heeled bedroom slippers struck a discordant note in her ensemble with their tufts of moulting purple feathers. It was strictly for their comfort they were being worn. She now held a small salver, with a jug on it.

'John,' said she, 'you must say truthfully what you think of this sauce. It's made with shallots, and butter, and Guinness. . . .'*

Someone remarked that he was only here for the beer.

Emma laughed. Then her face clouded. She said was it necessary to have such a high barricade of flowers all down the middle of the table? If she could not see the cameras, she was damn sure they could not see her.

'Hell! Take them away!' said Mike, in the control room.

'Shift the flowers, Speedy,' said Kay.

From the side of the studio, a man flashed across the front of the table, and away into the gloomy distances on the other side of the floor. He seemed to suck up the vases in his wake, for they vanished as swiftly as he did. Someone applauded.

'Let's have saucers with pansies in them,' said Harry.

'Coals to Newcastle!' said someone else.

At seven o'clock, the rehearsal stopped abruptly. And Mike came down from his eyrie to speak to his company in the studio.

'Lovely, everyone,' said he, with enthusiasm. 'It'll be a splendid show. Now – an hour to rest, freshen the make-up, adjust your dress, and etc. Relax, loves. I don't, under these circumstances, recommend having anything to eat. Perhaps a glass of milk, if you feel ravenous. You, Emma . . . you should. You're not going to be eating much tonight. No, I've got no notes for you. Have I, Jujube?'

At his elbow, his secretary shook her head so violently that her dark glasses fell forward on to the end of her nose, and she tossed them back into place with a practised gesture.

'No notes,' confirmed Mike. 'I'll see you all in the dressing-rooms, anyway. Off you go, now.'

The actors departed, chatting together. Mike and Kay and Jujube went off together, comparing the many notes which they really had made. The technicians left. The great studio stood empty.

An hour later, Chief Superintendent Stillman stood looking round the place. It was shadowy and sinister under its sparse working lights. It had a waiting quality. Waiting to come to life again, when the actors moved into place, when the cameras opened their eyes, when the lights sprang fiercely to brilliance, when the easy, natural-seeming performance began – that had taken so much work to prepare.

'Sir,' said Woolsey, 'are you quite sure this is a good idea?'

'By no means, George. I only wish I were. It may turn out to be a ghastly idea. But,' said the Superintendent, 'it's the only one I've got. If you've some better suggestions, as I'm sure you have, you should let me know.'

'Oh, I haven't, sir!'

But in the privacy of his own mind, he seethed with better suggestions. Anything, to divert Stillman from the collision course with professional disaster on which he was now set. Woolsey supposed the old man just did not care any more. In addition to the feebleness of old age, the collapse of authority, pride, ambition, he was about to retire in a matter of weeks. No need to take things too seriously. Just potter about, ask a few quite pointless questions, nod vaguely, and let your brain run down like an old clock. . . .

'Tomorrow,' said Stillman, kindly, 'they'll take me off this case. Bear with me till then, George. If I haven't come up with some sort of solution, you'll be working with a younger and cleverer man.'

'Sir!' exclaimed Woolsey, 'I'd *never* want to work with anyone else! It's . . . it's been an education, sir. You mustn't think. . . .'

'Oh, yes I must.'

Stillman led his junior across the dining-room set, through the wide unobstructed doorway into the kitchen set. Here they found three men lurking. Plain-clothes officers, detailed to stay in the studio from now on, and to keep their eyes well open. They told Stillman, in answer to his queries, that they were fed, happy, and prepared for anything. The Superintendent said he was glad to know it.

He left them arranging among themselves who should lurk where for the show.

Going back across the other set, he paused for a quick look at the banquet table. He examined the low silver bowls of artificial posies, the elegant cutlery, glasses, and napery, and smiled wryly at his Sergeant.

'I don't know how they do it,' he said. 'The thought of sitting here, under all those lights, eating real food, and chatting gaily – watched by millions of people – it would give me hiccups.'

Woolsey hazarded a guess that the actors felt the same. Only nerves of steel, long practice, and the thought of the money got them through.

The two men left the studio, and made their way through apparently endless curving corridors. Through various windows in the outer wall, they could see into a huge courtyard, with lights spilling from the building that surrounded it.

'Talking of food, George, did you get enough to eat?'

'Oh, yes, sir. Very nice.'

'But quite different from the stuff they're going to be gobbling down at this feast tonight, eh?'

Woolsey said rather them than him. He preferred fish and chips.

They came to a square hall, with four lifts. And here they were accosted by Miss Amy Barr. She gave them a nervous smile, and said she was just coming to look for them.

'People do get lost in this place,' said she. 'I've done it myself, when I first came to work here. I thought you might need a guide.'

The Superintendent said they were very glad of her company. He could easily, according to him, have gone round in circles for months . . . found in remote future ages, still wandering. She tittered feebly, and looked more than usually distraught. Noticing Stillman's eyes on her as they went up in the lift, she suddenly burst out:

'Today's been *awful*! B. L.'s raising hell about the police all over the place. He says you're going to arrest half the personnel of the B.B.C.'

'Why, what have they been up to?'

She laughed, relaxing a little. Some floors up, they went along another corridor, and she stopped by a door.

'Here we are,' Amy said. 'It's a cut above the ordinary viewing-room. We call it a Hospitality Room, and it's for special people. Special occasions.'

She ushered them in with the air of one entering the inner temple of some spooky religion. Yet the place was more like a smallish and impersonal sitting-room than anything else. Easy chairs and couches faced a large television set. Small tables were dotted about, with two larger ones against walls. On these were set convenient trays of drinks, glasses, syphons, canapés, olives, nuts, and sweets.

'I'm saving those two seats,' said Amy, pointing, 'for B.L. and Mrs Locke. I'll have to be next to him, and then I thought . . . Sir Robin Randall. Now, you two. . . .'

'I'll sit here,' said Stillman, 'near the door. But Sergeant Woolsey doesn't need to sit down. Standing's good for his figure.'

'Oh,' said Miss Barr, gazing round-eyed at the splendidly proportioned Sergeant. 'If you say so, Chief Superintendent. I must go back to Reception now, to make sure no one else is silly enough to get lost. Ha, ha!' she added, quickly, turned bright pink, and shot out of the room.

'And now,' said Stillman, 'we'd better copy Mr Warrington, and touch wood.'

'Are you really expecting something to happen tonight, sir? Trouble?'

'My dear boy, I've got police all over the building, in every corner where they can lurk. I've got ten men with little B.B.C. bleeping machines in their lapels, each with its code – so that I can dial them from the telephone over there. I've alerted the gatekeepers. I've had a very lively chat with the presentation editor. He'll be watching the show like a six-eyed lynx – and, if anything goes wrong, he has a Tom and Jerry cartoon standing by.'

'That'll be nice,' said Woolsey. 'I like Tom and Jerry.'

'Then there's an extra camera,' went on the Superintendent, 'set to watch what I want watched. Yes, George, I think you might say I'm expecting trouble. Even if it's only with the Yard, and the B.B.C., when nothing whatever happens, and I turn out to have made a silly old fool of myself. Which is, of course, what everyone expects.'

'God help us!' said the Sergeant, piously.

He glanced at his wristwatch. According to it, the time was now ten minutes to six. But it had not been itself since its owner had helped to dredge that appalling croquet ball from the pool. Noticing his action, Stillman said it was now exactly seven minutes past eight.

'Blimey!' said Woolsey, a little over-excited.

'Indeed, yes,' said the Superintendent. 'I think you'd better go along to the dressing-rooms, George, and see how everyone's getting on.'

'Yes, sir. And you'll be here, from now?'

'Yes, I think so. Yes. Come back when they're in the studio. And, George – in an emergency, use your own judgement. In which,' said Stillman, 'we both have such faith.'

His Sergeant gave him a quick look. But the older man was scribbling rapidly in his notebook. As Woolsey left the room, the Superintendent looked thoughtfully at what he had written.

'Robinia "Frisia" . . . sunlight effect . . . far end of garden . . . about twenty feet. Never asked Hawley about cauliflower. . . .'

Sergeant Woolsey came to a slithering halt outside the open door of Emma's dressing room.

'No!' he heard her shrieking. 'Not the long ones! They'll catch in the fur and drag off my ear-lobes. Find the short ones . . . I wore them for the rehearsal, dear.'

She stared into her looking-glass, pulled a horrible grimace, flicked an immaculate wisp of silver hair, and caught sight of the lurking Sergeant outside the room. Her softly-painted face broke into a smile of warm welcome.

'Come in, darling,' said she. 'It's chaos, but then it always is. Come on in. There's lots of us here.'

And there did seem to be.

Harriet was rooting through a box of jewellery on the dressing-table, at Emma's elbow. Thumper was leaning against the window-frame, reading a script of the show, and laughing aloud from time to time. At least, Woolsey assumed these persons to be Harriet and Thumper, for little of their faces could be glimpsed behind their streaming hair. They were dressed more formally, for the occasion. Both wore what looked like Ugandan cotton shirts to the ankles, stitched in large patterns of purple, green and yellow zig-zags. On top, they wore three-quarter-length sheepskin tunics, that smelt a bit sheep-like. On their feet were thick white socks, and sandals. The only visual difference between them was the fact that one was taller, and seemed to have a moustache. Giles was sitting in an easy chair, writing hurriedly on a thick note-pad. He looked hot and bothered, which was not surprising, as the entrance of the Sergeant had filled the smallish room to bursting point. Any new arrivals would have to sit on the bath, in its partitioned corner.

'. . . have to find Mike Peel,' said Giles.

'Bless you, love,' said Emma. 'He'll be along in a minute, anyway. But try to catch him quickly, so that he can warn the others. Why ever didn't I change the line before?'

Giles shot from the room, with a quick half-smile to the Sergeant.

'Going to watch the show, Mr Woolsey?' asked Emma. 'It'll be frightful! I'm in no fit state to boil an egg, let alone present a star-studded blow-out. You'll hate it.'

Woolsey began to say something reassuring and complimentary, but the lady had moved to more urgent problems.

'Did anyone give Derek my list of last-minute alterations?' she was demanding.

Getting no immediate reply, she gave a heart-rending wail, and said that settled it. The thing would be a shambles from start to finish. Derek would not get one single cue right. Harriet then said Emma had given Derek the list herself.

'When he came in to wish you luck.'

'Yes,' sighed Emma, relaxing. 'I remember. When he brought that mad elephant.'

Without surprise, the Sergeant registered the large, plush creature, in delicate shades of mustard and tangerine, with green eyes and a tasselled tail, standing in a corner of the dressing-table. It had a yellow horse-shoe in its trunk, and an insane smirk. Emma was now asking Thumper if he had found the lines she wanted changed. He nodded, and read aloud, his tones slightly muffled by hair:

'Fillet of chicken, flattened murderously with a mallet, wrapped round slices of shallot and chicken liver that have been drowned in sherry. . . .'

'Shut up!' squealed Emma, shuddering. 'It's got to be changed. It was all that rush this afternoon. I'll just say "fillets of chicken, wrapped round shallot and chicken liver flavoured with sherry" . . .' She turned sadly to the Sergeant. 'I'm going to have the pool filled in. I'll put a stand of silver birches. . . .'

A tannoy opened up. It said she had another ten minutes. She gave a faint scream, and grabbed the earrings that Harriet was offering.

There was a tap on the door. A voice called:

'Ten minutes, please, Lady Randall.'

Bedlam now ensued.

Woolsey backed hurriedly into the corridor, followed by Thumper. Derek erupted from a nearby doorway and collided with them both. Then he ricocheted to the wall, crying that now he must do his hair again, and disappeared into a dressing-room. As he had become attached to a string of beads round Thumper's neck, these broke, and cascaded over the polished floor. Woolsey was brushing at a smear of make-up on his shoulder. Thumper said he thought he had better go, and went.

From behind another door, a voice said in beautiful tenor cadences that someone had taken its clothes-brush, which must be instantly returned. Emma shrieked that her nose was shiny. And Giles came running to her door, clutching a huge bunch of roses. He said they were from Robin, and he'd meant to bring them to her earlier. She said take them somewhere and put them in water . . . but not here . . . not now . . . ! He disappeared again, at an even brisker trot.

And Mike Peel galloped happily down the hall, flinging doors open, and calling good-luck to the inmates of the dressing-rooms.

'You'll be lovely, darling! John, you're beautiful. Yes, I adore you,

162

Judy. Have fun, all of you. Good luck. Emma, my angel, you're marvellous. Good luck, sweetheart. Be good, Harry, and don't overdo the gags, love. Thank you, Michael. I'm not even nervous . . . no, not a qualm. . . .'

As he passed the Sergeant, Woolsey could see the sweat on his forehead, and the look of despair on his face.

'Omigod! Omigod! Help me! Omigod!' he was muttering, as he vanished across the green-room, and out of a far door by the little snack-bar.

'Let slip the dogs of war!' said someone, and gave a high terrified titter.

And a deep and rolling baritone said:

'Oh, shit!'

Someone else seemed to be crying.

There came a sound of tannoys summoning everyone to the studio. And a man went by tapping on the dressing-room doors and saying that those within were instantly required on the set.

Sergeant Woolsey flattened himself against a wall as the rush began. By some swing-doors, he saw a plain-clothes man being swept away, and hoped he'd escape before he found himself part of the show.

Harriet joined the Sergeant as the place emptied.

'There's always high panic,' said she. 'But they've been called in plenty of time. Are you going to watch in the studio, or up in the control room, or where?'

Woolsey said he would be with the Chief Superintendent in the hospitality room, for part of the time at least.

'That is,' he said, 'if I can ever find my way back.'

'I'll take you. I've done this before,' said Harriet. 'It's not much fun, but it pleases Emma. I think it's all fairly sordid, myself. One day, when I'm immensely rich, I'm going to buy the television Centre, and turn it into flats for out-of-work circus clowns.'

'They should feel very much at home here, miss.'

Harriet lifted her curtain of hair at one side, and gave Woolsey a flashing grin. Then she padded ahead of him to some lifts.

The show was, as usual, about to Go On.

Upstairs, the hospitality room began to fill with people.

Amy Barr ensconced B.L. and his wife in the centre armchairs, small tables by their knees, and filled glasses in their hands. She left empty for herself the chair on his left, and smilingly guided Robin to the one beside it. But her seating arrangements were disorganised when Charles Picklehampton entered the room, and was beckoned by B.L.

163

'Over here, Charles. I've something to discuss with you. Amy can sit behind me. She can hear well enough there to take notes.'

'Oh, yes . . . of course,' said Amy.

Charles settled down to be given a lecture on studio photography by B.L. He nodded and murmured agreeably. He was not listening to one word. Amy found seats for Betsie Bloot and her husband, and cleverly set a box of chocolates before Mr Bloot. He fell on them like a famished vulture on a very small Prometheus. Then Amy gave Robin a packet of his favourite cigarettes, and treasured his thanks.

As more people came in, she hurried to her indicated seat before someone took it. B.L. would think nothing of ordering them to shift. And Giles dropped into the chair on Amy's right, as Maybelle Warwick sank gracefully into one on her left. Harriet sat on a couch by the window. Thumper joined her, and they helped themselves to chocolate mints.

Looking round the room, the Chief Superintendent studied the faces there. Two were unfamiliar to him. One of them, he knew, must be a policeman disguised thinly as an invited visitor. The other was something to do with the B.B.C., and Stillman had heard B.L. address him as 'Ah, there you are, Stringer.'

'Just going to start,' said B.L. as if on cue. 'Carry on, Stringer. Lights!'

The young man hastened to switch off the main room lights, leaving only a couple of heavily shaded lamps in corners. Then he pressed a button on the television set. Nothing happened for a moment. Then there rose a faint humming sound, turning into a voice. A black-and-white picture faded up on the screen. Someone said something about the Kasbah.

'Other channel, you fool!' barked B.L.

Red-faced, Stringer skidded to a halt by the set, pressed another button, and backed away. B.L. growled that a change of personnel was impending. From the box, music swelled for the finale of the feeble family programme. The bland face of an announcer – too heavily made-up, in glorious technicolor – made hopeful, though quite unfounded, forecasts of magnificent entertainment on the morrow.

'And now,' he concluded, 'here is the programme you've all been waiting for. Lady Emma Randall, in her marvellous, *live* show . . . "Sound the Gong"!'

The Chief Superintendent put on his viewing spectacles.

To the opening bars of the 'London Symphony', a caption appeared. 'Sound the Gong', the letters slowly spelled out, one by one, by a golden icing-nozzle on a huge snow-white cake (Emma had fought against this, but it was B.L.'s idea and he loved it) – followed by the names of Emma, and her illustrious dinner-guests; followed by a zoomed-in close shot of a menu, held in a visibly quivering hand. Then the screen framed Emma's face, in her most bewitching mood. The show was away to a flying start.

She was wearing the sable cloak over her grey dress. It looked magnificent, and had been carefully described in the *Radio Times* as expensive fake, to put those in their place who were outdated enough to fancy real furs. The myriad unpressed pleats of her gown flowed round her ankles – almost hiding the small grey shoes – as she moved about the kitchen set. Derek stood rigid beside a stove. His fixed smile twitched at the edges.

The chat to the viewers began. The bacon puffs were brought from the oven by Derek,* and Emma, talking brightly with him about the ingredients, carried them on heated dishes through the doorway to the other set. A blaze of lights gleamed on the smiling faces at the dinner table.

'I say, I say, I say!' chanted the cherubic Harry. 'What have we here? Cream buns?'

The banquet began.

It had been arranged that afternoon that a youngish actor, already in the show, and referred to by all as Dickie, should help Derek when necessary – with extra pay, of course. He now leapt up from the table, dealt out dishes like a pack of cards, and sat down quickly to eat his puff before it got cold. Derek forgot to be self-conscious; he even forgot to smile towards whichever cameras seemed to be looking in his direction. He became so intent on what he was doing that he looked almost pleasing.

As well as Emma's, one face after another was picked out as its owner said something witty and/or apposite. Sometimes, Emma wandered round the table, chatting to her 'guests' and telling them (and the viewers) about the food they were eating. Then she would go through into the kitchen, to attend to dishes being taken from their ovens, and pots. Always she had the performance completely in hand; her timing was perfect; she was a past mistress of the medium. It was a good show. Entertaining, and reasonably instructive – if anyone was contemplating giving a full-scale banquet.

In the viewing room, the audience was attentive. Apart from a few muttered remarks by B.L., noted obediently by Amy, no one spoke. Harriet and Thumper laughed a few times, at an amusing remark or

165

situation on the screen. The plain-clothes man gave a small guffaw once, but stopped himself with a gulp, remembering he was on duty, and in the presence of a Yard senior.

And Superintendent Stillman looked half asleep. Through one part of his brain was floating a list of names – 'Margil', 'Black Hamburg', 'Greengage' – and through another part went another list of names. He was an adept at thinking on two levels, and it was anyone's guess which mattered most to him.

'And now,' said Emma, smiling with inimitable charm at audiences everywhere, 'we take a slight pause for breath, and a mouthful of grape-and-lemon water-ice.'

Mr Bloot licked his lips. The chocolate box was now empty, and the sight of all that food on the screen made him feel quite ravenous. The fact that he had eaten a huge steak, with chips and mushrooms, followed by two helpings of treacle tart, cheese, and five cups of coffee with cream, made little or no impression on his appetite. Betsie glanced at him, groped in her handbag, and gave him an enormous slab of milk chocolate. He fell on it like another unfed vulture.

'Dearest Emma looks quite young in that shot,' said Maybelle Warwick, in not quite a whisper.

'Please!' said Giles.

He looked at Robin, who had not stirred. Amy Barr looked, too. She had been doing this fairly frequently since the programme started. She watched his handsome profile, with the sensitive lines of strain round his mouth, with deep admiration. She wondered, not for the first time, what life would be like, married to someone like that. He had spoken so kindly to her, on each occasion that they had met. Fate was entirely unjust, thought Amy sadly.

The banquet-party was now gorging itself daintily on small helpings of beef fillet with juniper berries, braised celery, and tiny potatoes. Emma was handing round a silver sauce-boat.

'. . . made,' she was saying, 'with shallots and butter, and Guinness. . . .'

An actor said he personally was only here for the beer, and Emma laughed merrily, and swept on with the show.

Derek came in from the other set, after a short while, and he began to clear the dishes, with the help of the actor called Dickie. Emma went out with them to the kitchen, and talked to the cameras while featherweight cauliflower soufflés were taken from the ovens and rushed to the table. Then she went to her seat there, and sat sipping wine, and chatting to the cast and the viewers.

166

A little later, the amateur waiters served tiny hot Castle Puddings, with cherry-plums in cream, and cherry-brandy.

Mr Bloot gave a strangled groan, and Betsie handed him a stick of chewing-gum. Maybelle murmured, just audibly, that no one had yet been poisoned. So far, so good, she added. And Mrs Locke asked her very nicely to be quiet.

Then Derek came triumphantly from the kitchen set, carrying a huge silver dish on which was placed the set-piece of the whole banquet.

There was a beautifully arranged wide ring of fresh raspberries, quartered pears, grapes, baked quinces and strawberries, soaked in red-currant jelly which had been allowed to set lightly. In this ring of fruit stood a towering ice pudding. It was in layers of differing delicate colours, decorated sparsely with candied rose-petals. It was huge.

The 'guests' were surprised into a ripple of applause. Emma smiled. She was rather proud of the appearance of this concoction.

Derek walked carefully to the front of the table, frowning slightly with the weight and importance of his burden. He had been told quite frequently what would happen to him if he dropped it. He went between two widely spaced chairs, and set the great trencher down on the table. Then he stood to one side, with a noticeable look of relief. And Emma, who had risen, now came to the centre, at the back of the table, and smiled into the cameras.

'Now don't anyone be put off by the size of this thing,' said she, lightly. 'It's just an ice pudding. Eggs and sugar and purées of various fruits. Cream, of course. But, truly, there's nothing in it.'

She was wrong.

Her silver slicer jammed, as she started to cut the pudding. She wiggled the blade from side to side, and the whole grand edifice fell apart. In its centre was a package, wrapped in polythene.

Emma gave a small yelp.

'Oh, no!' said Derek.

He went forward and took the package from the ruins of the pudding. He looked closely at the cold bundle in his hands.

'It's Lynn's diary,' he said.

Upstairs, in the hospitality room, there was a small uproar taking place. Chief Superintendent Stillman was on his feet. He had done it. The Furies were loosed.

So was all hell.

B.L. announced furiously that everyone connected with this fiasco would be sacked forever.

Sergeant Woolsey shot out of the room. Maybelle said in a shrill, and hitherto never heard, voice that it was not Emma's fault, and she should sue someone.

Giles, saying he must go to her at once, almost ran from the place. Harriet rose to follow him, but was restrained by Thumper who said better leave it all to the experts. Stillman was now beside the telephone on a side table, dialling code numbers.

And Emma's clear voice lifted through the confusion of the banquet-party on the screen.

'Now who,' said she, 'will have some pudding?'

'Me,' said Harry, 'but none of the stuffing, love.'

The show, amazingly, went on. 'Tom and Jerry' would not be needed.

The Superintendent left the hospitality room, and hurried along a curving corridor to a hall with four lifts. One of these waited with opened doors, as though expecting his custom. Indeed, it was. Down went Stillman . . . through the vast reception hall, with its wall of windows looking on to the inner courtyard, the long desk, the cushioned seats, and out into the chilly night air. The Superintendent hurried round the curved approach, down shallow steps, and across the drive to a confusion by the main gateway.

The barriers were lowered, and a keeper stood defensively before the left-hand one where a car had been forced to pull up. Round this stood a knot of policemen. And someone was shouting.

As Stillman came up, a man got out of the car and stood shaking. Sergeant Woolsey was trying to tell him that anything he said might be used in evidence. But the warning seemed to lack significance to the man who continued to shout through the impassive, formal words.

'I *had* to kill the stupid bint! Anyone would! She was bloody asking for it. Whining the whole time for marriage – the randy prig! Easy lay, with a wedding in the offing . . . the bitch . . . the bitch. . . .'

'Now steady,' said the Superintendent. 'I have a warrant . . .'

'Anyone would have done the same . . . !'

'. . . for your arrest. You're charged with the murder . . .'

'The bitch! The prissy whore!'

'. . . of Lynn Sanderson,' said Stillman, evenly.

'You'll have to come with us,' said Woolsey, staring at the frothing man with deep revulsion.

'Blackmailing slut!' bawled Giles, quite beyond control. His eyes showed their whites, rolling like those of a goaded bull. He was gulping for breath, red-faced, and striking his clenched fists together in a way that would have been most painful had he been aware of pain. 'So she

found out I'd taken some bloody charity money! I needed it more than
. . . And she finds out. So what? Does that make her God? To lay down
the law . . . threaten me . . . what could I do? Jesus Christ, I'd have lost
my job . . . lost my wife. . . .'

'Now come along,' said Woolsey.

'What could anyone do? Had to say I loved her . . . I'd marry her . . .'
gabbled the man, trying to jerk his arm free from the steady grasp of one
of the policemen. He stared round at them all, without apparently
recognising any of them. 'Had to kill her!'

Two police cars had closed in behind them, and a small crowd of
gaping spectators had collected on the pavement outside the lowered
barriers. Others were running down from the towering building of the
television centre.

'Don't say any more,' said Stillman.

His warning was ignored.

'But I'd have lost my job!' screamed Giles. 'Lost Harriet . . . all her
money. Only another twelve months to wait. What was I to do, but kill
the dirty, blackmailing sneak . . . !'

Stillman thought of the gentle, kind girl, Lynn. His mouth twisted.

'Take him away,' he said, abruptly.

He handed the warrant to a senior police officer, and said he would be
following them to the station very soon. Bundled into a car, still
screaming obscenities, Giles Warrington was removed.

'What now, sir?' said the white-faced Sergeant Woolsey.

'Not a pretty scene, George, was it? They seldom are, at this point.
Now? Well, now I must go and break it to Lady Randall that she's lost
another of her staff. I owe her a personal explanation. It won't be
pleasant, having to do it, so if you'd rather not come with me. . . .'

'I'll come with you, sir.'

The barrier at the near gate had lifted, and the police cars had gone.
The Superintendent and his Sergeant walked wearily back towards the
main entrance of the Centre.

'It's been a strain tonight, what with one thing and another,' said
Stillman. 'You did everything I asked of you, most efficiently. The rest
isn't going to take long. I'll have to go and get a statement from that . . .
from Warrington, as soon as I've finished here. But you can call it a day
and shove off, George. That'll be all right by me.'

'I'd rather stay, sir,' said Woolsey. He then added, with feeling: 'All
the way to red-hot blazing hell, and dark-blue ice! And back again! You
wily old senile slyboots!'

'Are you all right, Sergeant?'

'My God, I didn't say that aloud, sir, did I?'

'You didn't say anything. You crossed your eyes.'

'Just nerves, sir.'

Stillman gave him an interested look, and the two men pushed open the glass doors into the great rotunda.

*Chapter sixteen*

## BRANDY ALL ROUND

The evening was not over as quickly as the Superintendent had hoped.

Making his way, without much hesitation, to the studio, he found that by sheer habit and their sense of responsibility to their audience and employers, the performers had somehow fought the show to a reasonably sane conclusion.

As the result of a serious talk given by Stillman to both B.L. and Mike Peel, no one in authority had discussed the contents of the pudding with the cast. Mike had just said something vague about a slip-up, which would all be made clear at a later time. He went round the dressing-rooms, telling everyone how lovely and clever they were, and how splendidly the show had gone. And B.L. was coerced by his wife and Amy Barr into doing and saying much the same. He did it with an ill grace, but no one thought this strange. He did everything with an ill grace. Betsie had been promised a rattling good story for the following morning, and had departed looking thoughtful and dragging her husband at her heels. Derek had presented him with a hard-boiled egg, and had then burst into floods of tears. He was totally silenced by Sergeant Woolsey, who arrived on the scene and told him to be a man.

Maybelle Warwick, accompanied by the elegant Charles, descended on Emma in her dressing-room, and said no one could possibly have noticed the little contretemps, if they had not been watching like hawks.

'Which most people do not,' said she. 'They've got one eye on their knitting, or the cup of tea. And if they did happen to see something odd, they'd think nothing of it. *We* know,' she said, 'that the average viewers would only notice Judgement Day if they were charged admission. Forget the whole thing, darling. You were a huge success.'

Reverting then to normal, she said Emma had looked quite slender in that clever gown. Charles took her away, saying over his shoulder that he had a marvellous idea for a new studio study of Emma.

'In Greek costume,' said he, 'by a smoking shrine! "The Sibyl at Delphi . . . or My God, the Chop's on Fire!" Lovely.'

Harriet and Thumper told Emma they had been riveted. Never

before, they said, had food seemed at all interesting to them. They then went away, holding hands.

'Where's Giles?' Harriet asked Stillman, as they passed him in the corridor.

'I think he's occupied, miss,' said the Superintendent.

Harriet giggled under her waterfall hair, and said that as soon as he was free, she had some news for him. And she let go of Thumper's hand, and put an arm round his waist instead. Stillman looked sadly at her, and said he thought her news would reach him sooner than that.

Derek stuck his head through a doorway, and begged the Sergeant to come and sit with him while he took off his make-up. He said he felt unsafe on his own.

'You do that, George,' said Stillman, wickedly. 'Keep an eye on him. But don't be conned into doing anything you shouldn't.'

Abandoning the stunned Sergeant, he knocked on the star's door, and asked to speak to Sir Robin Randall, who was, he understood, inside. Robin emerged looking cautious.

'I've very unpleasant news, sir,' said the Superintendent. 'I think I should inform you, before letting your wife know.'

'Is it absolutely necessary that she *should* know?'

'Unfortunately, yes. It concerns her, very closely. And she'll certainly be called as a witness later. And, anyway, she must be asking questions already. . . .'

'Oh, she is! Of course you're perfectly right, Mr Stillman. Now, tell me.'


It was just on midnight. The Superintendent and his Sergeant (who, unnerved, was sticking to him closer than a Band-Aid) found themselves sitting by the library fire at Monksend. Both were nursing large glasses of brandy, and admiring Emma's fortitude. Her face lined with fatigue and shock, she sat quietly, stroking the grey cat on her knee as though the touch of his silky fur was comforting.

'How did you know that Giles was married to Harriet?' she asked.

'When I read the diary, I looked up the Register,' said Stillman. 'I thought he must have a strong reason for not marrying Miss Sanderson quickly. He only stopped her from telling you about the way he'd defrauded you, by making her think he loved her. That he was repaying the money he'd stolen from your charity funds. That he was sorry. That he meant to marry her.'

'Poor Lynn. If only she'd come to me.'

'She felt strongly about him, Lady Randall. Tragically, she had a gentle and trusting nature. . . .'

'And was killed for it!'

Robin sat on the arm of her chair. Chin-Chin stared at him morosely, but suddenly decided to forgive him, and nuzzled his hand. Robin suggested that the Superintendent should tell them the details, in sequence. Emma said it was all vile and hateful, however it was told. Stillman agreed with her. Then he sat for a few minutes in silence, marshalling the facts into some sort of order in his mind. Oh dear, he reflected, a selfish, feckless, greedy business. That lives could be thrown away for such petty reasons was a slur on humanity. Apes conducted themselves in far more seemly fashion. He began to speak, sombrely.

Time had been running out for Giles Warrington.

On June the tenth, Lynn had written in her diary: 'He is paying back the £1,000 in instalments, and I know he's terribly upset about what he did. He needed the money so badly, poor boy.'

No one knew what tale she had been told about these needs, and probably never would know. But the Superintendent had checked Giles's bank statements, and found unaccounted-for lump sums paid in over a period of eleven months. And in the account books dealing with Emma's charities, among other things, some very curious donations were listed in the names of untraceable Friends of This and That.

Stillman told his listeners that these things were not, in themselves, enough to warrant an arrest on suspicion of murder. Straws in the wind, rather.

In the same diary, Lynn had written: 'I'll be married by now!' right across the page relating to the third week in the coming October. She had not stated to whom she would be wedded.

Before driving down to Monksend tonight, in response to the pleading invitation of Emma, seconded by Robin. . . .

'I know you must be worn out, but please . . . Superintendent, I'll go crazy unless I hear the full truth of this ghastly business!'

. . . Stillman had sat for nearly an hour at the Station, listening to Giles's frenzied and rambling account of his activities. In spite of repeated warnings and advice about lawyers, the man had insisted on explaining what he had done. Appallingly, he seemed to consider himself justified.

'Lynn must have found the discrepancies, in my cheque-books and accounts,' Emma was now saying, slowly. 'She was very painstaking, and straight with money . . . as with everything else. The girl who worked for me before was a slipshod creature, and would never have noticed what was being done. *I* should have noticed! I'm such a fool about money. Why ever didn't Lynn come to me about it?'

No one answered her cry. It was only too sadly clear why Lynn had gone directly to the man she loved. And she had believed his assurances of repentance, restitution . . . and returned love. Robin sighed. He asked how soon the Superintendent had known the identity of the killer.

'I'm a slow sort of person,' said Stillman. 'I don't reach conclusions quickly. I just let people talk. Sometimes they say something that makes you think. Sometimes, they don't. You can never tell with talk. What I didn't like was that broken catch on the bathroom door. It didn't seem to match the way your house is run.'

It had also indicated to him that Lynn might have been the intended victim. That the poisoning of Emma might have been a blind, to make it seem as if Lynn had died by error.

'That stuff in my drink?' said Emma. 'Giles got it from the garden?'

'Oh, yes. He knew what grew among the herbs,' Stillman told her. 'He was very careful not to give too big a dose, when he put it in the – "Blood on the Rocks", you call it? – waiting in the hall to be taken up to you. The delay in your reaction to it was a great help in confusing the issue. He must have been crossing his fingers and wishing on the moon, for fear he'd given you too big a dose. It would have spoilt things if you'd died!'

'Yes, wouldn't it!' said Robin, dryly.

'I mean, sir, he would have had no cover. The resulting enquiries would have shown up the fraudulent conversion of funds, instantly. He explained all this in his statement to us. He was quite proud of his cleverness. . . .'

Giles had also explained the care with which he had planned the death of Lynn, and his brilliantly conceived alibi. In fact, it was not nearly as brilliant as he imagined. Luck had been with him, for two-thirds of the way.

He had arranged for the B.B.C. to telephone Emma at the exact time when Lynn would have gone upstairs for her customary bath. He had broken the bolt, to make sure the girl would use Emma's bathroom. This was a safe assumption. In any case, if things had not gone according to plan, no murder need have been executed. It could wait a more favourable occasion. The announcement to Robin of his parcel's arrival ensured that he would go at once to his study; this, Giles hoped, would leave him open to suspicion later.

The Sergeant shot a self-conscious look at his senior, who ignored it.

Giles himself had then gone up to his office, and used his house-phone to speak to Mrs Smart, knowing she was in the drawing-room clearing the tea-things. Then, while she went to find the address-book – carefully dropped among the plants to cause delay – Giles had gone to kill.

First to Emma's bedroom (where the cat, misguidedly liking the man, had not screamed at him), to snatch up the jade statuette. Then into the bathroom. Lynn, though undoubtedly surprised by his arrival there, would not have screamed, either. And then the savage blow . . . the bath-cap dragged over the shattered head by gloved hands. . . .

'Why that? Why the bath-cap?' asked Robin.

'An added indication that Lady Randall was the one who was meant to die,' Stillman told him, morosely. 'He'd taken the cap away, earlier. Out to the gazebo. I'm sorry to tell you this, but he made it look . . . right . . . by hitting it with a brick, after putting a cauliflower inside it. Analysis showed the vegetable traces, of course. Then,' went on the Superintendent, 'having made sure the girl was quite dead, he took the house-telephone from the marble bowl in the bathroom, where it's kept. . . .'

And had stood there, with Lynn's body in the reddened water beside him, finishing his brief chat with Mrs Smart. He had replaced that telephone, slipped cautiously across the landing to his office, and re-placed the house-phone there. He had taken up the main-line one, and been seen by Mrs Smart a few seconds later, apparently in the middle of a phone-call.

'He took some staggering chances,' said Stillman. 'Like most amateurs. The upstairs landing must have been like Piccadilly Circus.'

For Robin had been in his study while brutal murder was committed. Johann in Lynn's bedroom, and had missed by moments walking into Giles as that gentleman returned to his office. Mrs Smart had almost collided with the German on the stairs as she came up with the address-book. And Robin, coming to investigate the flurrying, had seen Mrs Smart on her way down again.

'Warrington got in a panic when he found Miss Sanderson's papers missing,' said the Superintendent. 'He must have rushed to get them, while Sir Robin phoned the police. It's lucky for us that murderers are fairly easily panicked. But that does tend to lead to further crimes, even stupider than the first! He didn't know what the poor girl had left on record about him, and he was stunned to find her diary missing. All her papers gone. It was dangerous in *two* ways. It pointed to Miss Sanderson as the intended victim.'

'But . . . I thought Giles must have taken her . . .' began Emma.

'No. Johann Schulter took the lot. When he found her room empty, he rushed in and just grabbed up all the papers he could find. He meant to sort out his letters and stuff at leisure. He was angry with her at the time, and wanted his poems back.'

While the Superintendent was speaking, Derek had been going round topping up everyone's glasses. He had drunk a fair amount himself, in an absent-minded way. His eyes were round and glassy with fatigue, and with the horror of what he was hearing, but they rested occasionally on Sergeant Woolsey with unmistakable tenderness. That officer began to shift uneasily. Derek then gave a convulsive sigh. He said he had been almost sure it was Johann who had killed Lynn.

'Really, Mr Hawley?' said Stillman. 'I believe my Sergeant thought the same.'

Woolsey flinched. He feared Derek might consider this a mystic bond between them. He also feared lest his senior go on to mention that he (Woolsey) had also suspected Robin, Giles, Derek, Emma, and the gardener. He need not have worried about the second contingency. Stillman knew when to stop.

'Why was Johann killed?' said Emma, flatly and almost without emotion. 'He knew nothing about any money troubles of Giles's. What possible harm could the poor boy have done to Giles?'

'According to what Warrington has told us, madam, he found the entry in the diary concerning the forthcoming marriage. He went to question Warrington about this. Thinking – rightly – that he might be the intended groom.'

And Giles had not bothered to find out how little the German knew. A lie, a shrug, a statement of innocence about the marriage – and Johann might even have handed over that dangerous diary to him. But Giles, faced with a source of betrayal, had killed again, without mercy, and without much thought. He was ready, said Stillman, to strike again and again, to cover the first crime.

'Like Macbeth,' said Robin.

'Just so. It's a very great pity that young Schulter was too scared to bring those papers to me. Once it was known they were out of his hands, he wouldn't have had to die.'

'Did Giles get the diary from him?' asked Robin.

'No, sir. Schulter took it, with the letters and other papers, to his room. He hid them in the paper jackets of cookery books. I blame myself,' said Stillman, 'for not finding them right away. After his death, I made a more thorough search.'

'I blame *me!*' cried Derek. 'If I hadn't fought with him, he might have told me. . . .'

'Not anyone,' soothed Stillman. 'He was too frightened of being implicated.'

'And nervous of authority,' added Robin. 'Papers were very important to him. Passports, visas, identity cards . . . all his life he's been made over-aware of them.'

'How horrible that he was killed for so little!' said Emma, shuddering against her husband's arm.

'Murder's always horrible,' Stillman told her. 'And, in most cases, done for greed, and in muddled thinking. Giles Warrington was simply hell-bent on getting hold of a sizable chunk of his wife's money.'

'His sole objective!' said Emma.

'Yes. Your niece will inherit a great deal, at eighteen.'

'I, personally, place entire confidence in Thumper,' said Robin. 'He may talk her into refusing it.'

'Whatever will James say?' gasped Emma.

'My dear brother will probably faint. And serve him right,' said Robin. 'Harriet's worth a lot better than his plans for her. Hooray for Thumper! Sorry, Superintendent. Please go on.'

'Well . . . Warrington married her secretly, she being under age. He meant to get a deal of money from her when she got to be eighteen. Twelve months to wait, only. But the arrival on the scene of Master Thumper made it likely she'd want her freedom earlier. Warrington then decided to make her father pay through the nose for this, by going to him with the truth of her marriage.'

'He would have paid,' said Emma, scornfully.

'Then he found himself in a cleft stick, Warrington, I mean. He had to fob off Miss Sanderson. And he couldn't let either of the girls find out about the other. Being straightforward people, they would have got together. All the lies and frauds would have come into the open. And once Miss Lynn knew him for a liar . . . already married. . . .'

'He must be insane!' said Emma.

'I think he'll be found fit to plead, at his trial,' said Stillman, quietly. 'He'll go up for life, of course. And that,' he added, 'is the third life thrown away for nothing. As soon as I was sure that bathroom bolt had been tampered with, that the girl was the intended victim from the start, it was only a matter of proving the reason for her death. And once I had the diary, with that entry in it . . . I knew. . . .'

Emma suddenly sat bolt upright, dislodging Chin-Chin who slid to the carpet hissing.

'Good God!' she exclaimed. 'The pudding! How did the diary get into that? It's not possible. I made the thing a week ago, before any of this . . . it was in the deep-freezer! Who on earth . . . ?'

'It was I, madam,' said the Superintendent.

'What?' said everyone else.

'I put the diary in the pudding, for you to find. I was sorry to surprise you, Lady Randall, and make difficulties for your show; but I hoped the result would startle Warrington into making a run for it. Luckily, he did. I had quite a job to persuade my superiors to let me play the matter my own way. They'd have been pretty cross, if it hadn't worked.'

'Now just a minute, Mr Stillman,' said Emma. 'How could you possibly cut a deep-frozen, moulded pudding in half, scoop out the inside, stuff in a bulky parcel, and clamp it together again, without spoiling it? Without leaving any signs? It would all break to pieces. And it was perfect, when it came to the table tonight.'

'Well, thank you, madam. I made that pudding,' said the Superintendent. 'I made it last night, at home. We've got a tiny deep-freeze. And I changed it for yours just before the performance started.'

In the silence that followed, he smiled modestly round.

'I'm a keen cook,' said he. 'I kept the recipe for that special pudding, when it was published in a magazine article that you wrote months ago, madam.'

Emma drew a long breath.

'Would you care for a job as my assistant, Mr Stillman?' said she.

'That's a great compliment, thank you. But I'm retiring in a few weeks, with a lot to do, to make a garden for my wife and myself. Now your Mr Crawford has very kindly offered to come and help me with the lay-out,' said the Superintendent. 'He's got some splendid ideas to include all the things we want.'

'Oh, good,' said Emma, weakly.

Derek refilled the glasses, almost to overflowing. He was thinking about something else. Wondering what complicated and imaginary crime he could report, to get the Sergeant back to Monksend.

Woolsey was gloomily wondering if he could get himself transferred to duty on the top of Rockall. He also wondered how to remove his senior officer from the house before he lapped up all that brandy.

'That's all we need!' said Woolsey, to himself, crossly. 'Pulled in on a drunk-and-disorderly charge! Tossed out on his ancient ear! No retiring gracefully under his own steam!'

Stillman was wondering if he dared suggest to Crawford a very tiny, stone-flagged terrace. About four foot by two, with a miniature urn, and one little step down to the three square yards of lawn.

Robin wondered how to hint politely at the departure of the police. He could then talk Emma into taking a sleeping-pill, and trying to forget the recent tragedies.

Emma, eyes swimming with tears again for her much loved, and now lost, young employees, stooped to stroke Chin-Chin.

The cat gave an ear-splitting yell of protest and shot under a chair.

Everyone started. Everyone gulped. Everyone collected wits and smiled feebly. The policemen rose, and said they must be going.

'Thank God the day is ending,' thought Robin. 'Not before time!'

'Come on, you awful old soak, before you start singing and staggering,' said Woolsey to himself.

'Are you all right, Sergeant?' said Stillman.

# APPENDIX

1.  BLOOD ON THE ROCKS: p. 7.

    1 part Campari.
    2 parts Vodka.
    2 parts Grenadine syrup.
    2 parts water.
    Ice to taste.

2.  SAUCE GIBBLEORANGE: p. 10.

    2 pints water.
    3 onions, medium-sized, chopped.
    2 carrots, medium sized and young, chopped.
    1 young leek, chopped.
    A small bunch parsley-stalks.
    Duck giblets, and neck.

    Simmer all these together for two hours, until reduced by at least a third. Strain. Add grated rind, and the juice, of two oranges. Simmer for another half-hour. Strain again. Add one tablespoonful brandy.
    When duck is roasted, remove from baking-dish, and keep hot. To the fat in the dish, add two tablespoonsful of plain flour and cook together. Pour in the sauce and stir well. Return it all to the saucepan. If liked, just before serving, add a small carton of Yoghurt.

3.  SHRIMP BUTTER; To serve with hot or cold fish: p. 13.

    Equal quantities of peeled, cooked shrimps and unsalted butter.
    1 teaspoonful chopped mixed fresh tarragon and parsley.
    Fresh black pepper.

    Shred the shrimps, mix well with butter and herbs and a pinch of pepper.
    While still soft, shape (with forcing-bag or fork) into decorative

180

pyramids about the size of half a hard-boiled egg. Refrigerate until needed.

The sole fillets, with which these were served at the first dinner-party, were curled carefully into individual scrolls, packed into a baking-dish, covered with fish stock, and baked for 10 minutes in a pre-heated oven at Mark 4.

The shrimp butter should, with hot fish, be served on separate dishes, but can be set on top of cold fish.

4.   REAL MUSHROOM SOUP; Only field mushrooms should be used. Others are not worth the bother: p. 111.

½lb peeled rinsed field mushrooms.
2oz chopped streaky bacon.
1 pint white sauce. (3oz butter, 3 tablespoonsful plain flour, 1 pint of milk.)
1 pint of water.
Pepper and salt. (Do use fresh peppercorns, milled, and Malden table sea-salt.)

Boil the water. Add the mushrooms, chopped, and the bits of bacon. Cook for 5 minutes.

Melt the butter in separate saucepan. Add the flour, and cook together. Add the milk.

Cook till the sauce thickens.

Strain the mushrooms, and add their cooking-water to the white sauce. Then boil up again until the mixture has a creamy consistency. Add the mushrooms and bits of bacon. Season well.

5.   BACON PUFFS: p. 165.

For Choux pastry:
¼ pint milk-and-water, in equal parts.
2oz butter.
Pinch of salt.
2½oz plain flour.
2 standard eggs.

Sift flour and salt together. Put butter and liquid in saucepan, and cook slowly so that the butter melts just before the mixture begins to bubble. Remove pan from heat, shovel in the flour and salt all in one go, and stir vigorously with a wooden spoon until the stuff leaves the sides of the pan and becomes a thick smooth ball. Let it cool, then add the eggs one at a time, and beating well after each. Set the lot aside till quite cold.

Use forcing-bag to make little blobs of the mixture on a buttered baking-sheet. Cook 25-30 minutes in oven Mark 7.

For the Filling:
4oz streaky bacon, chopped small.
½ teaspoonful of paprika.
1 tablespoonful finely grated Cheddar cheese.
1 heaped dessertspoonful plain flour.
½ pint milk.

Fry the bacon until it is crisp. Add to it the cheese and paprika, and stir well. Add flour and stir again. Pour in milk, still stirring until the mixture is thick and creamy. But if too thick, add a little more milk.

When the Puffs are cooked, make small holes in their sides and fill them with the bacon mixture. Keep nicely hot until ready to serve.

6. GUINNESS SAUCE: p. 157.

2 pints stock (or 2 pints water with 3 beef cubes).
1oz streaky bacon, chopped.
1oz butter.
1oz plain flour.
2 shallots, chopped.
6 mushrooms, medium-sized, chopped.
1 carrot, chopped.
½ teaspoonful chopped parsley.
¼ teaspoonful chopped thyme.
1 bay leaf.
½ pint Guinness.

Melt butter in a saucepan, add bacon and fry till fat runs from it. Add vegetables, mushrooms, and herbs. Stir together over low heat for 5 minutes. Put in flour and stir, letting it all brown a bit together – with care not to burn! Add stock and Guinness and bay leaf. Stir well. Set on low heat to simmer very slowly for about an hour. Strain through coarse sieve, re-heat and serve.

7. CAULIFLOWER SOUFFLÉ: p. 166.

8oz cooked cauliflower.
1½ozs melted butter.

182

2½ tablespoonsful milk.
Pinch of nutmeg.
3oz fine breadcrumbs.
6 eggs.
¼ pint thick cream.

Drain cauliflower well, and mash it roughly.
Make a thick white sauce with the butter, flour and milk.
Add cauliflower and breadcrumbs and nutmeg. Stir together well.
Separate eggs. Beat the yolks lightly, and the whites stiffly. Then
stir the yolks and cream in to the mixture in the saucepan, and tip
the lot into a large bowl. When it is cooler, fold in the egg whites –
not too thoroughly. Pour into buttered soufflé-dish, being careful
the mixture only comes three-quarters of the way up the sides. Set
the dish in a pan, half-filled with hot water, and cook for 30-35
minutes in preheated oven at Mark 7.


8.  ANCHEESE OBLONGS.

Toasted and buttered brown bread.
Anchovies, tinned.
Cottage cheese.
Chopped fennel. Brown breadcrumbs. Parmesan cheese.

Drain anchovies and shred well. Mix with cottage cheese, and
fennel. Cut the toast into oblongs 2in. by 4in. (or to taste), and
spread with mixture. Sprinkle breadcrumbs mixed with Parmesan
cheese over the tops, and place in oven for 5 minutes at Mark 5.


9.  MENU FOR BANQUET.

Hors d'oeuvres: Bacon Puffs.
Soup: Pumpkin, leek and pheasant soup.
Fish: Sussex Sole, with oyster sauce.
Entrée: York ham, sliced, coiled round artichoke heart for each
portion.
Lemon water ice.
Remove: Braised beef fillet with juniper berries, and served with
Guinness sauce.
Roti: Chicken breasts, sandwiching sliced shallot and chicken
liver, roasted in butter, then cut for serving lengthways, like Swiss
Roll.

Entremets:
    Vegetable: Cauliflower Soufflé.
    Hot sweet: Castle puddings with cherry-plum, cream, and cherry-brandy topping.
    Cold sweet: THE PUDDING.
    Savoury: Ancheese oblongs.
Dessert: Fresh fruits.
Coffee.
Brandy.

Side dishes for Roti and Entrée of broad beans, runner beans, roasted potatoes, creamed potatoes, and young marrows.